also by Martin Lloyd

The Passport
The Trouble with France
The Trouble with Spain

The Chinese Transfer

best wishes
Martin Lloyd

Martin Lloyd

Queen Anne's Fan

First published in 2006 by Queen Anne's Fan
PO Box 883 Canterbury Kent CT1 3WJ
Reprinted 2008

ISBN 978 09547 1502 1

Set in New Baskerville 11 on 12pt.

Printed in England

Queen Anne's Fan

1
Paris in the 1970s

When the second truck flashed its headlights at me I began to take notice. I was grinding up the climb from the Porte d'Italie to join the Autoroute du Sud, overloaded with tons of the ancient entrails of Paris to be dumped on the landfill site at Sauvigny. My Berliet tipper truck was maintaining a steady 20 kph in the third of its eight gears. The black smoke belching from its exhaust almost obscured the crocodile of frustrated vehicles crawling behind me.

I glanced across at the other truck as it rattled down towards Paris and my heart sank. Having flashed his lights, the driver was holding up his papers against the windscreen and waving them at me. That could only mean one thing — he had just seen a police check. Another week and I would have been clear. Why did they have to choose today? Perhaps they would not pick me out. I knew that I was only kidding myself. The moment the cop saw the mound of earth appearing over the brow of the hill he kicked his motorcycle into life and as I fumbled the roaring engine up a gear, he waved me to follow him down the slip road.

Parked in the courtyard of the police HQ were two other trucks from the Turbigo site. One was loaded like mine, the other was empty, they were parked side by side, their hoppers touching. I eased my truck to a stop and switched off. The roar of the engine died away to a relative silence. Beyond a single line of scrawny poplar trees the traffic on the autoroute swished by. I leaned forwards onto the steering wheel and gazed morosely through the dirty, fly encrusted screen.

'Merde!'

The hot air rising from the engine rippled the view as if I were looking through a cool mountain stream. It was 28 degrees Celsius. Behind me a vague haze of dust and pollution hung over the city, before me the sky was blue and unencumbered by anything that would provide shade.

'Merde!'

I recognised the truck in front. It was Janacek. He had rumbled out of the bowels of Paris half an hour before me, wagging his fingers in a rude sign at the foreman. Now he was stripped to the waist, bent double in the hopper of his truck, languidly shovelling sour-smelling earth into the empty truck alongside as it baked in the sun.

'Merde!'

I booted open my door and clambered down the iron steps to the yard. The heat and smell from the tarmac cloyed at my throat. I looked at the back wheels. Even stationary, it was obvious from the eight tyres of the twin back axle that I was overloaded. I wondered by how much. Probably eight or nine tons. They always overloaded the trucks — it was the only way they could expect to shift the soil. I didn't care. It wasn't my truck. I had needed the job and I had known they would not bother to ask to see my licence. It would have been impossible in any case. I didn't have one.

'Merde!'

I kicked savagely at the wall of a tyre. The cops were in no hurry. Three of them lounged in the shade of the guard house, drawing cruel spectator amusement from making a man try to shovel eight tons of earth. They would get around to me, eventually. They would ask to see my papers. I would hand over my I.D. card and start to search for my missing licence. They probably would not recognise the name. The court case had been nearly a year ago but their filing cards would betray me.

'Merde!'

In another week, the court was due to return my licence. I would have been legal then. I suddenly realised the fix that I was in. Driving an overloaded truck whilst disqualified. Another suspension, a fine which I would not be able to pay and so a prison sentence. I had to do something.

I climbed back up into my oven of a cab and thought rapidly. My light blouson was hanging on the back of the seat. I emptied the pockets into my jeans and left it hanging there. I grabbed a rag from the locker and wiped the steering wheel, then the gear lever, then the door handle on the inside. I leaned an arm casually over the window ledge and surreptitiously wiped the outside door handle. Keeping the rag in my hand I opened the cab door and climbed down the ladder. Once at the bottom I threw the rag back into the cab through the open window. Pushing my hands into my pockets I ambled away from the truck.

'Hey!' One of the cops called me.

'I'm going to the toilets!' I shouted back and pointed towards a dirty grey concrete building. The cop eased his shoulders from the wall and started towards me. His colleagues turned their attention from Janacek's sweating back.

'We haven't done your papers,' he shouted above the drone of the traffic. I continued shuffling away. I waved a vague arm back at the truck.

'In my blouson,' I shouted.

He glanced across at my truck where my jacket could be seen hanging on the back of the seat. I only had a lead of about ten seconds. Not enough to get lost with. If he went for the jacket it would take him time to examine it. Out of the corner of my eye I could see him diverting towards the truck. I rounded the corner and immediately stepped briskly out towards the officer at the pole barrier. He watched me from inside his glass box. His glance was slow and heavy like treacle. He must have been cooking in there.

'I need some more smokes.' I made a mime with my fingers of puffing at a cigarette. 'Where's the nearest tobacconist mate?'

He pointed down the road. The shops were two hundred metres down a straight road with no cover. Merde! Nobody runs in 28 degrees to buy a packet of cigarettes.

'Thanks.'

'You're welcome.' He was not even looking at me.

The sun beat up from the white gravelly soil with merciless brutality. Spanning the road, thick black cables looped limply like liquorice laces. A fawn-eyed dog was squeezed into the shade of an iron gate and lay panting on concrete.

I lengthened my stride and paced along as fast as I dared, listening intently for sounds of pursuit. At the first small junction I glanced quickly down the side streets right and left to assess the possibilities of flight or concealment. Nothing. Rows of red tiled villas, drooping trees and cream rendered garden walls. I stopped and looked again to my right. About fifty metres down the road a brown Rolls Royce was parked. A portly man was crouching by it. He was straining at the wheel wrench, trying to change the wheel.

As I approached I could see madame sitting in the front seat. Dark glasses and wide brimmed hat, pale lipstick and pastel blue dress.

'Do you want a hand?'

The man looked up at me.

'Blasted things,' he said, 'they must have put them on with a pneumatic spanner.'

He straightened up stiffly and flexed his fingers. From a distance I had thought him portly. I could now see that although he was past sixty he was squarely built and strong with it. Brown eyes inspected me rapidly from beneath a bristle of grey crew cut. His light grey suit was not the uniform of a chauffeur, it was an expensive lightweight. He was obviously the owner of the car.

'See if you can budge them if you like. I'll get you a beer if you can.'

I nodded and then got down on my knees to check that he had installed the jack properly. Looking under the car I saw a black and white Renault cruise slowly over the cross roads, the cops peering out of the windows on both sides. I stayed down a little longer.

'You don't think I know how to put a car up on a jack?' The accusation was good natured but his regard was piercing.

'Two tons of Rolls Royce dropping onto its axle ends would not be funny,' I replied and then added, 'Even when the Rolls is not mine.'

He grunted.

'I've also chocked both rear wheels,' he said.

'I noticed.'

He had left the wrench on a wheel nut. I grasped it firmly. The bars were still warm.

'You've not loosened any of them?' I asked.

'No. The buggers! Two of them moved a bit but then stuck fast.'

I tested the nut. It was as if welded to the stub. Then something of what he had said made me remove the tool and stand up again. From the cool inside, madame gazed placidly out at the suburban avenue as if it were a different planet but of no particular interest and I were a non threatening alien life form which she had just discovered upon it.

'You don't exactly exert yourself do you?' he said testily. 'Give me the wrench and let me have another go.'

I could see that the heat and the effort was trying his temper. His silk tie was loose-knotted and he had grime on the cuffs of his jacket. He moved to take the spanner from me but I absently drew it out of his reach.

'Now look here,' he protested, 'either you give me that wrench...'

'Just a minute! I'm thinking.'

'I don't want a thinker, I need a doer,' he snapped.

'No, that's your problem, mate.' I was purposefully insolent. I disliked his tone. 'You are the doer not the thinker. You'll never get that wheel off without me. It's not Hercules you need,' I tapped my forehead with my finger, 'it's Einstein.'

'Stop talking crap and give me that wrench.'

I passed it across to him and watched him as he fitted it over a wheelnut and braced his legs.

'I wouldn't if I were you,' I said.

'You what, sonny? Do you think I don't know how to take the wheel off a car? I didn't start life with a Rolls, you know.' He tugged at the bar.

I could not prevent myself from wincing.

'I'm sure you know how to take the wheel off a car but I don't think you know how to take the wheel off a Rolls.'

That stopped him. He looked at me. I waited.

'Go on,' he said.

'Left hand thread.' I pointed at the wheel. 'Rolls Royce put right hand threads on one side of the car and left hand threads on the other so that as you drive along the motion of the car tightens up the nuts on all four wheels. You've got the left hand side.'

'You're not joking are you?'

'No. You've just tightened up all the nuts as tight as you can get them. On a hot day,' I added.

'Well I'm buggered.'

'Probably.'

He took the wrench from the wheel and dropped it to the ground. It raised a small puff of white dust. I watched it drift slowly away like an arthritic genie. The sun was burning the skin on the back of my neck. Away over the roof tops a jetliner was descending to the runway at Orly like an old lady lowering herself gingerly into an easy chair.

'All right then.' I heaved a resigned sigh. 'Show me your tool kit.'

It took me thirty minutes of gentle tapping on the wrench to get all the nuts off. By the time I had got the spare wheel on, my black hair was plastered down on my forehead with perspiration and dust. Ignoring his light-weight suit the man sat on the redundant wheel and offered me a can of beer. The passenger window slid down silently.

'Raoul! Your suit!'

I took the beer. It was cool.

The man grinned up at me.

'There's got to be some advantage in owning a car with left hand nuts,' he said. 'Fridge in the cocktail cabinet.'

I held the can against my neck, revelling in the coolness. Forcing the cold beer down my hot throat was like swallowing knives. The man flapped his hand vaguely.

'Well, thank you,' he said. For me, that was enough. It was genuine. 'What do you do for a living?'

'Driver. Coach driver.'

'Who for?'

'Well I used to drive for a small company. Sort of one man show affair.'

'But you're not now?'

'No.'

'Not working?'

'No. I haven't driven a coach for a year.' It was the honest truth. I had lived the first three months by driving taxis on Sundays so that the owners could have their day off. Then I had turned up at the Turbigo site one day when they were short of truck drivers and had started within the hour. God knows what they were going to do with the hole when they have finished with it. Some say it is going to be one of those underground shopping centres like they have in America. At the moment it is a quarry in the centre of Paris, down below third basement level and still descending. A never ending string of trucks await their turn, night and day. You get the flag. You pull forward, your wheels slithering across the clay which is perpetually wet even in this heat. You stop. There is a noise like thunder and your truck squats. Clods of earth the size of television sets rain down on either side and you get the flag again and hope that you have enough teeth in your gearbox to drag you and your burden up to the street level. Four times a working day for the last nine months they had tried to bury me alive.

'Drink problems?'

'No.'

'Boss's wife?'

'No. My face just doesn't seem to fit at the moment. It happens like that.'

'But you're a useful sort of chap to have around. A bit pig headed.'

'But right.'

His face screwed up into a laugh.

'Yes and cheeky with it. Bosses don't like that.' He fumbled in his pocket and pulled out a business card. 'You don't know who I am do you?' he asked as he wrote on the back of the card. I shook my head. 'Thought not.' He handed me the card.

*Raoul de Mello, President of the Coach Operators'
Federation.*

'Ah,' I said.

Raoul de Mello had started at the bottom, sweeping
the garage floor and cleaning the coaches. With his wages
he had paid his fees at commercial college. He had come
back as management. In thirty years he had built up a
prosperous business whose fleet of fine coaches had been
the envy of all others. Film stars, cup-winning sports teams,
top business groups had all insisted on a Car de Mello.
Then at the height of success, some say with characteristic
shrewdness, he had sold out to his rival and bought a
fishing rod. He now divided his time between mountain
streams of the Pyrenees and his responsibilities as President
of the influential federation for coach operators.

'Go and see Artur.'

I flipped the card over and read the name.

'Artur Fromme? Autocars Fromme? He certainly
won't want me.'

'You can drive?'

'Of course.'

'Bit of a mechanic?'

'Fairly good.'

'Well that's what he wants. A garage dogsbody. It
didn't do ME any harm.'

I smiled ironically as I echoed his words.

'You don't know who I am do you?'

'You're a cheeky fellow who knows how to change
the wheel on a Rolls and does it without asking and you're
an out of work coach driver.'

'Called Simon Laperche.'

He looked at me as the name sunk in. Then he said
quietly, 'Papa Coursamel was an old friend of mine.' He
held my gaze unblinkingly. I suppose his reaction was what
I should have expected. I shrugged and offered him back
the card. He added, 'He was also the biggest fool this side
of Christendom. I had warned him years before.'

'You didn't speak in my defence.'

'I was not invited. It was not my affair. Anyway, you
were a fool as well. I trust you have learned by it?'

'I've learned how far people can push their hatred.'
'And that's why you don't get coaching jobs?'
'What do you think?'
'That's taking it too far. You've paid the price. Go and see Artur. Get back into coaches.'

I did not go to see Artur. I went to see Daniel. He was the tours manager for Cityscope. I had known him a long time. When I had worked for Coursamel we had occasionally helped him out in an emergency, supplying a coach for a city tour or a transfer. The Cityscope offices were just off the Place de l'Opéra — a large double fronted shop whose windows were hung with posters of Versailles and Chantilly and the Eiffel Tower. This was the tourist quarter. The pavements overflowed with the hideous dress sense of brightly coloured foreigners, usually bunched around the free map they could get from Galeries Lafayette. Daniel worked at a desk inside the window, sheltered from the public gaze by the hanging posters which he had cleverly arranged so that, whilst providing the privacy, they did not obscure the strategic views he needed.

I walked briskly past the agency and glanced through the poster gap between the Trianon and the Musée Grévin. His desk was empty. I went to the corner and listened to some Americans arguing over their free map. I walked back past the window. The desk was still empty so I stopped at the newspaper kiosk and pulled the papers about until the old cow told me to clear off if I was not buying anything.

I'd try just once more.

Daniel saw me. The shock on his face was instant. I lifted my hand before my mouth, suggesting a drink. He looked quickly behind him, put up a handful of fingers to mean five minutes and then angrily waved me away out of sight. I went to Charlie's Bar down the narrow street at the back of the Opera House. It was where I used to meet Daniel and listen to his incessant complaints about his wife. He loved his wife but did not know it. Charlie's was a poky place, gloomy and none too clean. It was run by an ancient Moroccan. I had asked him once if he had brought the flies with him from Rabat. He had given me a yellow toothed grin and swatted at them ineffectually with a cloth. Charlie's had one big advantage as far as we were concerned. It was not used by coach drivers.

I took a pastis with a large jug of water and sat at one of the two tables that the patron had managed to squeeze onto the pavement. Daniel came by about ten minutes later.

'You've got a bloody nerve,' he said, 'showing your face around here.'

'How's Amélie?' I shouted above the noise of the Volkswagen that was rattling like a badly adjusted chainsaw as it tried to reverse into a space near our table.

'Don't you know that...? What?'

'I said, "How's Amélie?"' I pointed to the chair.

'Oh, she's fine, fine.' He sat down and ordered a drink. 'She wants another kid.'

The car had pulled out into the street to make another attempt. The driver was a woman in her late twenties. Quite pretty. Her dark hair hung to her shoulders and swirled around her neck like a ballgown as she flung her head anxiously from one side to the other.

'She wants another kid,' I said. 'I want another job.'

'For Christ's sake, Simon, you don't think I can give you a job do you? I could probably lose mine just by being here.'

She was not going to make it this time. The nose of the car stuck out too far and the rear wheel had hit the kerb. She revved the engine to try to mount the pavement. A pointless manoeuvre — it would only make her position even worse.

'If you can lose your job that easily it's obviously not worth having,' I said.

'We can't all afford the luxury of being single. I've got mouths to feed.'

'Tell me about Autocars Fromme.'

'Fromme?'

'Yes. What kind of set up is it?'

He fiddled with his glass. He was drinking Vichy water and peppermint. The young woman had realised her mistake and pulled out again, but she had left her rear wheel too close to the other car. She would not make it next time either.

'Their garage is up in La Villette. Behind the Paris City Abattoirs.'

'What's the old man like?'

'Artur Fromme?'

'Yes.'

'Nobody's fool. He's a bit cautious — won't take risks.'

'Which is why he still has a small garage but is still in business I suppose.' That engine was still racing.

'Yes, probably. Why do you want to know?'

'Just a minute, Daniel. I can't stand this any more.'

I got up and opened the door of the car. The woman looked up at me with startled eyes. She was wearing a neat linen suit and high heeled sandals.

'Monsieur!' she started.

'Move over!' I ordered her.

'But monsieur I didn't ask...'

'Stop protesting and move over. We were enjoying a quiet drink till you came along.' I pointed to the passenger seat.

She opened her mouth; neat white teeth, and then clamped it shut and moved across. She had freckles on her nose and her thighs were suntanned. I parked the car in three moves and switched off the engine. She was saying something as I got out but I just waved my hand in dismissal and went back to Daniel at the table.

'Who was that?' He nodded at the linen suit as it disappeared down the street.

'Some woman who couldn't park a car.'

'Do you know her?'

'No,' I replied, surprised, 'do you?'

'No, of course not. I thought you knew her from the way you went up to her.' He gazed after her and I could sense an envy in his manner. 'So why do you want to know about Fromme?'

'I'm going to ask him for a job.'

His glass stopped in mid air and descended to the

table top. He stared at me. Now he really did think I was mad.

'Oh that's rich! That really is rich! You're going to ask Artur Fromme for a job? Doing what?'

'Mechanic, dogsbody. Whatever he will give me.' I remembered de Mello's instruction. 'I've got to get back into coaches.'

'Why Fromme? Why should he take you?'

'He's looking for someone.'

'But not you.'

'I come with a recommendation.'

'You?!'

I took the card from my pocket and dropped it onto the table. He picked it up. His eyebrows shot up and he looked searchingly at me as if he expected me to have grown horns or scales.

'Read the back.'

He read it.

'Well,' he said, the relief flowing over him like a cool breeze, 'with friends like that you don't need me.'

'Did I ever?'

I could smell the diesel even before I could see the coaches. Outside the garage an ancient Saviem was parked with two wheels on the sidewalk. Once a proud excursion coach, the dark green paint was now patched in several versions of green and the outdated, elaborate lettering of *Autocars A. Fromme* was faded to beige. Underfloor mid engine, gear lever in the dashboard, four wheels, plastic seats and spongy brakes. Simple, reliable, unbreakable. The jack-knife doors were open and the engine cover was ticking as it cooled down. I reached in and scooped up the driver's orders from the padded dash. *06.00 G.E.C. Nord; 07.30 Hotel de Ville - Lycée St. Ouen; 08.45 Gare de l'Est - Postes.* Factories and schools. A bread and butter coach for bread and butter work. This coach was thirty years old and had now sifted its way to the bottom of the pile.

The garage was three long sheds with vaulted part glazed roofs through which a grey light filtered to the oil-stained concrete floor below. In the pit in the corner, the electric blue crackle of an arc welder lit the chassis of a fifty three seater as a shadowy figure cursed the spark into tricks that Ampère had never dreamed of. An unused driver was perched on an oil drum, kicking his heels and watching the mechanic. He was probably the pilot of the ancient Saviem I had inspected outside, waiting for his next job. He watched me as I approached.

'Looking for the boss,' I announced.

'That's him there.' He indicated the figure in the pit. 'He's in a bad mood so don't try to sell him anything.'

'I won't.' I only had Simon Laperche to sell and the product was not in demand.

I sat on a crate and we watched the completion of the job in silence. If the driver had any curiosity about me, then he did not show it. Artur Fromme laid down the shield, turned off the power and then spat on his weld. It was a welder's signature. He climbed out of the pit.

'I'll finish that off tomorrow,' he said to nobody in particular. 'Shouldn't you be on your way to Le Plessis?' he said to the driver.

The man hopped smartly off the drum.

'I'm on my way Monsieur Fromme.'

Artur Fromme turned to me. 'What do you want?'

Standing there in his blue overalls, with his ruddy face and ginger moustache he looked more like a farmer than a coach operator. He pulled off his heavy gloves to reveal clean hands with properly clipped nails. That was not something that I could flaunt. His blue eyes pinned me.

'Well?'

I decided to go in with the big gun.

'Monsieur de Mello sent me.'

'Ah yes,' he sighed. 'I've been expecting you. Come into the office.'

He led me to the glass box which served as his office. It was the same as garage offices country wide. The nerve centre of the entire operation. In this glass box, coaches were bought and sold, customers were pampered or insulted, all the bills were paid, all the routes were devised, the wages were doled out, the arguments were settled and drivers were sacked and hired.

He flicked a switch and a vast electric fan wobbled into life on its perch on the filing cabinet and began to swing back and forth, pausing at each end of its sweep as if sluggishly following an endless argument or watching a game of lethargic tennis. Monsieur Fromme sat in a polished wooden rotating chair which creaked dryly with his every movement. The top of his desk was entirely covered with a sheet of heavy glass below which a map of France had been spread out. A map which could be consulted or ignored but which never got greasy finger marks on it.

'Sit down.' I sat. 'I'll tell you now that I don't want you. Sit down!' he roared as I made to get up. 'I don't want you but if you are any use I will take you.'

'Thanks.'

'Any trouble and you are out.' He drummed his manicured fingers on the table and inspected me. 'You've got a powerful friend in Monsieur de Mello.' I said nothing. 'Hmm!' he muttered, annoyed that he had learned no more. 'I owe him nothing and he owes me nothing but I respect his judgement. He's a very shrewd man. If he says you are all right then I'm willing to take the risk. Got your licence?'

'Yes.'

He held out his hand for it then sucked on his teeth as he examined it.

'Suspended for a year weren't you?' There was no point in denying it. I nodded. 'What did you do for a year?'

'Bit of this and that. Odd jobbing. I coped.'

'Awkward, not being able to drive.'

I fell into the trap.

'Yes it was.'

He pointedly looked at my bare forearms. First the right, then the left.

'So what have you been driving then without a licence?'

I opened my mouth to protest my innocence but before uttering a denial, I, also, looked at my forearms. My left arm was tanned dark brown from leaning on the window of the truck, my right arm was much paler.

'I drove a truck. A tipper truck on a building site.'

He threw the licence back at me.

'You've got to play straight with me Laperche, you've got no room for manoeuvre. If you cheat, I'll catch you and you'll be out.'

'I understand.' I understood that there were no flies on Artur Fromme. If he was still running his own show when others had gone to the wall then it was not by luck.

The phone rang. He picked it up. I could hear the voice of the driver resonating in the earpiece like a tinny bell on a cheap toy. He was at Le Bourget, Monsieur Fromme. He was doing the UTA staff, monsieur. His coach had been blocked.

'What do you mean it's been "blocked"?' Fromme's voice thundered.

'There's a protest or strike or something. It's the public transport union. They've blocked the exit from the police pound. I can't get out. Nobody can. They're only letting through the RATP buses. What shall I do?'

'What are you doing in the pound?'

'The police sent all the coaches over to clear the front of the terminal. We're all stuck.'

'Ring me back in half an hour if it's not settled.'

'Yes monsieur.'

Monsieur Fromme dropped the receiver to the cradle with one hand whilst the other pulled the order book across. He flipped back to today's page and then glanced up at the clock.

'Imbeciles!' he said. 'Lebrun!' he shouted through the open door. 'Oh yes, he's gone to Le Plessis,' he said to himself. He pushed the book away. 'Right. What can you do?'

'I can spit on my welds like the Army taught me.'

'I see.' His tone was even.

'And the usual mechanical stuff, injectors, filters, servos, pumps.'

'What about air conditioning units?'

'Not yet. But have you got any?'

His mouth twitched. 'Not yet.'

The phone rang again. The amused smile left his

face as he listened to the ranting voice. It was the station manager of UTA at Le Bourget explaining none too gently that Fromme had the contract for staff transport and was expected to fulfil it, come hell or high water. He would not accept the excuse of a few placards and a handful of striking bus drivers for a non-execution of the service for which Autocars Fromme were contracted and, he might add, quite generously paid. Autocars Fromme, he took the liberty of pointing out, was not the only fish in the ocean.

Monsieur Fromme placed the receiver back on the cradle with an exaggerated gesture as if it were Sèvres porcelain. He strode out into his garage and stood tapping his pen on the palm of his hand. I followed him out. Apart from the sick coach squatting over the pit and a school bus lurking in the corner, it was empty.

'Am I right in thinking that you have got a staff transport to do for UTA and that your coach is immobilised at Le Bourget?'

'That's about the strength of it.'

'Use another coach?'

'How do I contact the driver? Courier pigeon? Anyway my nearest coach is on a service at the moment. I could have done without this happening at this particular time.'

'Where does the coach pick them up from?'

'Outside the terminal. At Departures. They are a mixture of office and airside staff. They're a good bunch. It's only the station manager who's an idiot.'

'I could take that.' I nodded at the school bus. It was actually an ex-RATP bus, still in the green livery. It was not an uncommon occurrence for a coach company to buy a couple of Paris town buses secondhand at the official auctions because they were ideal for school services; they were robust and they had the reputation of having been kept in tip-top working condition.

'Yes you could. If I gave you a job. Can you drive it?'

'Semi-automatic gearbox? No problem.' We walked over to it. 'If I took down the *schoolchildren* signs and took a UTA board with me... Do you have a spare one?'

He looked at me for an instant, indecision wavering

in his eyes. I remembered what Daniel had said about him not taking risks.

'I'll look.'

He walked over to the storeroom door and I jumped up into the open bus and insinuated myself under the steering wheel. By the time he came back carrying a UTA signboard, I had taken down the school signs, started the engine, checked the fuel gauge and was waiting for the compressed air cylinder to fill up to release the brakes.

Monsieur Fromme looked to the doorway.

'We could wait for Lebrun to get back.'

'As you like.' I shrugged. It had been too good to be true. Looking in the rear-view mirror and seeing lines of seats stretching out behind me I had nearly believed it. Even if they were brown plastic and interspersed with vertical grab poles. It had so nearly worked. Suddenly he said, 'Go. Go on. We can't wait. Lebrun will be years.'

I raised my hand and eased the bus forwards towards the open doorway. I paused on the threshold for a second to allow my pupils to contract and then drove out into the sunlight.

I was back in coaches.

2

Mine was not the only vehicle travelling north on the Avenue Jean Jaurès. The traffic was crawling. At that speed the bus waddled on the pavé, wiggling its empty body on its suspension. I swore loudly at a dented Simca as it suddenly lurched out of a side street before me. I had forgotten that kind of driving. When I had flaunted wheels the size of taxicabs and had carried twenty tons of rubble on my back, nobody had got in my way. Two ladies on a bench tut-tutted at my language which had come undiluted at them from the open door. I wondered what on earth they were doing just sitting on a bench, watching the cars go past. They were metres from two lanes of slow moving traffic, breathing in the fumes and deafened by the motors but they seemed quite happy. Each to his own, after all, I was happy. I was prepared to overlook the fact that I was not driving a real coach, only a school bus. The important point was that it would soon have people in.

But when we got to Quatre-Routes at Aubervilliers then everything stopped and we sat looking at each other. Some lunatic began blowing his klaxon as if it would make the street wider. The man in front of him got out of his car, walked back and banged angrily on his roof. The idiot horn player got out, pushing the man with his door as he did so. The man pushed him back against the car. Shove, push, shout, swear. A blond haired man in a green jacket climbed menacingly out of a German registered Mercedes and walked up to the arguing drivers. He took each by the collar and pulled them easily apart. Horn player turned and socked him in the face and he went straight down as if his legs had melted. The two men stopped arguing and gaped in amazement. A sound like a factory siren came from the Mercedes and a muscular woman in grey trousers with her yellow hair tied up on her head, leaped from the car and ran noisily to the succour of her warrior. It was a mixture of Wagner and Léhar and it was all so utterly pointless.

The traffic now began to move again and suddenly the contestants and spectators were hurrying back to their cars to gain a few more metres of avenue.

The traffic ground on and at last the flags of Le Bourget came into view. And the placards. And the picket. It was being held back by a small contingent of police who were unable to stop them from flowing into the road so that they could hurl their catechism at the passing vehicles. This was not what Monsieur Fromme and I had understood by 'a few placards and a handful of bus drivers'. It had the components of a full scale industrial uprising.

One of Lecaplain's coaches ahead of me was trying to get into the airport but the crowd would not let him and the police were angrily waving him past to try to clear the road. I knew immediately what I had to do. I yanked the UTA board from its position in full view on the dash and dropped it behind me into the gangway. Whilst the police dealt with Lecaplain I slipped from my seat and pulled open the route blind box which showed through the glass above the windscreen. I madly wound the handle through a stream of the route history till I came to 'Service Spécial'. I swung the blind back up into place in its window and jumped back into my seat. As an afterthought I shut the door. I did not want any uninvited guests.

With my heart thumping I drove forward. I now looked as much like a Paris bus as I could. Enough to fool the police. If there were any bus drivers amongst the demonstrators they would know that I was not a normal service bus. I had to hope that they would suppose that I was a mechanic who had come straight from the garage to offer solidarity. In an attempt to distract them from noticing the absence of an RATP fleet number I switched on my headlights, signalled to turn into the airport and then slid open my window and sang out, 'Allez les gars, allez les gars, allez.'

The policeman blew his whistle furiously and waved me in as the crowd took up my chant.

'Let him pass! Let him pass! Reinforcements!' they shouted as they parted to let me through. To maintain the deceit I grinned and called out acknowledgments to imaginary friends in the crowd.

Once I was safely through the cordon, the crowd's attention turned out to the avenue again and I drove sedately up the terminal approach road. I could see no sign of the unfortunate Fromme coach, but then if he had been sent to the police pound as he had said on the phone, he would be across the avenue. I glanced in my rear view mirror and noticed one or two individuals gazing after me as if wondering what I intended to do. I was not so sure myself. It is not that easy to hide a bus but the obvious place presented itself. I pulled into the bus stop behind a couple of empty town buses, switched off the engine and jumped quickly out, closing the door behind me. I needed to get into the terminal building and somehow to contact my passengers. So engrossed was I in this problem that I nearly knocked over the drivers of the two buses who were gossiping on the paved forecourt. They looked at me in curiosity, they in their blue uniforms, me in my tee shirt and jeans, all three supposedly Paris bus drivers. I thought quickly.

'Where's the nearest bog? I've just eaten a duff choucroute.' Why, when I needed an escape stratagem did my mind always think of a bowel-related excuse? Their eyes flicked up from questioning my clothes to an amused perusal of my grimacing face.

One of them directed me inside the terminal. 'It's in the middle,' he said and then shouted at my rapidly disappearing back, 'Underneath the main staircase.'

Inside the long concourse the air was cool and shady. I preferred Le Bourget to its younger southern usurper, Orly. Le Bourget was an airport at the scale of man; one long line of low buildings lying along the main road to Senlis. It was simple and unpretentious. Aeroplanes took off and landed on one side of the buildings, passengers came and went on the other. The terminal building was there in the middle merely to effect the changeover. It did not have the jazz and acres of glass of Orly and to my mind it did not need them; it had history. Lindbergh, Costes, Bellonte — all the early pioneers had flown from this field.

I walked rapidly through the sparse collection of travellers who were drifting about the floor like random molecules in some giant microscope. On my right the kiosks were occupied by car rental companies and hotel and tourism people. The airline check-in desks were ranged along the wall to my left. I carried on up the hall to Departures. There was no group of UTA staff waiting there for a coach. Damn! I turned and walked back towards a UTA desk at which a line of passengers were checking in for the Tananarive flight. Some were softly fanning themselves with their tickets as they queued. According to the airport information board, it was cooler in Madagascar than it was in Paris. Two desks along, a statuesque Martiniquan was preparing a pile of boarding cards for the next flight. I waited till she had finished counting and then said,

'I'm the driver for your staff bus. Where can I find my passengers?'

She opened a mouth full of pink tongue and white teeth and then called over her shoulder, 'Monsieur Dupertuille!'

Through the open doorway of the back office bounced a little bundle of a man with a round head set with black darting eyes and an equally black moustache. He was sweating inside a uniform jacket laden down with a golden spaghetti of braid. The moment I saw him I knew he was trouble.

'Well my sweet, you can't do without me?' he said as he passed his hand over the Martiniquan's uniformed bottom. She rolled her eyes till the whites showed her contempt and moved away from his pressing contact. Opening a brown and beige hand like a tropical flower, she indicated me.

'The driver for the staff bus.'

The face immediately assumed an expression befitting the station manager of an international airline who needed to exert his authority over another male and before the audience of his harem. I watched the eyebrows sink and the lower jaw slide forward and I began to ask myself what was it that I had found so unsatisfying about shifting mounds of earth.

'Who are you?' he spat at me.

I glanced insolently in the direction of the check-in girl who had just told him who I was.

'I'm the driver for your staff bus.' I kept my voice even.

'No you're not. Where's Patrick?'

'The police have put all the coaches over in their pound till the demonstration is under control. I imagine he is with his coach.'

'That's not my problem. Why isn't he here?' He squeezed through the gap between two desks to confront me on the concourse. I shrugged. 'What time do you call this, anyway? Your contract is for half past one.' He stabbed his hand at the enormous clock. 'It's now two fifteen.' I swung an interested gaze towards the clock and then ostentatiously adjusted my watch. Behind his back I caught a glimpse of the big pink mouth opened in surprise before a brown hand covered it. As I had intended, Dupertuille was not amused. 'Don't you try and be funny with me.' He poked me in the chest with his finger.

'Just show me where my passengers are, Monsieur Duberville.'

'Dupertuille!' he screamed. 'I am Monsieur Dupertuille! I am the UTA Station Manager. I don't take orders, I give orders.'

'Oh good, I've come to the right person then. If you will give me my orders I can get on with my job.'

His little face was becoming redder. He looked like a radish. His smouldering eyes blistered my casual dress. When I had gone to see Monsieur Fromme I had assumed that I would be sweeping out the garage for the first few weeks, there had seemed no sense in putting on my best jeans for that.

'Where is your coach?'

'Outside Arrivals.'

'Take it up to Departures and wait there.'

'Yes sir.'

As I turned away I winked at the Martiniquan. She glanced nervously at Dupertuille.

I stepped outside and the kerosene laden heat slapped me in the face like a swing door. I stopped to take a breath and saw the two RATP bus drivers making a slow inspection of my bus. I turned my back and watched their reflections in the terminal windows until they walked down the far side then I turned and sprinted across the road and banged open the air doors. I jumped into my seat and glanced in the mirror. They had just found the small *Autocars Fromme* plaque down by the rear wheel. When I started the engine they both looked up and as I pulled away one of them smacked the side of the bus with the flat of his hand to tell me to stop. I ignored him and roared off towards the Departures canopy a hundred metres away where I pulled up alongside the kerb with squealing brakes.

I jumped out and hurried into the terminal. Dupertuille was marching across the concourse at the head of his column of staff like a general on parade, the gold braid on his uniform adding to the illusion. Behind him straggled an uneven line of check-in staff, office girls, baggage loaders and cleaners. Some were chatting in pairs, some carried their newspapers or lunch bags or uniform jackets. They were hot, tired and fed up but bore it all with a resigned good humour. All they wanted to do was get out of the airport and go home.

'You!' Dupertuille clicked his fingers at me. 'Take us to your coach now that you have deigned to arrive.'

I theatrically looked over my shoulder as if I had thought that he was talking to somebody behind me and then addressed the group directly.

'Ladies and gentlemen if you would please follow me to my transport I shall endeavour to drive you home.'

A couple of the staff smiled.

'At last!' a baggage loader said. 'That's good news.'

'You don't need to talk to my staff, just drive your coach.' Dupertuille was containing his anger behind clenched teeth.

I looked over the top of him as if he were not there.

'This way please ladies and gentlemen.' I led them through the doors to the bus. Dupertuille stopped dead on the pavement, his jaw working fiercely as if fighting a guerilla attack by chewing gum.

'Ah no. No. I will not permit it! I will not permit it!'

His staff ignored his posturing and flowed both sides of him like metro travellers round a beggar.

'This is a bit of a laugh,' a girl in a short pink skirt said as she skipped up the steps.

'Ladies on first please,' I announced. 'Seats are a bit limited. Some of you gentlemen may have to stand.'

Dupertuille bustled forward and pushed out his arm to bar the way.

'This is preposterous. Your contract clearly states...'

'Oh don't be such a pig's bum, Du-Du, we just want to go home.' The voice was cultured and came from a magnificent negress, squeezed into a tailored suit. She pushed his arm aside and wafted up the step in an expensive haze of Chanel. Then in the commonest Paris accent you could expect she called, 'Pass right down the bus, elbows in your pockets and breathe in.'

A wave of laughter ran down the bus. Dupertuille turned on his heel and scorched the marble floor into the terminal.

'Waste of time,' a voice said behind me. 'They'll all have to get off again.'

'He's a cheerful blighter,' a lad observed as he passed me to get on the bus.

I turned to find the two RATP bus drivers looking very pleased with themselves. The thinner one said, 'You didn't fool us, you know.'

I quickly sized up the queue. About a dozen left.

'I didn't try to fool you, mate. I just did what I was told. Take the bus to the airport, collect these workers and take them home.'

'Blackleg!' the other driver said.

'Don't be ridiculous. How can I be a blackleg? I'm not in your union.'

'Taking our jobs,' the thin one hissed.

'Now you are being stupid. This was never an RATP contract.'

'You'll never get out of the airport,' the thin one insisted. Then he shouted into the bus as the last passenger boarded, 'You'll never get out of the airport!' This last announcement was met with a chorus of jeers and whistles. His temper was not assisted by the voice of the cultured negress exhorting him to go and play with himself. He turned to the other driver. 'Go and tell Red Mike!'

'Look,' I said to the thin one as his mate busied his way across to find Red Mike, 'I've got no argument with you. I'm just doing my job.'

'And I've got no argument with you. Just get your passengers off and you will be free to leave.'

'And who is going to stop me?' I looked him directly in the eye. 'Are you going to stop me?' I cracked my knuckles and took a step towards him. 'Are you?'

'Oh!' He backed off in an exaggerated manner. 'Playing the tough guy now are we? Well we'll soon see about that.' He turned and began to walk purposefully across the taxi lanes to the picket. 'We'll soon see about that!' he threw over his shoulder.

Somebody rang the bell inside the bus and everybody laughed again. I was not laughing. Walking in a direct line across the approach road, that driver would easily reach the picket before I could get to the exit. I would try nevertheless. I jumped into the bus and slid into my seat.

'Hold tight everyone,' I shouted as I started the engine. 'We may have to take some avoiding action.'

I pulled away from the kerb and in my mirror saw about a dozen men running across to cut us off. Zigzagging through the taxis on a tangential course, they just managed to drum on the side of the bus with their hands before I outsped them. The noise was startling. Two of the women screamed. To make matters worse I had just noticed that somebody had picked up the UTA sign from the floor and propped it up in a side window. We had run up our colours.

Paddling across the road before me, a pair of lime green Americans towing matching Samsonites suddenly stopped to consider Plato, or the meaning of infinity or whatever it is that people do when they stand in front of an accelerating bus. I blew my horn and aimed behind them. They started to retreat, nearly falling over their suitcases in the process and then realised their mistake. The draught of our passage took the woman's straw hat off and bowled it along in our wake.

'Look out! Here they come!' the man in the front seat warned me.

And come they did. Once Red Mike or whatever his name was had been appraised of the situation he had obviously decided that action was just what the men were waiting for. As one mass the picket turned from the main road and surged across the airport approach road towards the terminal building. Jumping over fences, vaulting the walls, stumbling up and down kerbs and across the scrawny flower bed, they were aiming at one point: the top corner where the exit road turned through one hundred and eighty degrees. I would be a sitting duck there.

'Is there another way out?' I yelled to the bus.

'Through Cargo,' a voice shouted but just as quickly another said, 'It's too late, they've blocked it.'

It made no sense to pound towards a crowd blocking the road and they had already begun to link arms. I could only intimidate the front fifty: the five hundred behind them would not let them move aside. I had to do something so I stamped on the brakes. The top surface of the hot tarmac rolled up like the skin off a boiled beetroot. The bus slithered crookedly to a halt.

'All clear behind?' I shouted.

'No. Yes. Go!'

'Hold tight to the poles,' I instructed them and we lurched off backwards at 30kph, the reverse gear screaming like a banshee. I had a vague idea that although the ground clearance was not as good as a coach, I might be able to jump a kerb and turn the wrong way up the entrance road but a white lorry suddenly driving up behind me, flashed its lights and I had to ease up to avoid a collision. He went past me, blowing his horn and then turned left down an alleyway between the buildings. It looked like some sort of delivery van.

The crowd was now jubilant with its assured success. With arms tightly linked, it chanted and stamped its way towards us with an intentionally slow menace. We were trapped.

'Follow the van. Follow the van. Go airside!' the man in the front seat suddenly shouted. 'Quick, the barrier will be up!'

I could see myself in court again as easily as winking.

I started off forwards again at full pelt as if I intended to drive straight into the picket line. I had to reach the alleyway between the buildings before the crowd did. As I roared towards them I could see the front line wavering but as I had expected, it was not allowed to stop, urged on by the ignorant hundreds behind.

'Chrissake you'll kill 'em!' someone protested.

'Left by the bins.' The calm voice of the man in the front seat came to me. 'Down the alleyway.'

'Hang on to everything!' I yelled.

RATP buses are built narrower than coaches and with a tapered front and rear so that they can filter through the traffic easily. As we leaned hard into the corner and lurched into the alleyway a bare twenty metres before the picket, I was thankful for those dimensions. I nevertheless clipped a drainpipe with the bumper.

The van ahead of us was just passing through the control point which prevented unauthorised persons from 'going airside'. The airside section of an airport is subject to all kinds of rules and regulations. It is a strictly reserved area controlled by the Tower Control. The vehicles which are permitted to circulate on the same aprons as the aircraft have to be fitted with an orange flashing light and have a radio link with Tower Control. Their every movement has to be authorised, their radius of operation is strictly laid down. Baggage handling vehicles can only move within certain lines painted on the concrete; passenger buses, aircrew buses, maintenance and refuelling vehicles all have to be marshalled to avoid accidents, to concur with customs regulations and to maintain the security of the airport.

'What do I..?'

'Put your emergency flashers on,' my mentor said,

then turned to the group. 'Settle down, straighten up, look bored,' he instructed them. The barrier was beginning to descend after the passage of the van. 'Blow your horn once.' I did so. The barrier lifted. 'Don't rush. 20kph is the limit.'

I glanced in my mirror. The staff had recovered from their excitement and had tidied themselves up. I crawled past the check point ready to stop if challenged. The security officer looked up questioningly and his hand reached across the desk for something. I lifted my hand from the wheel in casual salute and the UTA board came into his view and he thought better of whatever he had intended doing and touched his cap instead. I drove on through.

The van made a sharp right turn ahead of me and ran along the airside edge of the passenger terminal building. Before me opened a vista of concrete and grass, uncluttered and open to the horizon. To my left, three or four airliners were nose on to the terminal, multifarious vehicles nudging in and out with hoses and fork lifts, platforms and containers.

'Which line do we take?' the man in the front seat called up the bus.

'Take the red. Take the red,' a voice replied.

I picked out the red line painted on the concrete apron and stuck to it, trying not to let my nervousness show. We described a gentle curve which took us way out behind the aircraft. Nobody seemed to take any notice of us at all although I was stupidly aware of the wide slow sweep of the radar scanner on the tower.

'Look out Jaquel has seen us!' a warning came from someone in the bus.

'Who the hell is Jaquel?' I asked my mentor. He shrugged.

'He's the apron marshal,' a baggage handler said.

In the mirror I could see a miniature baggage tractor detach itself from a group and bounce across the concrete behind us, orange light flashing and thin horn sounding. It was then that things began to go haywire as helpful suggestions were fired at me from everywhere.

'Speed up, he can't catch us on that scooter.'

I put my foot down.

'Look out the 058 is moving off the stand!'

'Go behind it.'

'Go in front. It's a Caravelle. Engines at the back.'

'Jaquel's catching us up. He's waving.'

I flung the bus off the red line and swerved around a train of baggage trolleys.

'Where do I go now?' I pleaded as I passed before the startled gaze of the tow tractor which was just disconnecting from the Caravelle.

'We've lost Jacquel. He's arguing with the trolley tug.'

'No he isn't. He's come round it.'

On our left now opened up two lines of hangars facing each other across an untidy jumble of planes. I could see a complete engine swinging slowly on a mobile crane and fitters in orange overalls wandering about on various errands.

In desperation I shouted, 'What about down here?'

'Yes, go down through Maintenance.'

The tyres whistled on the shiny apron as I swung the bus down between the hangars.

'No, stop! There's a security jeep at the far end.'

Merde. This was getting worse.

'Look,' I shouted, 'You lot work in this bloody airport. Get us out of here before we all get put behind bars!' The servo on the steering groaned and clunked as I pulled the bus around on full lock again. In the midst of all the mayhem I found myself calmly making a note to myself to tell Fromme about it when I got back. It would need checking. 'Where do I go now?' I yelled.

'Straight ahead! Go up to the beacon and turn left. We'll take the perimeter road.'

We were now leaving the buildings behind and striking out on a broad concrete track. On either side of us stretched the vast green nothingness of the field itself. I felt as conspicuous as a penguin on an iceberg.

'Turn left!' a voice instructed.

'No, not here,' another contradicted.

I turned left and was relieved to see that it brought the perimeter fence into view, albeit in the distance, and that there was a line to follow on the concrete.

'I'll follow the orange line shall I?'

'What orange line? There shouldn't be an orange line.'

But I was not listening. I had just looked in my mirror and my heart had nearly stopped.

'There's a bloody plane coming up behind us!' I screamed, my voice rising an octave in fright.

'Don't worry! There's nothing to worry about. We are on a taxiway, that's all.'

'What do you mean "a taxiway"?' I shrieked as the nose of the aircraft began to fill the mirror.

'It is sure to turn off soon. It's just going to the runway to take off.'

'Oh it's one of ours,' a woman exclaimed.

'Oh goody! That makes all the difference, being run down by one of your own planes.' My sarcasm was wasted.

'The 2022,' somebody else confirmed. 'Pass the UTA board down.'

My foot had automatically pushed the accelerator to the floor the moment that the nose of the aircraft had appeared in my mirror but for all the qualities designed into the Paris bus, the ability to outrun an airliner across an airfield was not one that the RATP had considered necessary to specify. I seemed to have entered a dream where time had slowed down. The bus was bucketing down the taxiway at the limit of its governor but the sheer expanse of nothingness in which we were travelling gave the impression that we were standing still. And then a surrealist aspect was introduced when the airliner began to flash its landing lights at me as if it wanted to overtake.

I heard my detached voice coming out of a void at me, as I said to no-one in particular.

'He's flashing his lights at me. What do I do?'

'It's alright. It's Jean-Michel. He's saying hello.'

'Saying hello?'

I looked in the mirror. Two of the girls were holding up the UTA board to the deep back window and waving and blowing kisses at the pilot. Every time they waved, he flashed his lights. The world had gone mad. I snapped myself back to reality.

'I can see the perimeter fence ahead,' I shouted to the man in the front seat.

'When you reach it I think you should turn right and go up as far as that green shed. I have a feeling there is an emergency access gate there.'

I nodded and then with a numbed relief, watched the plane disappear from my mirror as it veered down a taxiway at rightangles to ours to reach the end of the main runway. I eased up the speed and the noise in the bus descended a few decibels. One of the girls swung back up the aisle from the back.

'That was fun!' she said.

We had lost the apron marshal somewhere in our flight, I was not sure where, but we were still not out of the airport. As I gingerly drove along the track towards the green hut I cast my eyes about but could see no pursuit, no vehicles with sirens screeching and lights flashing. Perhaps they were waiting at the green hut.

'Going out the Dugny gate?' A man appeared at my elbow.

'Is that what it is called? By this hut?' I slowed the bus to a crawl and edged past the hut. Sure enough, there was a gate which seemed to give access on to a minor road outside the airport. What was more surprising was that there did not appear to be any form of lock to it.

'Yeah, that's it,' the man confirmed and then produced a large screwdriver from his jacket. 'You'll need me to fix the alarm.'

'Alarm! What alarm?'

'Well you didn't think they'd put gates around the airport without detector alarms on them did you? Wouldn't make sense.' He shook his head as if talking to a simpleton. The possibility that the gate might have been alarmed had not entered my mind. 'Can you get through just one gate?'

I quickly estimated the width.

'Just.'

'Good. Come on then,' he said to the man in the

front seat. 'I'll need you to open the gate whilst I disable the alarm.'

'How do you do that? Won't they notice?' I asked.

The look the man gave me really did show what an imbecile I was. He stood on the step in the open doorway and pointed with his screwdriver.

'You see that grey box? There's one at each hinge end.' I nodded. 'There's a peg on the gate which fits in there and holds closed a switch. As soon as a gate is swung, the peg comes out and off goes the alarm.'

'How do you know?'

'I'm a maintenance electrician.'

'So what are you going to do?'

'Easy. I stick my screwdriver in the slot alongside the peg and I hold the switch closed. But I need someone to open and close the gate. I can't do everything, I'm not a bloody octopus.'

I held my breath as he jiggered his screwdriver into the grey box and the man from the front seat unlatched the gate and gently pulled it open. I edged the bus through the gap. I had about ten centimetres on each side. As we cleared it, the staff cheered good humouredly. It all seemed a picnic to them. We had just escaped a riot, made an unauthorised incursion into a restricted area, been pursued by airport security and chased up a taxiway by an airliner and now we were calmly disabling the electronic security system of the airport.

The gate was closed behind us and the screwdriver slowly withdrawn. Nothing happened. The man climbed over the gate and back into the bus to another round of cheering.

'Well the alarm didn't go off,' I said.

His words fell like a sack of cement on my toe.

'Oh you can't tell. You wouldn't hear it from here.' He pointed his screwdriver back towards the airport. 'It goes off in the control tower.' He grinned and nodded. 'Better get moving, just in case.'

I would not have been able to describe the suburb of Dugny to save my life. To employ an appropriate metaphor; I drove through it on automatic pilot. The staff were unconcerned with my state, they were buzzing with laughter and anecdotes, still high from the excitement which they merely saw as 'fun'. I only began to take notice of my surroundings when we passed under the Périphérique and entered Paris proper. By the time that I drew up at their contracted destination — the Invalides Air Terminal in the centre of the city — they were calling me 'Simon' and inviting me to parties.

I waved the last one off the step and wearily closed the door. The journey back through Paris with the slow crawl up the rue Lafayette and the knot of vehicles around the Gare du Nord just about finished me off. It was nearly six o' clock when I drove the bus back through the big doors. Monsieur Fromme stood and watched me reverse it into its place in the corner of the garage then he pointed to his office.

'I've had Dupertuille on the phone. Twice.'

'Ah.'

'He was nearly having a fit.'

'I did the job.'

'You were also very rude to him.'

'Who says so?'

He ignored my reckless challenge.

'If you are going to work for me you are not going to insult my clients.'

'Am I going to work for you then?'

'No matter how stupid they are. Do you understand that Laperche?'

'Yes Monsieur Fromme.'

'Be at the garage tomorrow morning at seven.'

'Yes monsieur.'

'I have also received three telephone calls from your passengers who seem to think that you are some kind of a hero.' I smiled. 'You're not.' I stopped smiling. 'Now get out and be on time tomorrow.'

3

Monsieur Fromme strode out of his office. 'Laperche!' I put the file back down to the workbench and turned, wiping my hands on my overalls as I did so.

'Never mind that,' he indicated the track rod end clamped in the vice, 'Get your tools.' He pointed at a coach parked by the open door. 'Take the fifty three up to Orly. LeGuennec has got a faulty compressor on the nine nine two. He's doing a Pan Am transfer.'

I was already throwing loose tools into my bag.

'How does he know it's a duff compressor?'

'No air. He can hear the compressor running but he still gets no air.'

It was one of the new Saviems with air assisted everything — steering, gear change, clutch. No air and the coach was crippled. I scrabbled in my box of bits, found some odd clips and lengths of hose and stuffed them into my bag, just in case.

'Where is he?'

'Orly arrivals, baggage pickup.' Monsieur Fromme watched me as I unbuttoned my overalls. 'You'll need those. You'll have to repair it on site. It's undriveable.'

I rolled the overalls up into a ball and pushed them between the handles of my bag.

'I'm taking them with me, don't worry. I'll put them on when I get there. He won't want grease smeared on the driving seat.' Fromme nodded. He knew. He was testing me. 'When is the flight due in?'

'In ten minutes.'

Orly was forty five minutes away on a good run.

'I'd better get going.'

It was a bad run. When I pulled up alongside LeGuennec's coach it was an hour and a quarter later. The stranded coach was sitting with the doors open, utterly empty. I slung my tool bag well inside and then went off in search of the driver. I got about five metres.

'You can't leave that coach there. You'll have to move it.' The policeman stood with his hands on his hips and nodded over his shoulder at the coaches. 'Only three allowed in the bay at a time. You're the fourth. You'll have to go over to the coach park and wait. They'll call you on the tannoy when there's a space.'

'Which coach do you want me to move?'

The policeman looked at me carefully.

'How many have you got?'

'Two. One working and one not. Can you give me five minutes to find the driver of the working one?'

'But it's you. I saw you drive up.'

'No, I'm the mechanic who's been sent to mend the broken down coach. If you'll let me find the driver I can get him to take the coach I've just brought.'

'Five minutes, then you get a ticket.'

I thanked him but could not see why. As I walked along the front of the terminal building I saw LeGuennec through the glass. He was talking on the phone. I rapped on the window with a coin. He turned around, the irritation on his Breton face immediately changing to recognition. He said something quickly into the phone and put it down. He waved me to the nearest door.

'That was the boss. I'd wondered where the hell you'd got to.'

'Top end of the Boulevard Raspail was choc a bloc. Where's your group? Have they arrived yet?'

'Yeah. About half an hour ago.' He began to shoulder a path through the travellers on the concourse. 'I'll go back by the boulevard Montparnasse then.'

'Yeah, good idea.'

'What have you brought me?'

'The fifty three.'

'O.K. There's my guide over there.'

He pointed at a girl dressed in a sky blue two piece

suit and toting a Pan Am bag slung over her shoulder. She was surrounded by a group of brightly coloured Americans of gargantuan proportions.

'Jesus! They would bugger the suspension on any coach.'

The girl spoke a mostly correct French with an open American accent. Pan Am imported students from the USA each season. It paid them peanuts and did not bother with work permits and the girls perfected their French and broadened their horizons. That was the theory of it.

When the girl saw us coming she turned to the group, clapped her hands for attention and then began quacking at them in American. They arose and dragged their cases out towards the coach. These cases with wheels on the bottom were still a novelty for us Parisians but were mightily unpopular with the airport porters. One of the latter had cornered me in the basement bar one night and explained to me through a haze of pastis and garlic just how these suitcases were a devil's invention, product of the international capitalist conspiracy to deprive the proletariat masses of an honest day's crust. Or something like that. The porters at Orly were quite a bolshie lot.

We strode out of the terminal to find the policeman standing before the coach, notebook in hand.

'Merde!' LeGuennec said.

'Why did you say "murrd"?' the girl enquired.

He jerked his head in the direction of the cop and then bent to open the luggage doors on the coach.

'Tell them to just put their cases here in line and get on the coach,' I said to the girl, 'And then go and chat to the cop.'

LeGuennec and I began to load Samsonites into the boot. They were a bloody nuisance. They would not stack because they were all rounded corners and slippery plastic. It was like trying to build a garden wall with blocks of wet soap. At last the cases were stowed, the pavement was clear and we were both drenched in sweat.

The girl's tinkling laughter came to us as we straightened up.

'All right, no need to have an orgasm,' LeGuennec muttered.

I glanced at the distracted cop.

'That kid's doing all right.'

'Yeah I suppose so.' He called to her, 'Come on. On the road!'

She gave the cop a dazzling smile and broke away as if she were being dragged off against her will. It was quite a performance.

'Don't forget this!' I unplugged the microphone from the dashboard of LeGuennec's old coach and handed it across to him.

He pulled a face. Each driver was responsible for his own microphone.

'Thanks.'

I watched as LeGuennec drove away and then nodded to the cop.

'I'm going to try to get this one going so that I can get it off the bay, O.K.?' He shrugged. There was not much he could do about it.

I got uncomfortably hot working outside in overalls. I would normally have taken my jeans off but the gaping holes in my top layer would have been a trifle too indiscreet for the public and so I swore and sweated instead. My temper was not helped by twice having to turn passengers out of the coach. They insisted that mine was the Air France shuttle coach to the Invalides Air Terminal. In the end I shut the doors and let it cook.

It took me half an hour of bending, prodding and stretching to find the problem and another thirty minutes to repair it. The compressor was functioning perfectly; LeGuennec had confirmed that once you had got the engine cover open you could hear it working. It was compressing the air beautifully and pushing it into the reservoir from which it was leaking almost as quickly. I bled the remainder of air from the reservoir, making sure that I kept my eyes covered so as to avoid muck and dust being blown in, then I unbolted the valve. I sat on the kerb and inspected the mechanism carefully, working all the bits that I could move. A rumble of retrothrusters rolling around the building announced the arrival of another airliner. In about thirty minutes the passengers would wander out through the many sets of automatic sliding glass doors and then fight for taxis or pester me to take them to the Invalides Air Terminal despite the fact that my coach was not blue and white and did not have *Air France* written on it anywhere.

My reverie was rudely interrupted by the Estournet coach which was parked next to me. It started up and threw an oily bucketful of diesel fumes into my face. I staggered upright, coughing the gases out of my lungs. The driver had not noticed and there was no point in making an issue of it. I was stupid to sit on the kerb with my head at the same level as an exhaust pipe.

I replaced the washers in the valve, adjusted the seat clearance and then bolted the valve back into place and connected the hoses. I started the engine and ran it for a while and was gratified to see the needle on the manometer slowly rising as the compressed air reservoir began to build up pressure. I took off my overalls and slung them on the floor in the gangway. I left the coach with the motor running and went back inside the terminal to wash my hands. The toilets were in the basement, presided over by the usual sour faced matron with a saucer of twenty centime pieces. I worked the liquid soap well into the grime of my pores and under my finger nails before turning on the taps. That was the secret of efficient hand cleaning. Let the soap get at the grease first, then rinse the whole lot off together.

As I rode up the escalator to the ground level again I seemed to register the noise of the airport for the first time. The high echoing roof under which the bing-bong announcements reverberated themselves into an incoherent symphony; the dull rhythmic thudding of the escalator steps as they metamorphosed into flat steel and then disappeared under the floor; the jingling rattles and squeaks of luggage trolleys being pushed into ankles; the clack-clacking of heels on the marble tiled floor; they all came together with the shrieks and calls to mix with the babble of a dozen languages and make the unmistakeable multi-layered cacophony that was an airport terminal at full speed. It was a magic for me. I loved the vitality of it just as I loved the incongruity of its night-time somnolence.

A small collection of men were grouped around a couple. They watched with embarrassed interest as the man and woman argued; the man, waving his grey-suited arms vaguely in the direction of Paris and the woman in her lightweight linen suit, standing calm and aloof and replying in monosyllables. I looked again. I had seen that suit before. And that swinging dark shoulder length hair. It was the lady who could not park a Volkswagen. Small world, I mused as I circumnavigated them.

'You don't seem to care,' the man's voice was raised, 'This is an important technical team. Find some way! That's what you hostesses are here for isn't it? Facilitation?'

Now that I was nearer I could see that the hostess was not aloof, she was almost on the brink of tears.

'I don't understand,' she said, 'I've tried ringing Buisson but the number is unobtainable.'

'Well do something. We can't leave them here.'

I slowed down and turned towards the group.

'I hope you don't mind me interrupting,' I said.

The man looked up my jeans to my open-necked shirt and said, 'Yes we do, we're busy,'

'What do you want? Oh!' the hostess said as she recognised me. 'It's you again.'

'Clear off!' the man said and then looked quickly at the woman. 'He's not a friend or anything is he?'

'No, just a man who parks cars.' Her voice had a tinge of disappointment in it as if I had not come up to the mark.

'OK,' I said. 'Please yourselves. You won't get Buisson on the phone and you won't get his coach but that's no concern of mine.'

I walked away. Some people just don't want to be helped. I was almost at the automatic doors when I heard running heels and her hand plucked at my sleeve.

'Monsieur, please, wait.'

I turned around and looked into her freckled face. It was flushed with the running and her hair was still swinging from the movement.

'What did you say? What did you mean?'

Her breasts rose and fell gently in her silk blouse as she tried to recapture her breath.

'Well how nice it is to meet again so soon.' I held my hand out and she gingerly shook it. Her face was hot but her hand was cold.

'Yes, look Monsieur, what was it you said about Buisson?'

'I presume we are talking about the same Buisson? Autocars Buisson et Frères?' She nodded. 'And I suppose that you booked them for your transfer?'

'Yes, they should have been here an hour ago. We've been waiting ages and the Minister is very angry.'

'The Minister? That oaf in the grey suit?'

'Shh!' She winced. 'The Minister of Commerce and Industry.'

'Well Buisson can't send you any coaches because he was forced into administrative liquidation two weeks ago. The garage is under seal and the services have probably been cut off which is why the phone is out of order.' I could see the comedy of the situation. 'It's a bit ironic isn't it? Buisson was probably closed down by one of your Minister's inspectors.'

'Oh.' Her face crumpled.

I turned away and the door swung open before me, wafting in the bouquet of kerosene and diesel fumes from the real outside. I needed to keep my job and wasting time at Orly was not the way to do it.

'Just a minute,' I called at her retreating back, 'Mademoiselle!'

She stopped and turned. 'Madame,' she corrected.

I made a mental note. She saw me do it.

'How many in your group?' I asked.

Don't be an idiot Laperche.

'Twenty two.'

'Where are you taking them?'

Don't do it.

'Lunch at Maxim's.' I looked at my watch and raised my eyebrows. 'We're already late,' she added.

'Have they got any baggage?'

'It's gone direct to the hotel in a van. Calberson's.'

You're a fool Simon Laperche. An utter fool. Don't do it.

'That green coach there. It's mine. I'm going down empty to Paris. I'll take you but make it snappy.' She looked out of the window and then stared at me as if uncertain. 'Go! Go! Go!' I said and flapped my hand.

They were from Romania, apparently. Under her directions they chattered and smiled their way onto Fromme's coach as if it were the most normal thing in the world to wait an hour. Perhaps in Romania it was. Now that his train was back on the rails the Minister was going to play engine driver, guard and signalman. He turned on the charm, choosing to overlook my jeans and casual shirt. Wonderfully flexible these politicians.

'Straight to the Rue Royale, my man, we've got a lunch appointment and you've got plenty of lost time to make up.'

I turned sedately in my seat to point out that it was not me who had lost the time but caught sight of the woman behind him, frantically shaking her head to me.

'Yes sir,' I said.

Hell, it was too hot to argue anyway. I would go down to Paris, dump them in the Rue Royale and that would be that. The rest of the day would be their problem.

The hostess moved down the coach, tending to the comfort of the delegation. In my mirror I watched her linen bottom as it wriggled down the aisle between the Romanian businessmen. The Minister had taken the front seat with the best view, naturally.

We caught up with the Air France shuttle as we came up through the underpass and I mentally prepared myself to sit and look at its squat rear end all the way to Paris but it turned onto a slip road which ran down to the old Route Nationale Seven. Perhaps the coach was not in service after all. But it had people on board. Even through the smoked glass I could see them. I realised the significance just in time.

'Hold on!' I shouted over my shoulder as I braked

hard and swerved down the slip road behind the shuttle.

'What the devil?' the Minister blustered.

Despite my warning, the sudden manoeuvre caught the hostess off balance and with the balletic finesse of a person losing a slow motion battle with centrifugal force, she swivelled on one foot and gracefully sat on the lap of a surprised but otherwise contented Romanian engineer.

'Where the devil are you going? Don't you know the way to Paris? Go down the autoroute!' The Minister was obviously accustomed to giving orders.

I bit my lip and said nothing as we joined a sporadic stream of vehicles rattling over the patchy tarmac and cobbles of the Nationale. The Air France coach was about fifty metres ahead. The woman made her way back up to the front of the coach where the Minister remained slouched across the two seats that he thought befitted his station in life.

'The idiot's going the wrong way,' he said to nobody in particular. 'If we are any later for our lunch you will be in big trouble.' He addressed the last remark to the standing woman.

'There's a guide seat under the dash,' I said as I steered around a wobbling mobylette. 'Just pull that white handle. It folds out. Unless you prefer to sit on my lap as well.'

She scowled at me, unfolded the seat and squeezed herself onto it.

'There's no mike, I'm afraid.'

'No matter.' She shrugged.

'We were supposed to be giving them a view of the new Rungis market on the way in to Paris,' the Minister pointed out testily. 'You can see it from the autoroute.'

'If you think we've got the time I can turn down this next avenue and show them the perimeter. It'll only take five minutes.'

'No, no, we can't risk it. We're late enough as it is.'

He was beginning to grate my cheese. I turned left towards the market. The woman's eyes stared at me pleadingly.

'What the devil do you think you're doing now?' he

spluttered. 'I said we haven't got time.'

'We've got all the time in the world,' I replied and nodded at the overbridge as we passed under the autoroute. 'That is where you wanted to be, up there. Eight lanes of traffic going nowhere fast.'

'A temporary delay. It'll soon clear.'

'There's the market on our right. I'm going to turn right and right again and rejoin the Nationale into Paris.'

Two minutes later we passed back under the inert autoroute.

'That beige coach sitting up there,' I pointed to the Estournet that had spat diesel fumes in my face, 'left Orly half an hour before us. He will be in Paris half an hour behind us.' I glanced across at the politician. One doesn't often get the chance, so what the hell? 'I don't tell you how to run the government. Don't tell me how to drive a coach.' It wasn't very original, but satisfyingly offensive nonetheless.

'I always find it very interesting,' the woman spoke up quickly and loudly to cover the Minister's puffing, 'to pick up the little tricks of different trades.' She looked at me with a plastic smile welded to her face. 'How did you know the autoroute was blocked?'

'Only guesswork!' the Minister exploded. 'Pure guesswork.'

'Partly guesswork,' I admitted, 'but partly brains.' It always annoys powerful people to be reminded that they only have the same reasoning organs as other mortals. 'Air France run shuttle departures to the Invalides Air Terminal every twenty minutes. We were following one of their coaches out of the airport but he did not go on the autoroute. Why not? Air France, being a state financed monopoly...' I glanced across at the Minister, '...it can afford to equip all its coaches with two way radio. The coach we were following had just received a message from the coach which had left twenty minutes before him to say that it was stuck in a jam on the autoroute. So he decided to go down the Nationale. I followed him. Simple.'

'Sounds very clever to me,' she said.

The Minister looked out of the window and said nothing.

I took them across the Pont Alexandre III and up between the Grand Palais and the Petit Palais, pausing as I crossed the Champs Elysées so that they could get a good view up to the Arc de Triomphe and down to the Concorde. As I continued straight across and up the Avenue de Marigny I knew that the Minister wanted to tell me that I was going the wrong way but did not want to be made to look a fool again. Taking the right into the rue St. Honoré and right again into the Rue Royale I pulled up on the correct side of the street, directly outside Maxim's. I would let him work out for himself how he would have turned a thirteen metre coach around in the Rue Royale.

Parked in the taxi rank in the middle of the street were two blue and grey Citroen Safaris — the long load carrying estate cars favoured by any enterprise that wanted to move a ton at one hundred and eighty kilometres an hour. When you spend as much time as I do in the streets of Paris, you become accustomed to seeing the vehicles of the ORTF — the national radio and television company — in the most unlikely places. They were probably doing a documentary in the Tuileries Gardens.

One of the two doormen turned and went quickly in to the restaurant to warn the maitre d' of our arrival whilst the other came forward to welcome the group and usher them in. First out of the coach behind the hostess was Monsieur le Ministre whose professional eye had obviously spotted something that I had not. He stood on the step of the coach and began to spout fluent unctuousness into the microphone whilst smiling confidently into the bug eyed lens of the camera.

'...cementing the already strong technical relations with our Romanian friends... splendid opportunity for an overdue rapprochement of East and West...' He stepped down to the pavement and steered a balding Romanian technician towards the lens. '...building on the historic links between the two powers...'

This was the last thing I wanted. I caught madame's eye and tapped my watch with my finger. She glanced at her boss and then slipped around the front of the coach to my window.

'I would like to thank you sincerely monsieur for...'

'Forget that, will you? Just get the blighters off the coach. I've got a life to lead.'

'Yes, yes of course. I'll try.'

She began to coax the edge of the group towards the restaurant entrance. The Minister calmly turned his back to conceal the movement and continued his discourse to the network. I had to admire, grudgingly, the skill with which he managed to ensure that he was always in the frame no matter what was happening. As the last Romanian foot left the step I pushed the doorshut button and let in the clutch. The hostess made forward as if to say something but I dismissed her with my hand and roared off towards the Place de la Concorde. I briefly caught the image in my mirror of a desolate figure in a linen suit staring at the back of my coach and then I was fighting my way around the square to get to the Quais.

Monsieur Fromme was sunning himself in the vast open doors of the garage and once again he reminded me of a farmer, perhaps standing at the doors of his barn. I parked the coach where I had taken the fifty three from and climbed out with my tool bag and overalls.

'Did LeGuennec get off all right?' I nodded. 'And this one?' He patted the side of the coach.

'The compressor was OK but the air reservoir was leaking. I've reseated the valve and replaced the seals and it's holding pressure now. How long it will last I don't know.' He grunted. 'I think as a matter of priority I should check the other two new Saviems when they are free.'

'Hmm. Do you think it's a design fault?' He tugged at his moustache absent-mindedly.

'I don't know. I just think that if we can stop it from grounding your other two coaches we should try.'

'I'll look at the roster. And I'll phone that bloody Renault sales rep and give him a piece of my mind. Latest technology my arse.'

Monique slipped onto the bench seat opposite me, picked up my glass and took a swig at my beer.

'Buy me a beer Sisi?'

'Buy your own beer, you're earning more than me.'

She raised a painted eyebrow and crossed her legs a metre above the knee. Her miniature leather skirt climbed up towards her navel. Her pink fluffy bolero stretched vainly down to the same dimple. She tapped her rolled umbrella on her boots and pouted at a man leaning on the bar. He grinned, shook his head and flicked his eyes back to the football match on the television.

'Bloody intellectuals!' she complained. 'They buy with their eyes and spend with their tongues.'

I frowned at the crescent of scarlet lipstick which was now decorating my glass.

'You can be a nuisance sometimes Nikki, do you know that?' I cut another piece of my minute steak and stabbed three chips onto the fork with it. When my room got too small for me I liked to wander down the rue Blanche and eat a leisurely steak on the terrace of the Terminus Bar. Monique was one of the girls who worked the station. She had probably endured a brutal childhood and a vicious exploitation if I had ever bothered to listen, but I hadn't. One night, under the staggering shadows of the arches, I had struggled a knife out of a man's hand and pulled him off her. She had run away and I had kicked the man down the steps to the metro. By way of thanking me, she cadged beers off me.

She was now watching the last streams of workers trickling into the Gare St. Lazare on their way home.

'All going the wrong way,' she observed obscurely. 'Can't they see me?'

'They could hardly miss you in that hideous get up. Is that the latest?'

She looked down at her cleavage and then tugged her bolero back and forth several times as if to cool herself down. If anybody had doubted it before, they could now be certain that all she was hiding underneath the garment were two breasts.

'Have you seen my pépin?'

She swung her umbrella upright and opened it. It was shaped like the dome on the Sacré Coeur and was fashioned from transparent plastic. She stood up.

'See!' She twirled it around. 'I can shelter from the rain but my friends can still see me. Now that's the very latest *truc*.'

'Very nice.' I said. I thought of Nikki standing on street corners for hours on end in the rain, waiting for somebody's husband. Hoping for a rich aristocrat and getting a furtive clerk or a disbelieving tourist. What a life.

'Whilst you are up, get yourself a beer. Tell Marc to put it on my tab.'

'Thanks chéri!' She blew me a kiss and waltzed up to the bar. She wore no stockings. The weather was too hot. Just the minimum clothes for work.

I dug my knife in the mustard.

'Oh, it's Sisi,' she suddenly shrieked. I looked up wearily, expecting to have to confirm with Marc that I had offered to buy her beer.

Every other country in Europe has 625 lines on its televisions but not France, oh no. We have 819. Naturally, none of the giant foreign electrical corporations can be bothered with such a quirky system so all the televisions sold in France are made by French companies. We declare, of course, that 819 lines is not a trade barrier, its pushing the boundaries of technology towards the goal of a better defined picture. Sometimes it can be too good. The Minister's face did not quite fill the screen. Behind him, in glorious 819 line definition, at the wheel of a Fromme coach, sat Simon Laperche in scruffy jeans and shirt.

Merde.

'So you're not driving your wheelbarrows any more then?' Monique asked as she plonked her beer glass down on my table. 'You looked like a right tramp in that shirt.' She pulled at the collar of the clean one I was wearing. 'This one is nicer. I'm surprised they let you drive coaches dressed like that.'

Her crimson painted hand snaked across the table and stole one of my chips. I did not care. I had suddenly lost my appetite.

4

'The old man's in a foul mood. You'd better keep your head below the parapet.'

Noel Lebrun, the driver whom I had met when I had come begging for a job, pulled a face and nodded towards the glass office. I could see Monsieur Fromme's head bent over his desk.

'Thanks Noel.'

He grinned. I did not. I set to work on the power steering of the Paris bus and found myself wishing I had not mentioned the problem. More than once I abused the anonymous person who had perpetuated the myth that maintenance on these buses was simplicity itself.

There was no room to get the bus over the pit. I was lying on my back on the concrete when somebody kicked my feet. I screwed my head around to see a pair of brown suede shoes.

'Are you Laperche?'

I scraped out from under the front of the bus and looked up at the man. My view was distorted from below but I had an overpowering impression of a thin mouth, a sharp nose and very clear blue eyes. It was one of the drivers whom I had seen vaguely over the last few weeks but not had occasion to speak to. Rather like coaches, drivers are a mixed bunch. Every garage has its clown, its lawyer, its grumbler and its shirker and I was certain that Autocars Fromme would be no exception.

'Yeah,' I said, wondering which stereotype he was.

'Simon Laperche?'

'That's my name.' I kept my voice even. I did not like the way the conversation was starting.

'THE Simon Laperche?' I said nothing. 'Widow Maker Laperche?' I clenched my fist around the wrench.

'What's your name?' I said.

'Pradel. Monsieur Pradel to you.'

'Now the introductions are over, Pradel, do you have anything else to say? I am rather busy at the moment.'

'We don't want you here, Laperche.'

I suppose I should have expected it but nevertheless it came as an unwelcome surprise. I pulled myself into a squatting position and looked up at the sneering blue eyes.

'The day this coach,' I casually tapped the wheel behind my back with the spanner, 'has "*Autocars Pradel*" painted on the side of it then you will be able to get rid of me. Not until then.'

'You'll go before then Laperche, we'll see to that.'

'Fighting talk, Pradel, fighting talk.'

His gaze shifted across the garage and he stood up straight.

'Has Laperche come in yet?' Monsieur Fromme's voice demanded curtly.

'He's here, Monsieur Fromme. Hiding under the bus.'

Monsieur Fromme appeared not to notice the malice in the remark. He looked at me and then at Pradel.

'What are you doing Laperche?'

I stood up.

'Power steering servo.' I jerked my head at the bus.

'What are you doing Pradel?'

'Cleaning my coach, monsieur.' Monsieur Fromme looked squarely at him. He wavered. 'Right then Laperche, I'll er... I'll see you later.'

I gave a short nod and he turned and walked off across the garage.

'Come into my office,' Fromme said to me as he turned on his heel. It was not a suggestion. It was an order.

He sat behind his desk, creaking the wooden chair, and laid his broad hands palm downwards on the glass. One hand covered Paris, the other, the Breton peninsula.

'Shut the door.' I shut it. 'Laperche, you are here because I gave you a job. I didn't have to give you a job.'

'No monsieur.'

'And you don't have to work here if you really don't want to.' He tugged at the end of his moustache.

'I do want to work here, monsieur.'

Monsieur Fromme looked pointedly out into the garage where Pradel was sluicing the front of his coach.

'Any trouble of any sort and you'll be out. Understood?'

I nodded.

'Have you understood, Laperche?'

'Yes Monsieur Fromme.'

'I don't think you have.' His eyes bored into me. I could not read their message. It was not anger. It was not hate. 'Monsieur de Mello rang me up last night, Laperche.'

I wondered whether the president of the Coach Operators' Federation had changed his opinion of me. I cleared my throat.

'Oh yes?' I said.

'Yes. He had just watched the news on television. He thought it was very funny — Autocars Fromme putting their tramp mechanic into the starring role.' I focused on the map of France on his desk and chose some place else to be. 'I had missed the news report of course. I was getting a bottle from the cellar and Madame Fromme would not have recognised one of my coaches even if she had passed it on the stairs.' That was some relief. At least he had been spared the sight of me in my grubby shirt and jeans, scowling at the hostess who was just out of the shot. 'Luckily, like the other twenty million viewers in France, I had another opportunity when they repeated it on the late news after the film.'

Merde

'Just what did you think you were doing Laperche? A bit of private hire to line your own pocket was it? Hmm? Or did somebody put you up to it?'

'No. Neither. I was just helping someone.'

'Oh, so Autocars Fromme work for free now do they? That will make us popular. And since when have you counted government ministers amongst your friends to do favours for?'

'I didn't know who he was.'

'You didn't know who he was? The Minister of Commerce and Industry? He who could shut us down with a blink of his eye and you did not know who he was? What was he doing on your coach?'

'They were stuck at Orly. They had a transfer booked with Buisson. You know, Buisson have...'

'Of course I know. Why were they on your coach?'

'I told you. I was helping out.'

'For nothing?'

'Look, if it's the money you are worried about you can take the hire fee from my wages.'

'You still have not understood have you Laperche? What did I send you to Orly for?'

'To repair a coach and bring it back.'

'Empty. To bring it back empty, Laperche. Do you fully understand the significance of that word?' I said nothing. 'How many passengers did you carry?'

I thought quickly. What had the girl said?

'About twenty.'

'ABOUT twenty? You don't know how many?'

'I think it was twenty two. Yes I'm sure she said it was twenty two. Plus her and the Minister.'

'Her?'

'The hostess.'

'Pretty was she? Worth losing your job for?'

'Look, just give me my card and I'll go now.'

He shook his head slowly.

'Oh no, it's not as easy as that Laperche. I shall need a body to hand over when they come looking for you. Where is the journey sheet for that job?'

'Well I could not have had one because...'

'Oh you had a contract did you? It would have to be one or the other because without them, you would be driving a coach of uninsured passengers and you would not do that would you, Laperche? You would not pick up a non-scheduled group, one without any protection in law, one including the government minister responsible for the legal requirement for every job to have a correctly completed journey sheet, and then transport it to the centre of Paris, free of charge and do it on television would you Laperche? You would not be that cretinous.'

I slowly realised just how stupid I had been. Monsieur Fromme jumped up from his chair, leaned over me and bellowed, 'You of all people, Laperche, you should know better than anybody what happens when you flout regulations. Now get back to your work.'

Pradel smirked at me as I crossed back to the bus.

A couple of days later I was eating a biftek-frites, tucked into a corner table at Chez Jean — the bistrot that all the drivers used — when Madame Aurélie plumped herself down on the chair opposite. Madame Aurélie was the overweight, middle-aged gossip who came in three days a week to type and file for Monsieur Fromme. It was she who made up the work book for the next week and sent out the invoices for the various accounts and acknowledged all the customers' orders.

'How's the back?' I asked. Last time she had cornered me I had submitted to fifteen minutes of her medical problems.

'I'm a martyr to it.' I glanced up from my steak to see if she was being flippant but no, she was serious. She prodded her bouffon of violently henna'd hair. It did not budge a centimetre. 'The quack said that he had never seen a spinal distortion like mine.'

'Plat du jour and a pichet of rouge?' Jean called from the bar.

She nodded and continued in the same breath.

'Quite extraordinary, he said it was. Of course I had always said that there was something wrong about it. I mean, for years I have been in absolute agony.'

I masticated the leathery steak as Madame Aurélie prattled on about her back. I was not listening and she knew that it did not matter. It was therapy for her just to be able to talk about it.

The front of the café was soaked in the flat black shade cast by the drab awning yawning over the pavement. Not a breath stirred its fringe. It hung limp and still and hot. I watched Pradel arguing with a woman on the corner of a side street opposite. She was poking him forcefully on the chest. If that was his wife, it was no wonder that he tried to throw his weight around in the garage, he certainly could not do so at home. As if he suspected that he was being watched, he moved her further from the main street. Poor Pradel, a hen-pecked husband. Who would have thought it? She poked him again and he shrugged his shoulders and then turned away and walked towards the garage.

What was motivating him, I wondered? With his sharp face and darting eyes he looked a bit like a weasel. What was behind it all? Was he going to try to make trouble with the union? Acting like a tough guy yet he liked his brown suede shoes and his blue cotton jacket. I measured him up as he disappeared inside the vault of the garage. He would be no trouble to me. I could knock the stuffing out of him. I thought about his slick dressing and tidy hair and decided that somebody like that would probably carry a knife and know how to use it. That would account for this self assurance. I would have to remember not to give him the opportunity to prove my hypothesis.

'You're not listening to me are you Monsieur Laperche?' Madame Aurélie speared a radish on the end of her fork and pointed it at me. Anybody else would have eaten it with their fingers. 'I said that Monsieur Fromme phoned the Ministry and got the name of the group and then told me to send them an invoice.'

'An invoice?' I was still thinking of the armoury that I had invented for Pradel.

'For your famous television appearance. If we invoice them for a transfer and they pay, then that lets us off the hook. It makes it all legal. Not that it was illegal before, if you understand me.'

'Well that's a relief.' I looked at my watch. 'I must get back before Monsieur Fromme.'

'No dessert? No coffee?'

'No time.'

It was a pointless courtesy, trying to make sure that I left for lunch after the boss and returned before him but I stuck to it. I knew that I needed to keep an absolutely clean sheet. Autocars Fromme was my very last chance. Monsieur Fromme had taken me on against his better judgment and, so far, it seemed that I had proven to him that his reluctance had been well founded. If I messed up with Fromme, nobody would employ me.

I was too late. He was already back. As I stepped across the threshold I heard him slam the drawer of the metal filing cabinet in his office. I scurried quickly around to the coach I had been working on before lunch and resumed the adjustment of the gear lever linkage. With luck, he would not have noticed me.

In dribs and drabs, the eight or so drivers whose day's tasks had allowed them to be near the garage, returned from lunch. They ambled back, feet slow and heavy on the hot street, perspiration running down the spines of their shirts. Doors hissed open and slammed shut. Engines roared black smoke. Power assisted steering churned tyres easily from lock to lock on the garage floor as the coaches manoeuvred around each other. First out was Georges with a Mercedes, the beat of the V8 reverberating around the garage as he paused at the entrance. Then Armand in one of the pneumatic Saviems and then Pradel in an older Mercedes with an exhaust pipe which rattled on the overrun.

As the silence descended I heard the clip clip clop of reinforced heels and the murmur of voices. I glanced across and saw Madame Aurélie and Monsieur Fromme entering the garage side by side, deep in discussion. I wondered if he was getting the full medical diagnosis that I had managed to dream through. It was not until much later that I asked myself who it was, then, who had slammed the filing cabinet drawer in Monsieur Fromme's office when I had returned from the café. But by then, the damage had already been done.

I finished the gear linkage. It took me until mid afternoon. Even in the cool of the garage the spanner kept slipping in my sweaty hand. Then Noel asked me if I could repair his nearside mirror and so together we fashioned and drilled a stabilising bracket from a piece of scrap alloy and screwed it into place with self tappers.

'A bit System D but it works.' He stood back and surveyed our efforts.

'It's the result that's important.'

In a burst of engine noise, Georges' Mercedes erupted into the garage. We turned and then stood agog. It had changed colour, or rather, it had been decorated.

Georges jerked to an abrupt halt in the middle of the garage. He banged on the parking brake and tumbled out of his coach.

'Look at it! Just look at it!' He was furious. His normally protruding eyes seemed to bulge out of his florid face like the headlights on a 2cv. 'The connards. Connards!' He spat.

We looked at it. It had been transformed into a political billboard. All down the nearside and across most of the rear, strident slogans marched in lurid spray paint colours.

'*Down with authority.*'

'*The streets for the people, the people for the streets.*'

'*Force will vanquish all.*'

'That's not how you spell, "vanquish",' Noel observed.

'What do you expect from illiterate parasites? Parasites and connards, that's what they are!'

'What happened?'

'The students were demonstrating down near the Panthéon. Marching up and down waving banners like the salvation army. We were at a standstill all along the Boul'Mich.'

'What were you doing in the Boulevard St. Michel?' Noel asked. 'You should have taken the Boulevard Raspail.'

George's eyes bulged dangerously as he filled his lungs for an energetic explanation.

'Well, never mind that,' I said hurriedly, 'let's see if we can clean this up a bit. It's aerosol paint isn't it?'

'The connards. If I get my hands on them!'

I walked over to the Citroen van that served as the knockabout do-all for the garage. As I searched in my tool bag I heard Noel asking Georges why he had stopped in the first place. He really was unconscious to danger.

'Noel! See if you can find a bottle or a can to put a drop of petrol in. Georges, can you get some rags or waste from somewhere?'

I ferreted out a length of the spare air hose that I had taken to Orly and threaded it down the filler pipe of the van. I siphoned off about half a litre of petrol into the can that Noel held for me.

'That should do. If we work quickly we might be able to get this paint off before it hardens.'

'It's been baked in the sun for an hour,' Georges grumbled as he tied an overall around his portly midriff.

'Even with that, this spray paint does not go hard for about twelve hours so let's get scrubbing.'

It was unpleasant and arduous work, and we were soon uncomfortably warm with our exertions and nauseous from the fumes but neither Georges nor Noel would give up whilst I was still scrubbing and so we worked on. Gradually the original livery of the coach began to reassert itself through the graffiti. I dragged the ancient stepladder to the back of the coach and gazed up at the window in wonder.

'How the devil did they get to write up there?'

Georges tucked his rag into his belt and stomped down to me.

'Some buggers climbed up on other buggers' shoulders.' He held the ladder as I climbed. 'Can you get it all right?'

I paused before assuring him that I could because I was watching a man get out of a black Renault. It had D plates which meant that he was an official of some sort. And he was looking at the sign above the garage doors.

'It looks as if Monsieur Fromme is about to get a visit from the tax inspector.'

Georges poked his head around the back of the coach and I nodded at the blue suit that was picking its way towards us across the scrubby sand and broken kerb stones which served as a pavement in this district of Paris.

'Well he certainly hasn't won the lottery, that's for sure,' he said.

We watched the man knock on Fromme's office

door and Madame Aurélie let him in then we returned to our scrubbing. For the next few minutes all that could be heard was grunting and the squeaking of rag on paintwork. Then Georges muttered to himself, 'I could do with a fag.'

'That would solve all our problems,' Noel called out. 'With these petrol fumes you'd have no coach left, never mind the decoration.'

'Petrol fumes?' Fromme's voice echoed around the rafters in query. 'Where are they coming from? Is there a leak?'

'No Monsieur,' Noel replied quickly, 'we're cleaning some paint from Georges' coach.'

Fromme was there, bouncing up and down gently on his toes, surveying his bespattered property and sucking his top lip.

'How did this happen Georges?'

'Students! Connards in the Boul'mich. They held up the traffic and then sprayed us all. Connards! If you think this is bad you should have seen Lecaplan's new Setra. They plastered the windscreen, the driver couldn't see a thing. At least I could drive the coach.'

'Is it coming off all right with petrol?'

'Petrol and elbow grease.'

'Where did you get the petrol from?'

Georges shrugged.

'Simon got it,' Noel half explained.

'Simon?'

'Laperche,' I added. 'And I siphoned it from the van. I only took about half a litre.'

'Ah Laperche,' Fromme said as if he had just noticed me, 'Just the person I was looking for. I need you in my office.'

'Now? I haven't finished this cleaning.'

'Now.'

I handed my rag to Noel.

'Don't throw the rags in the waste,' I warned as I walked after Monsieur Fromme. 'Stick them in the sand bucket and I'll get rid of them.'

I could see Fromme's head nodding short approval. He probably did not know he was doing it. He took a final glance at the violated coach as I caught up with him. 'That's not how you spell "vanquish",' he said.

I agreed.

The official in the blue suit was sitting in Fromme's office.

'This is Laperche,' Fromme said.

The man looked me up and down as if I were a hat stand.

'Monsieur,' I nodded.

Fromme smiled at me and explained.

'Monsieur Knopf is from the Ministry of Commerce and Industry.'

I suddenly felt that sinking feeling. What was it that he had shouted across the desk at me? "I shall need a body to hand over when they come looking for you".'

'Oh yes,' I said.

'Mr. Van der Leeuven specifically requested that Autocars Fromme supply the coach for this present task and that you be the driver.' Knopf made it quite plain in his manner of speech exactly what he thought of the idea himself.

'Mr. Van der Leeuven?' I said.

Knopf pressed his lips tightly together in a show of exasperation and glanced across at Monsieur Fromme.

'The Minister,' Fromme explained.

'Oh yes,' I said again, thinking as I did so, that thus far, my contribution to the conversation had managed to make me look the utter moron that Knopf thought I was. But in the back of my mind a cautious jubilation was arising. It seemed that I was not being castigated. Monsieur Fromme's trick of sending an invoice for my transfer must have cleared me and jogged the Minister's memory. My jubilation was cautious, however, because I could not help but observe to myself that although I had apparently favourably impressed a customer, I still found that customer an obnoxious boor.

Knopf cleared his throat.

'Monsieur Fromme has the details. He will explain them to you and the importance of this task.' He stood up and cradled his brief case in his arms. They shook hands. Monsieur Fromme opened the door and with the merest nod in my direction, Knopf stalked out.

'Wait here,' Fromme said and followed Knopf.

I edged into the area swept by the electric fan and studied the photograph of one of the latest tenders depicted on the Fire Service Calendar. I had worked my way back to the escape ladder at February before Monsieur Fromme returned. He paused in the doorway and looked at me. I looked back.

'Madame Aurélie, go and get some fresh air.'

She knew better than to argue. She switched off her electric typewriter and scooped up her handbag.

'Sit down, Laperche.' I sat. 'What you did at Orly was stupid and recklessly dangerous,' Fromme said. 'Whatever comes of this job, you cannot expunge your cretinous behaviour. So Van der Leeuven asks for you in person and I have to hope that you don't bugger it up for us all. This job could lead to others.' His gaze wandered out into the garage where Georges and Noel had just finished cleaning the coach. 'We need it,' he said quietly. 'It's not easy, running a coach company.'

'Knopf is a conceited toady and Van der Leeuven is a megalomaniac bully and what about you, Laperche? Are you really as stupid as you pretend?' I said nothing. 'I somehow think not.' His eyes bored into mine. 'Perhaps Monsieur De Mello saw something that is, so far, hidden from me.' I shrugged. He grunted, then said briskly, 'Right, this is the job. A Chinese group. A delegation of some sort. An official visit. The Minister is very concerned that everything should go as clockwork.'

'Just the transfer to the hotel?'

'To start with, Laperche, to start with. If we don't cock that up he might ask us to do some day visits for the delegation.'

I watched Monsieur Fromme imagining their finest coach appearing regularly on television news clips and then saw him struggling with the realities of the situation.

'The trouble is, Van der Leeuven insists that the only driver we use is you.'

'Why?'

'Because he's an idiot who's been educated beyond the limits of his self-confidence.' He glanced at me. 'You don't follow politics do you, Laperche?'

'No.'

'No,' he repeated. 'The government is worried that all this student trouble and union agitation could flare up into another '68.'

'It wouldn't take much.'

'Van der Leeuven is a very ambitious chap. And so is his opinion of himself. He wanted the job of Minister of the Interior in this cabinet and because he wanted the job he assumed that he would get it.'

'He was wrong then.' I could still hear Van der Leeuven's bullying anger.

'So he's stuck with showing coach loads of foreign visitors around chicken farms and glass factories. That is why he is a pain in the arse. Everything has to be just right for him. He's got to show everyone what he is capable of.'

He picked up a pencil and began to fiddle with it. I realised that he was worried about something. Just how badly did he need a contract with the Ministry? It would be guaranteed money, no defaulting customers.

'When is this job?' I asked.

'They arrive at Orly on Thursday morning.'

'This week?' I asked. Monsieur Fromme nodded. 'That's cutting it a bit fine.' It was two days away.

'I would imagine that this is another casualty from the Buisson collapse.' He paused and reflected. 'I wonder how many more there are. No doubt we will find out in good time. Let's get down to work. It would suit me if you'd take your day off tomorrow.' It didn't suit me but I did not argue. 'You will need a decent coach.' He looked out into the garage. 'You'll take Georges' Mercedes. They should be happy with that.'

I knew somebody who would not be happy about it.

'What about Georges?'

'What about Georges?' he asked.

'It's his coach.'

'It's my coach. I decide who drives it. Just you make

sure that you bring it back all in one piece.' He pulled a scrap of paper across the desk. 'Madame Aurélie will not be typing your orders for this group. There won't be any orders. Knopf wants it kept quiet. No fuss. What a buffoon! Anyway, I don't want you talking about it. Georges will do what I say.'

I did not doubt that.

'What's the flight number?' I took out my diary.

'China Airways, 2007, arriving 11.20 at Orly Ouest.'

'Orly Ouest? From China?' Orly Ouest was the new terminal set at right angles to the original Orly Sud. It was reserved for short hop journeys, Air Alger and Alitalia and such like.

'The Ministry feels it will be cosier if they arrive at Orly Ouest.' Monsieur Fromme glanced at my incredulous expression and added, 'I think that is their way of saying that it will be more secure.'

'Where am I taking them?'

'Hotel du Louvre.'

'And why not?' I said. A five star hotel would impress the disciples of Mao. 'What is so special about this group?'

'I don't think there is anything special about it. All that security stuff was probably invented by Knopf to make Van der Leeuven look important.'

'What is the group called? How do I find them?'

'Amongst all those Maghrebins on flying carpets a group of slit eyed rice eaters should stick out like a baguette in a salad bowl. You shouldn't have any trouble but in any case there will be a Chinese courier — a Madame Chan.'

'Let's hope she can speak French.'

On Wednesday morning I took Georges around to Chez Jean to stand him a drink. He was morose and belligerent at the same time and I knew perfectly why.

'I don't understand what all the Captain Zorro stuff is in aid of. It's stupid.' He took a sip from his beer. 'And why you? It's my coach.'

I dared not repeat what Monsieur Fromme had said about the proprietorship of the vehicle.

'Georges, I didn't ask for this job.' He threw me a disbelieving look. 'How could I? I am a nobody. It's nothing to do with me and it's not a question of you not being good enough.'

'I should hope not.'

'It's just a whim of Monsieur Fromme's and you have to admit that there is no way that anybody can influence that, least of all me.'

'I suppose so. But why all the bloody secrecy?'

I shook my head.

'Search me, Georges, search me.'

'You could tell me.'

'I've got nothing to tell. I don't know anything. And why do you want to know, anyway?'

'Because you won't tell me.' He laughed. 'If you bounced in here and started to talk about your next job I'd tell you to shut up.'

'That's always the funny thing about secrets. Drink your beer.'

'I hear you're going up in the world.' The sneering voice came from behind me and I did not have to turn to know that it was Pradel. 'Like a rocket! One minute you're sweeping the floor, the next, you're at the top of the list for the best coaches.'

'Go away and play with your pram,' I said. It was not very original but it was too hot for thinking.

'Oh very funny.' He addressed Georges. 'Are you happy with handing you coach over to this...'

'Just watch what you say next, Pradel,' I interrupted. 'It could involve you in a visit to the dentist's.'

'Of course I'm not happy,' Georges said. His eyes were beginning to bulge. 'But what the devil has it got to do with you?'

'Well I'm first in line for your coach when you get a new one, not some upstart from a building site.'

'Building site?' Georges was confused.

'Go on Laperche, tell him what you were driving before you came here.'

I turned slowly to face him.

'I made no secret of it. I was driving a tipper truck.'

'On a building site, Georges. Now ask him why he had to stay on the building site.'

Georges looked at me. Pradel smirked. I wanted to smack his teeth down his throat.

'So?' Georges asked.

'Twelve months suspended licence.'

'Oh is that all,' he said.

I nearly kissed him.

'No it's not all,' Pradel bounced back.

'Just leave it alone,' I suggested but it was Georges who shut him up.

'Actually, Pradel,' he said, 'my new coach is also a Mercedes — Yours.'

'What?'

'Madame Aurélie was typing the orders as I came out. I'm having your Mercedes and you're moving down to a Saviem.' He took my elbow and pushed me towards the door. 'I don't suppose you've got time to fix the exhaust pipe before tomorrow have you? I've noticed that it always rattles on the overrun. Of course, it could be the way he drives it...'

5

It was well after eight at night by the time I had fixed the exhaust pipe on the Mercedes. I wheeled the tool dolly back to the wall and wiped my hands on some waste. I felt dog-tired. I pulled off my overalls and threw them into my locker and slammed the door. I stopped and thought. Then I opened the locker door, picked the overalls up and hung them up properly. Throwing them on the floor was making work only for me.

One of the drivers was sweeping out his coach to the accompaniment of Edith Piaf on his radio. I waved, pointed at him and then screwed my hand right and left to show him that he was locking up. He nodded to acknowledge his responsibility and pointed to the top gang of lights. I switched them off as I passed the fuse board. It would save him walking across the garage and back.

Outside, the residue of the daytime heat was coming up from the tarmac and radiating from the brick walls of the Post Office. I glanced up at the fading sky. Ten tenths cloud cover. The atmosphere was heavy and oppressive. I felt as if I were eating the air, not breathing it.

The pole was already hooked into the steel blind at Chez Jean, ready for closure. I ducked under and slapped some coins onto the counter. The barman turned wearily from his broom.

'We're closed,' he said.

'Just give me a beer, Paul, in a bottle. Any beer will do. I'll take it away.'

He stooped to the fridge and pulled out a bottle by the neck and gave it to me. In one swift movement he scooped the coins into his pocket.

'We could do with some rain,' he said.

I could not face the suffocating heat of the métro so I sat on a bench, slowly drank my beer and watched the passers by hurrying homewards in the advancing gloom. The traffic was sparser now. A blonde drove by in a Renault convertible. She was pulling irritably at her hair, failing to get the slipstream to lift it and cool her.

One by one the street lights flicked on.

I thought about the minister, Van der Leeuven and his conceited ignorance. I was not looking forward to the transfer at Orly. If that stupid woman had not looked so despondent I would not have been in this situation now. As I saw it, it was all her fault. She couldn't even park a car.

I heard the distinctive whine of a six cylinder Fulgur engine and looked around for the source. There would have to be an old Saviem SC somewhere. Then I saw that it was one of ours and it was going westwards. I jumped up and whistled. It was Noel. He swerved over to the kerb and in a hiss and clatter the jack-knife door rattled open. I jumped in and he pulled away without stopping.

'Where are you going?' I shouted above the noise of second gear.

'Home. Argenteuil.'

'Which way?'

'Where do you want to go, Simon?'

'Gare St.Lazare or thereabouts.'

'Drop you at the Place Clichy?'

'Brilliant.'

I stood in the doorwell and allowed the breeze from the open door to flow over me as we swayed and lurched through the quickening traffic. Above us a lethargic snake of red and green coaches grated heavily along on the elevated section of the métro. I jerked my thumb at the humanity crammed against its yellow lit windows.

'That's where I should have been. Cooking.'

'May God be blessed for Autocars Fromme!'

'Amen,' I endorsed his facetious remark. I was surprised at my sincerity.

At the Place Clichy Noel brought the coach alongside a road island and I jumped out.

'*Ciao* Simon!' he shouted and then roared away northwards up the avenue.

I skipped through the traffic and entered the tranquillity of the rue de Leningrad. It seemed cooler here. It was probably an illusion. I knew I was nearly home. As I ambled down towards the Place de l'Europe I amused myself by trying to name the six towns which had given their names to the streets of the square. The trick, of course, was that the famous one, the rue de Rome, does not actually touch the square.

I could hear a train squealing over some tight points as it ran in the cutting out of St Lazare station. When you do the Paris tour, the guide always makes you slow down as you cross the square so that she can point out the trains running underneath and explain about the Batignolles tunnel; for the cutting had been made by removing the top from the original tunnel after a disastrous fire. I tried to remember the date of the fire but failed. I must have heard the commentary scores of times but I could not recall the date. I did not have that sort of a brain.

A dark saloon drove slowly by and stopped on the corner. The driver got out and left the keys in the ignition. Some people ask for trouble. He walked up towards me and I knew he was lost. As long as he did not ask me to name the six streets of the Place de l'Europe in their correct order I would be alright.

'I wonder, monsieur, could you tell me...' he began, then he looked over my shoulder and nodded. Before I could react somebody hit me on the back of the neck, hard. I blacked out momentarily and woke as my knees jarred on the pavement. Dazed, I was watching a shoe swing round to kick me in the face. It seemed to take all afternoon so I spent the time abstractedly reflecting that if my assailant had used his knee he would already have laid me out. I threw up my left arm and gasped as the shoe cracked into my forearm and slammed my head against the railings. In a flash of electric arc, a commuter train rumbled below me in the cutting. I got one knee up before my befuddled brain reminded me that my assailant had a mate behind me. From a one knee crouch I launched myself head first at the car driver whilst he was still off balance. He crashed backwards to the ground and I fell onto him. He smelt of stale cigarettes and sweat.

'Get him off me!' he screamed.

Then I got mad. As his mate's hand grabbed my shoulder to drag me off, I decided to put at least one of my attackers out of action to even up the contest. I cracked my forehead down with a smart chop onto the driver's nose. It exploded in blood and I was wrenched backwards against the railings. The driver was squealing and lashing out with his legs. His mate was a bit more stolid and began to lay into me with blows that made up in force for their lack of accuracy. I dodged them as best I could and tried to get up but he kicked my legs away. Another blow thudded into my chest, knocking out all my breath. I could feel myself losing out.

In an ear splitting screech a pink furry monster suddenly leapt in front of me and began hitting his head with a rolled umbrella.

'Bugger off you bully!' Monique screamed at him and then in one vicious lunge she stabbed her umbrella point into his crotch.

As the man doubled up he lashed out with his arm and sent her sprawling on the sidewalk. I struggled to get up but my head swam and my legs would not work. The driver was already hurrying back to the car, holding one hand to his face. With what little breath he had left, his mate swore and then shambled off after him, half bent with pain.

I twisted my head around to the tangle of bare thighs and leather skirt.

'Are you all right Nikki?'

'Look what he did to my pépin,' she said, holding up her bent umbrella. 'The brute.'

In a squeal of tyres the car took off and disappeared around the corner.

'Good riddance!' Nikki jumped up and rubbed her elbow. 'Got a bit of a graze there. Not good for business.' I marvelled at her resilience. She came over to me. 'You're a mess, Sisi. You're covered in blood.'

'Not much of it is mine,' I boasted.

''Soon see about that. Hold still.' She retrieved her bag and wetted the corner of her handkerchief. 'You can say "ouch" if you want to.' She squatted down and dabbed at my face.

'Ouch.'

'There's a big brave boy.'

'Nikki?'

'What?'

'Don't you ever wear knickers? Ouch.'

She looked at her leather skirt.

'Not part of the uniform. I wear them when I go to the clinic.'

'Ouch. Why?'

'Gives me something to take off.' She studied my face. 'You know, you're not bad looking for an old man. If you had more money I could fancy you.'

'If I had more money I would buy you a pair of knickers. Now help me get up.'

Monique was wiry rather than strong. It took too much of my energy to get me staggered to an upright position against the railings. She looked at me closely.

'You O.K.?' she said.

'Be alright in a minute. Feel a bit, er...' I gulped, turned suddenly and vomited down through the railings as another train rumbled out towards the suburbs. The SNCF was taking a pasting tonight.

'Come on, lean on me and we'll get you home.' She took my arm.

'Not that one.' I winced and offered my right arm. 'I got kicked on that one.'

'Charming. Do you know who your friends were?'

'No idea. They just jumped me.'

'Did they get anything?'

'What do you mean?'

'Well, they were trying to rob you weren't they?'

'I suppose they were. I don't know why they picked me. I don't exactly look rich.'

She giggled and held up her banana shaped umbrella.

'Well whoever they were, one of them won't be bothering us girls for a while.' She draped my right arm around her bare shoulders. 'Come on. You can pretend you're a client.'

'Oh thanks!'

We stumbled off down the street. To all the world I looked like a drunken mug being taken upstairs to be fleeced. We wobbled along in a silence interspersed with grunts from me and short instructions from Monique such as, 'kerb, up'.

'Here we are,' she said at last.

I looked through quickly puffing eyes at the unfamiliar carriage entrance. 'Where?' I said.

'My place, Sisi. I'm going to bathe your wounds and lavish tender care and affection on you.'

'What about your landlady?'

'I can deal with her.'

I thought that she probably could.

I woke up in a strange bed, in a strange room. For a moment I gazed around at the unfamiliar wallpaper, the dainty porcelain door knobs and the polished floorboards. I tentatively moved my head and was pleased to discover that it did not fall off and roll across the floor. Monique had spent half the evening kneading the muscles and tendons at the back of my neck. It must have had some effect.

I frowned. My eyelids felt as if they had been stretched over my eyeballs. The last thing that I could remember was lying fully clothed on the bed whilst waiting to see if the knockout pills she had given me would have any effect. I looked cautiously around. To my right, on a boudoir chair, neatly folded, lay my clothes. All my clothes. To my left, on a chaise longue, neatly curled, lay Monique. Monique asleep in printed cotton nightdress and clutching a teddy bear.

I gingerly sat up. Not much problem there. A bit stiff on the thighs and my left arm ached a bit. My chest was purple and yellow but everything seemed to be working more or less. I lowered my feet to the floor and stood up.

'You've got a nice bum.'

I began to turn around, then thought better of it.

'Just avert your eyes, little girl, whilst I get dressed.'

'Why? You haven't got anything that I don't know about. Who do you think undressed you?'

'That's not the point.'

'I've seen your point as well.'

'Nikki! Behave yourself little girl. I'm an old man, remember? And a pauper.'

'You're thirty two. I looked at your identity card.' She sat up and sighed heavily. 'But you're right about being a pauper. What a shame.'

'Shame? You don't know the meaning of the word. I don't suppose you possess a razor do you?'

I began to pull on my clothes.

She jumped up from the couch. 'Of course I do.' She went towards the bathroom.

'Nikki.' She turned at the doorway. 'You've got a nice bum as well.'

She grinned, flirted up the back of her nightie and went into the bathroom.

My face did not look too bad. My eyes only felt like tennis balls, most of the swelling had subsided. Nikki's bags of frozen haricots had helped that. I had two more cuts on my face by the time I had finished shaving. Nikki had not warned me that although she had a razor, it was one of those dainty instruments that ladies use and the confounded thing was too small for me to grasp properly. But all in all, I looked quite presentable and if I did not move my limbs too violently or turn my head too quickly, I thought that I would be able to carry it off. I had before me the whole of my rest day in which to recover and I intended to do nothing in particular all day.

She poured the coffee and we broke bread. It was fresh from the oven.

'Where did you get fresh bread from?' She was still in her nightie.

'Bread shop of course.'

'You didn't go out like that?'

'I put my coat on.' She nodded at a thin housecoat

hanging on the back of the door. 'Anyway, they know me. They see quite a lot of me.'

'I should think they see all of you.'

'You sound just like my father.'

'Sensible man.'

'He was a bastard.'

She switched the radio on and we listened whilst we ate. The weather forecaster told us that today would be hot, like yesterday and probably like tomorrow.

'Don't need to be Einstein to work that out,' Nikki observed sourly.

Another hot, oppressive, Parisian summer day.

Now the news. The students would be out at the République for a rally on human rights. Well what a surprise! Two forest fires were consuming acres of scrub in the Midi and a small bomb had blown in the windows of an airline office in Athens.

'Can't see the point in that,' Nikki said.

'What?'

'Blowing up offices. What do they do it for?'

'I don't know. It's a funny old world.' I drained my cup. 'Thanks Nikki.'

'That makes the score fifteen-all. You rescue me. I rescue you.'

'A great team.'

'Do you like haricot beans?'

'Hate them.'

She looked at the two defrosted bags.

'I shall be eating the bloody things until Christmas.'

I was in the garage by half past eight on the Thursday morning, wearing my smartest trousers and a freshly ironed shirt. Monsieur Fromme did not like uniforms for drivers. He reasoned that he only employed drivers if they wore the right clothes. The drivers said that it was to save money. A uniform would have to be provided by the employer, along with a regular allowance for cleaning and replacement.

Noel came out of the office with his day's orders in his hand.

'Let me warn you.' He waved a paper at me. 'If they give you the Lycée Jean Jaurès, slit your throat. It's a nicer death.'

I swept the dust into the pan on the step of the Mercedes.

'I'll bear that in mind,' I laughed.

He watched me, puzzled.

'What is so special about Georges?'

'Nothing.' It was my turn to be puzzled.

'So why do you clean his coach out for him?'

'Oh haven't you heard?' Pradel appeared at his elbow. 'Georges has been deposed by a criminal truck driver.' His blue eyes glinted at me.

I remembered watching from the café as his wife poked him vigorously in the chest.

'Ignore him,' I said to Noel. 'He's just henpecked.'

Pradel's face turned into a snarl but before he could respond, Monsieur Fromme's voice boomed out.

'Pradel! Move your coach, it's blocking the 229.' Pradel hesitated. 'Now!'

'Just watch it!' he hissed at me and strode off.

Noel watched him go.

'What was all that about?'

'Pradel is upset because he's now got a Saviem.'

'So who's got his coach?'

'Georges.'

'Georges? But Georges drives a better Mercedes. Why should he...?'

'And Georges is upset because I have been given his coach.'

Noel looked at me strangely.

'You're doing alright for yourself.'

'Oh don't you start, Noel. I didn't ask for this coach. Monsieur Fromme decided that just for this one transfer, I was to use it. What could I say? He is the boss.'

'So what was all that nasty stuff about, "criminal truck drivers"?'

'Just Pradel being petty. As I said, he's henpecked, he's got to work it out on somebody.'

'Henpecked?'

'Yeah. Haven't you seen his wife? She'd frighten me in daylight.'

'Wife? That'll be the day. He's a poof. Lives with a waiter from the Café de la Paix.' He walked towards his old Saviem. 'I'll leave the doors open. Just do the windows and brush the carpets will you?'

I said something rude and he laughed.

I was rubbing a final polish on the inside of the awkward back window when I felt the coach rock as somebody climbed in.

'Time to go,' Monsieur Fromme said.

I looked at the clock above the windscreen. It was only half past nine. It would not take me two hours to get to Orly. He saw my glance.

'We cannot afford to be late, Laperche. Better forty minutes early than four minutes late.' He pulled at the end of his moustache.

'As you wish, Monsieur.'

'Fuel OK?'

'Three quarters full. Should get me to Orly and back with no trouble.'

'It would get you to Brussels and back with no trouble. I had long distance tanks fitted on this coach.'

It made sense. It was Georges who generally did the three and four day tours: Brussels and the Dutch bulb fields, the Chateaux of the Loire, that sort of thing.

'Right. I'll get going then.'

On the road out to Orly I thought about the violent assault on me and the more I thought, the less I understood. What came back to me was the bizarrely detached observation that I made as I was kneeling in stunned limbo, waiting for the driver's foot to kick me in the face. Why had he not used his knee? It was level with my chin. He could have knocked me out stone cold. And that terrified screaming of 'Get him off me' was not the behaviour of an experienced thug. And why were they not three — one to sit in the car and drive? It all seemed very amateur. But the thing that I really found unfathomable was the glance and nod that the driver had given to his mate behind me. It had been a nod of confirmation. He was making sure that he had the right person. The more I thought about that, the less I liked it.

I was still musing on it when I swung off under the autoroute and joined the stream of vehicles for the two air terminals. I swept past the chaos of Orly Sud and onto the relative calm of Orly Ouest. This terminal took so little traffic that it was like visiting a village. The coaches could park outside for as long as they liked without being moved on by some dyspeptic cop.

I still had a good three quarters of an hour before my flight was due to arrive, without adding the thirty minutes for them to disembark and get through customs, so I went to the concourse bar. It was deserted. I sat on the high stool and sipped at a *double express* and chewed a cardboard croissant. After serving me, the barman disappeared through a panelled door at the back. He was obviously not expecting any more customers. Compared to the bustle and noise of Orly Sud, this terminal was eerie. An empty cathedral and no congregation. I had not heard a tannoy announcement since I had been here.

I made my coffee last as long as I could then I slipped from the stool and wandered up towards the arrivals board. I checked the flight number in my diary and joined the handful of individuals gawping up at the board. *'Cancelled, cancelled, cancelled, diverted, cancelled, diverted, diverted, cancelled.'* Every flight? I looked for my China Airways 2007. There it was. *'Cancelled'.* I half turned to the person at the side of me.

'What's going on?' I said.

The woman turned towards me. It was the hostess who could not park a Volkswagen. She was wearing a navy blue suit tailored in what was probably a thin cotton and navy blue high heeled sandals. Her dark hair was pulled back from her face by a light blue band. Between her feet stood an attaché case.

'Hello,' she said. 'It's the air traffic controllers. They're on strike.'

'Since when?'

'Since this morning.'

'Oh brilliant.   That's all I needed.' I thought of Fromme tugging his moustache with anxiety lest the transfer go wrong. 'Well what are they doing with the planes that are up? They can't just tell them not to land.'

'Those that are in the air are being diverted.   Those that haven't taken off are being cancelled.'

'But who's looking after the planes in the air if the controllers are on strike?'

'The Belgian controllers are handling the diversions to Brussels and the Italians to Milan.' She shrugged as if it were obvious.

'I'd better phone the garage,' I muttered and as I turned a thought suddenly occurred to me. 'It's your fault I'm here.'

'My fault?'

'I nearly lost my job by taking your obnoxious minister to his lunch.'

'I'm very sorry,' she said quietly. 'It was very good of you to do it. It got me out of a nasty spot.'

'My boss saw me on television.   He thought I was trying to make some quick money on the side.'

'But you weren't.' An anguished frown crossed her freckled face. 'You were being very kind.'

'I was being very stupid. And this group is my punishment. But don't you worry, you won't catch me like that again. Au revoir madame.'

I walked brusquely away and nearly felled two Air Inter hostesses as they stepped from the lift.

As I waited for the numbers to click through on the public phone, I could see the traffic piling up around the Sud terminal. Then two of the notorious grey-green coaches used by the CRS arrived. Then stiff legged riot police climbed out of them and stretched their limbs on the hot tarmac. It was not going to be a picnic.

When I did get through, Monsieur Fromme's voice kept snapping on and off with the make and break of a faulty wire connection on my handset. Eventually I twisted it into a position which assured continuous speech.

'Is that Laperche?'

'Yes monsieur.'

'I've just heard on the radio. The controllers are on strike, correct?'

'Yes. Everything's cancelled or diverted.'

'What about China Airways?'

'It says "cancelled" on the board.'

'Who are the handling agents? Have you asked them?'

'I don't know who they are. Could be Alitalia, could be Air Inter.'

'Never mind. Stay there. Stay where you are. I'll ring the Ministry. Phone me back in half an hour.'

'Understood.'

I returned to the concourse bar and sat on a stool. The barman was still absent. I could see the bobbing hair of the hostess as she spoke on another phone in the bank. I took a spiteful comfort from the knowledge that she was in the same boat. I knew within me that it was not her fault that I had nearly lost my job; the fault could be laid fairly and squarely at the feet of Simon Laperche. When would he learn? Probably never.

She put the phone down and walked to the Alitalia desk.

'Monsieur?' a voice called behind me. I jumped like a propositioned priest.

'Christ, you startled me!' I said to the barman. He did not care. 'I'll have a beer. No, a coffee. Make it a coffee.' I did not want to smell of alcohol for Monsieur Fromme.

The barman slapped a saucer onto the counter behind me and threw two paper-wrapped sugars and a teaspoon onto it.

'Madame?' he called over his shoulder as he banged the espresso machine into life.

I glanced down the bar. Climbing onto another stool was the hostess. Her skirt was shorter when she sat and she had nice knees.

'A Vittel menthe please.'

'A Vittel menthe,' he shouted to the optics, as if they would serve it with no human intervention. He probably felt unease at the improper silence of the terminal and was trying to prove to us that really it was the thriving hub of a European crossroads and not the white elephant that we all knew it to be.

I drank my coffee.

She sipped her mint.

The barman picked his teeth.

At length I said, 'Has your flight been cancelled or diverted?'

'Cancelled,' she said over her glass. 'Yours?'

'The same.'

End of conversation. I turned away and watched the two Air Inter hostesses walk back down the concourse. They proudly stepped along in their new summer uniforms of cream and orange, unaware that every pool of sunlight they walked through made their dresses transparent. I followed them with my gaze until they were out of sight. I caught the barman's eye.

'There's some recompense for working here then?'

He grinned.

The girl in the blue suit scowled.

Time to ring the garage. I paid for my coffee and, to make the hostess feel uncomfortable, surreptitiously paid for her drink. I chose the phone that I had seen her using — it had seemed to work all right. Monsieur Fromme answered.

'Laperche? No panic.' I gazed around the torpor of the almost empty terminal. He had no idea. 'The news is that the flight has been delayed. It has not left Pekin yet.'

'Well that's alright then.'

'Yes. You'd better come back to the garage. You're no good where you are.'

'Not if they are still in Pekin.'

'Quite. We might have some more news by the time you get back.'

'OK'

'Oh, and is there any sign of the courier, Madame Chan?'

'I thought she was arriving with the group.'

'No, she's local. She should be there. See if you can find her and bring her down as well.'

I walked the length of the concourse and began to curse Madame Chan. I pounced on one Oriental who turned out to be a Vietnamese waiting for her husband who was in the toilet. I asked at the Alitalia desk and at Air Inter but nobody had seen a Chinese courier so I considered honour satisfied and made my way back towards my coach. The hostess had moved to a bench and was sifting through some papers in her case. She looked up as I approached.

'It was quite unnecessary for you to pay for my drink,' she said. 'Allow me to reimburse you.'

I waved away her purse.

'I'm looking for a courier,' I said. 'A Chinky. I don't suppose you've seen one have you?'

'A what?'

'A Chinese woman. Called Madame Chan. She's my courier and I've got to take her down to Paris.'

I thought she had not heard me for the moment because she carefully pushed the papers back into her case, snapped it shut and then stood up.

'That's very kind of you,' she said. 'I'm the "Chinky" you are looking for.' She held out her hand. 'I am Madame Chan. I can see we are going to get on well together.'

'But...'

'But I'm not slit-eyed and yellow skinned and dangling a pig-tail?'

'It was a manner of speaking.' We shook hands and I remembered that her hands were cool.

'An uninformed one.'

She picked up her case and I pointed her towards the nearest exit to my coach.

'Well I was told to look for a Chinese courier called Madame Chan. What do you expect?'

'From you? Probably not a lot more than that.'

6

Walking out of the smoked glass and air conditioning of the terminal into the heavy midday air was like stepping into a sauna filled with cotton wool. I could feel the sweat beginning to trickle down my spine and I knew that the time and effort that I had devotedly spent ironing my shirt would soon be wasted. Madame Chan walked alongside me, looking cool and comfortable.

'There's my coach over... Oh I don't believe it.' I shook my head pityingly. With all the parking space available on the terminal forecourt, someone had parked a coach right across the front of me. 'What an idiot!'

'What is wrong?'

'The green coach is mine, not the white one.'

'Oh, but you can't get out. He's blocked you in.'

'Exactly.' I unlocked the door of the Mercedes, turned the door release tap and pulled the doors open. 'I'll put the ventilation on and you can sit here in the shade whilst I find the other driver.'

She sat on the front seat. I started the motor and let it run for a while. I checked the charge of the batteries and then put the ceiling and floor ventilators on boost.

'You see that button there?' She slipped from her seat and leaned over my shoulder. I could smell perfume. It was *Eau de Roche*. Coach drivers soon learn the popular perfumes because the perfume houses give presents to tourist guides to encourage them to unload their coaches outside their shops. She looked at the board.

'The yellow one?'

'Yes. If you get too cold or you can't stand the noise of the fans, just push it once OK?'

'Just once. I understand. Will you be long?'

'I hope not. I've just got to find this idiotic driver. I'll leave the door open.'

She nodded, settled on the seat and pulled a *Le Monde* from her case. I walked around the white coach. It was an old model of Neoplan. I recognised the livery as the Autocars du Louvre. They had often supplied coaches to Cityscope, where Daniel worked; I had met them when I was with Papa Coursamel. I banged on the side of the coach in case the driver was asleep on the back seat. Nothing happened. The door was open so I stepped in. Empty. No keys on the board. Pity. I could have moved it in fifteen seconds with the keys.

I leaned across the wheel and blew the horn several times and waited. Nobody reacted. This was getting stupid. I jumped down and peered along the forecourt in both directions under the canopy. A couple of taxis were slowly stewing at Arrivals. A van driver was reversing with his head stuck out of the sliding door. I could see nobody who looked anything like a coach driver. I poked my head back into my coach.

'The idiot has disappeared. I shall probably have to put an announcement out in the terminal.'

'OK,' she said and turned a page of her paper.

The girl at the Welcome Desk in the middle of the concourse said she had no idea who did the speaker announcements, why didn't I ask at one of the airlines? I walked along to Departures. The Air Inter check-in girl said that they did not have the microphones but that Marise at Alitalia had a boyfriend who worked in that part of the office and he would know, so I crossed the hall to Alitalia. The Alitalia check-in girl said that she had not seen Marise but this was not surprising because Marise was scheduled to work on Arrivals today. I plodded back down the concourse, past the Welcome Desk, down to the other end of the building. The airport security man would not let me through into the baggage claim and did not know who supplied the metallic voices for the loudspeakers. I grabbed an Alitalia steward as he came out and he said that Marise had not turned in for work today and directed me to the Information Desk of the Paris Airports Authority. There, a self satisfied, smug, flesh-wobbling mound of a tartar haughtily divulged that she was the supremo of the tannoy and then gleefully regretted that she could not put out private announcements on the tannoy without the written permission of the Director of Communications and Public Relations.

'Success?' Madame Chan looked up from her paper.

'I'll tell you what, I'll read your paper and you go and find the driver.'

She folded the paper up and offered it to me.

'Would you like it?' she asked sweetly.

Sarcasm always backfires on me.

'No.' I suddenly had an idea. 'Not your paper. I don't want your paper. Lend me your hair band. It's elastic isn't it?'

'Yes.' Her admission was guarded. 'What do you want it for?'

'To get the driver. Come on.' I held out my hand.

She looked at me and then shrugged. With one hand, she peeled the band from her head, shaking her hair to her shoulders. She held it out to me. I took it and stretched it a couple of times to test its strength.

'Happy?' she asked.

I nodded. I skipped over to the Neoplan and climbed up the steps. I searched around the dashboard until I had located what I wanted. The sliding ashtray would do nicely. I pulled it half out and looped one end of the hairband under it. I then stretched the other end up towards the steering column. With a twang the band hooked over the end of the klaxon lever and held it down.

I ambled leisurely back to my coach and slipped behind the wheel.

'How long will that dreadful noise go on?' Madame Chan asked.

'Shall I close the door?' I pushed the button and the door hissed shut, cutting out some of the noise but not all.

'How will that childish prank advance us?'

'We are not going anywhere whilst he is parked in front of us. He must be in the terminal somewhere. This will alert him to the need for him to return to his coach.'

'But it's an awful noise. Look, people are staring.'

'That is what we want. We need the driver.'

'What happens if he does not come?'

'Then we will not go anywhere, but then neither will he because his battery will be flat and his air reservoir empty.'

She jumped as a hand crashed on the side of my coach and a voice shouted,

'All right Laperche, joke's over.'

He leaned into the Neoplan and flipped off the hairband from the horn lever.

'Well that's a relief,' Madame Chan said as the klaxon died.

It was Monceau. Nicolas Monceau. A tight faced man with a pulsing vein in his forehead and wet eyes. Restless, thin, living on nervous energy, he was capable of almost any excess once he had lost his temper which he did about twice a day. Our paths had crossed several times when I was doing excursions for Cityscope. Crossing paths with Monceau meant that he carved you up at the lights so that he got the unloading point that you had lined up for or he baulked you at the Pont Neuf so that his tourists got the view of the Seine and yours, the advertising hoarding. He used his coach as a tool, or more exactly, a weapon.

I opened our coach doors.

'Hello Monceau. I should have recognised your crap parking. Move your coach will you? Some of us have work to do.'

'I'd heard they had given you back your licence.' He stood there grinning spitefully at me and twirling Madame Chan's hairband around one finger. He offered it to me. 'Yours, Laperche?'

'Never seen it before in my life.'

'Or is it perhaps mademoiselle's garter?' He flipped at the hem of Madame Chan's skirt with his finger. She jumped back and slapped her newspaper down onto her lap.

'That's enough of that,' I snapped. His familiarity had riled me. The instant anger in my voice caused Madame Chan to give me a funny look. 'You're wrong on both counts,' I said. 'It's "madame" not "mademoiselle" and she is not wearing stockings. Just move your coach Monceau.'

'Who for? Simon Laperche? The most detested coach driver in Paris?' He addressed Madame Chan. 'You be careful with him, he's dangerous is Laperche.' I slid out from behind the wheel and moved towards him. 'Make sure you are insured,' he sneered.

Madame Chan looked at him with wide eyes. I came down the steps and pushed him off the coach.

'Move your coach Monceau,' I said through gritted teeth. 'I've asked you nicely.'

'I don't need to. I'm not going anywhere and neither are you Laperche.' He poked me on the chest with his finger. 'Don't try to push me around. You don't belong in coaches. You should never have come back.'

I gave him a shove that pushed him back a few paces and then jumped back into my coach and slammed the door. I started the engine and backed up onto the pavement, judging the distance by my reflection in the plate glass wall. The Mercedes was renowned for a tight turning lock and I gambled that with one quick manoeuvre I might be able to get free. The steering pump whined furiously as I edged the front of the coach sideways. A cloud of black smoke poured from the back of Monceau's badly tuned Neoplan as he revved up. Then he launched his coach at us like a lance. Madame Chan screamed as eight tons of metal lunged towards her. I swerved and then stamped on the brakes to avoid ramming a stanchion which supported the canopy. The coach dipped forwards on its suspension and crushed a wire waste paper basket attached to the girder. We had been that close to a smash.

'Right Monceau, that's it!' I yelled.

His laughing face mouthed victorious obscenities at me through the glass. I yanked on the parking brake and banged open the doors.

'Please, don't do anything. It's not worth it,' I heard

Madame Chan plead as I thundered down the steps.

On a whim, I slipped down the blind side of my coach so that Monceau could not see me. I was angry for allowing myself to be caught in such a dangerous game. I was also unwilling to admit the obvious — there was nothing that I could do. Monceau had won. His advantage was unbeatable. He could bend his Neoplan and laugh it off back at the garage. If I so much as scratched Georges' Mercedes, I would be looking for another job.

I stood at the back of my coach, listening to the V8 tick over and wondering what to do. If I stayed out of sight, Monceau would worry himself to death wondering what I was doing. That would give me time to think but I could not hide there all day.

Suddenly, Monceau's Neoplan revved up again and began to pull away. What the devil was he cooking up now? I crept stealthily back up the side of my coach and met a CRS agent in full riot gear.

'Are you the driver?' I nodded and tried to pretend that I had been doing something important at the back of my vehicle. 'You've got to move it.'

'Where to?'

'Anywhere outside the airport boundary. We're clearing the airport. Security exercise.'

'You've picked a good day for it. You must be fermenting inside those helmets.'

'Go on, move your coach.'

'I'm going, I'm going.'

He was disappointed that I was not arguing with him. He could not know that to move my coach had been my desire for some time. I climbed up the steps of the Mercedes. Madame Chan looked coolly at me.

'You friend also had to move.' She indicated the rear of Monceau's coach which was disappearing towards the autoroute. 'He said he was sorry he missed you.'

'It was a bloody miracle that he did.'

'It certainly was not your skill.'

I thought that she could have been a bit more thankful than that.

'Are you alright?' I asked a little belatedly.

'No I am not all right.' She slapped her newspaper down on her knees. 'I don't like your behaviour, I don't like your friends and I don't like the way you drive.'

'Well that's fine then.' I shouted back. 'I don't like your attitude, and I don't like your friends either and come to think of it, this all started because I didn't like the way you drove so that makes us evens.'

'Splendid!' She rustled her paper and pulled it up before her face.

'Right then,' I said as I slipped the coach into gear, 'I'll take you back to the garage as I have been requested and I shall unload you there with great pleasure. Next time I find you crying at Orly because you have booked a dud coach, I'll walk straight past, whistling.'

'I was not crying,' she said through clenched teeth.

I grunted disbelievingly.

Monsieur Fromme was in his favourite place, sunning himself on the concrete apron before the garage door. He was standing with his hands in his jacket pockets, thumbs pointing forwards and rocking backwards and forwards on his heels. When he saw me, he stepped inside and was swallowed up by the black shade. I swung the coach in. Fromme came up the steps.

'This is Madame Chan,' I said to his raised eyebrows and then turned to the courier. 'Madame Chan, this is Monsieur Fromme, my boss.' They shook hands.

'It seems we have had a lot of trouble for nothing,' Monsieur Fromme said.

'Yes... a lot of trouble,' Madame Chan said.

Fromme looked sharply at me.

'Any problems, Laperche?'

'No, none,' I said airily. 'Apart from the missing group of course.'

'Well we're working on that.' He turned and said over his shoulder, 'Come into my office both of you,'

I grinned at Madame Chan. She did not like his apparent assumption that she had no more status than a coach driver. I followed her into the office. The wobbly fan was still wobbling. Madame Aurélie was not at work today so Monsieur Fromme pulled forward her chair and offered it to Madame Chan. I leaned against the doorway and thought that she would probably be quite attractive if she were not so prickly and uncompromising. Presumably Mr. Chan had found her attractive.

'The last news I had from the Ministry was that their plane had not left Pekin yet. They are awaiting assurance before they take off that they will be able to land.'

'That sounds eminently reasonable to me,' I said. 'How long does it take to fly from China?'

Monsieur Fromme rubbed his temple and thought.

'Well it must...' he began.

'About fourteen hours,' Madame Chan replied. 'They'll come via Calcutta and Ankara to avoid flying over Russia.'

'I see, I see. Well that gives us plenty of warning.' He looked at Madame Chan and then seemed to suddenly remember his courtesy. 'Oh, would you like a coffee, Madame Chan?'

'That would be most welcome.'

Monsieur Fromme half turned towards Madame Aurélie's desk and then swung back. He looked at Madame Chan in consternation. She smiled back at him.

'Yes, make it two coffees Laperche.'

I jerked to attention.

'What?'

'Two coffees Laperche.'

'Black, no sugar,' Madame Chan added. Her smile was sweetness itself.

'Right,' I said. 'Two coffees.'

I heard the phone ring as I left the office. 'Two coffees!' I muttered. 'Two coffees!' as I strode over to the sink. The porcelain was cracked and stained, the taps, tarnished. I peered into the mugs. Somehow, I could not see Madame Chan drinking from these. I skipped out of the door and down the street to Chez Jean.   Several of the drivers were taking a relaxed lunch. Georges scowled at me over his plate.

'How did it go?' he asked.

'It hasn't yet. We've come up against a problem.' I

turned to the barman. 'Paul, could you do me three coffees and put them on a tray for me?' He opened his mouth as if to argue but then shrugged his shoulders.

'If you've bent my coach...' Georges began.

'Now be fair,' I said. 'It always pulled a bit to the left, the dent in the side is an old one and the back seat was ripped when I got it.'

'What!' Georges gagged on his pork chop. The other drivers jeered at him and he realised that I was teasing him. He pointed his fork at me. 'One day,' he choked. 'One day.'

The barman put the tray on the bar.

'Have you got any of those little wafer biscuit things? Just to make it look more genteel.'

The barman sighed.

'You are a pain.' He arranged a handful of wafers on a saucer and added it to the tray. 'Make sure I get the tray back.'

'I promise.'

I swept grandly in to Monsieur Fromme's office with the exaggerated swagger of an Italian waiter.

'Coffee madame, black no sugar.' I placed her cup on the Pas de Calais. She inclined her head with the beginnings of a smile hovering around the corners of her mouth. 'And monsieur.' I leaned across and lowered his coffee onto the Cote d'Azur. He stared open mouthed at me. 'Biscuits,' I said, covering the Massif Central with the saucer of champagne wafers.

'Thank you.' Her voice was deep and melodious.

Monsieur Fromme woke up in the real world again.

'Yes, thank you Laperche.' He stared at me again. 'Get a stool and sit down.' I did so. Madame Chan caught my eye for an instant. Her glance was infused with a hint of humorous curiosity. 'We've had news on the group,' he said. 'That clot Knopf has just phoned.' He shot an embarrassed glance at Madame Chan. 'Do you know Monsieur Knopf?'

'We have met.' The answer was neutral. 'Please don't trouble yourself, Monsieur Fromme.'

'Right. Right.' Monsieur Fromme looked relieved.

I thought that any woman who could embarrass Monsieur Fromme was worth some interest.

'So what is the news?' I sipped my coffee.

'They are flying in to Lyon tomorrow at 10.30.'

I took a wafer from the saucer and sat back.

'Well that lets us off the hook,' I said brightly.

'How?'

'Well, they will have to use a coach from Lyon. They can't expect us to drive down there.'

'They might not expect it,' Fromme paused and looked longingly at the biscuits. 'But I do.' He nodded at Madame Chan. 'We've talked it over. You can drive down this afternoon and pick them up in the morning.'

'But it must be five hundred kilometres.' I scowled angrily at Madame Chan.

He traced his finger down the map.

'Four hundred and sixty eight and it's autoroute all the way.'

'What about my hours? The tachograph?'

'That Merc will hold one hundred kph on an autoroute all day long. Even allowing for stops you could easily be there by eight tonight.'

I looked across at Madame Chan. She was studying her finger nails.

'What about you? Are you quite happy to...?'

'It's what I am paid for,' she replied.

'And driving coaches is what you are paid for Laperche.'

I caught the tone of his voice and it reminded me of dumper trucks and building sites and unemployment. I nodded in agreement.

'O.K.' I conceded. 'I'll top up the tank. I shall need every litre I've got.'

'I'll give you an agency card for good measure.'

This made sense. The card would allow me to fill up at any station with the bill being charged directly to Autocars Fromme. It was an essential introduction to a filling station. It guaranteed that they would be paid and would avoid Fromme having to give me a hefty float of cash.

'Madame Chan, how long will you need in order to collect some overnight things and get back here?'

She bit her bottom lip and looked at the ceiling.

'An hour and a half.'

Monsieur Fromme glanced up at the office clock.

'So you could be back here at about three o clock?' She nodded. 'Good. We'll do that then.'

She stood up, picked up her attaché case and turned to go.

'Thank you for the coffee, Monsieur Laperche.'

'My pleasure madame,' I said correctly and opened the door for her.

We watched in silence as she walked out of the garage and into the sunlight. I thought of the two air hostesses at Orly Ouest and found myself regretting that Madame Chan's skirt did not become transparent in the sunlight.

I looked at Monsieur Fromme. He looked at me.

'Hmm,' he said thoughtfully.

I took the tray back to the café and paid the barman. Monsieur Fromme had not offered to pay and, recalling the sight of his face as I had pirouetted into his office bearing aloft the silver tray had made the bill worth every centime. I stood at the bar and ate a rillettes sandwich. The drivers had gone back to work. The café tables looked abandoned and jaded in the heat. I turned to the barman and nodded at the scorching pavement.

'This weather must give your trade a boost.'

'Just the opposite,' he said. 'It's too hot to drink. All they want to do is sit with a glass on the table and wait until the shadows get longer.'

'Have you got any bread left?'

He pulled open the bin.

'Three or four.'

'Could you make me another couple of sandwiches? Rillettes with plenty of gherkins and a ham.'

He sighed and nodded.

'And could you wrap them up for me to take away?'

He looked at me and sighed again.

'Have you got any redeeming features?' he asked.

I shrugged. I just did not need a philosopher for a barman.

I filled up Georges' Mercedes at the garage pump and then walked around it to make sure that I had not marked it in any way. I discreetly rubbed the sole of my shoe over the scuff marks on the bumper where I had crushed the rubbish basket. I stood thinking quietly in the cool gloom of the garage. I had nearly lost my temper at the airport. I knew that what I had done was stupid. With a passenger in the coach, it had been reckless. I could still see the terror on Madame Chan's face as the Neoplan had charged towards her. I would have to be a lot more careful if I wanted to keep my job. I had no idea what Monsieur Fromme thought of me but I dared not force him into an assessment.

Then Noel rattled into the garage in his Saviem. 'Simon,' he shouted from the wheel, 'can you help me?'

I walked across to him.

'What's the matter? Schoolkids playing you up?'

'Very funny.' He nodded over his shoulder. 'Take a look.'

I did. The roof lining above the aisle was hanging loose, suspended by the wiring of the three ceiling lights. It swung at chest height like a ten metre long hammock.

'How on earth did you do that?'

He gave me a disgusted look.

'How old is this coach?' he asked. 'I bet it's older than me. It's falling apart that is what is happening. It ought to be stuffed full of poultry and dumped in a field.'

I ducked down the aisle and gingerly offered one end of the board up to its locating lugs.

'Poxy coach,' Noel muttered. 'The kids thought it was great fun. That was after all the girls had stopped screaming, of course.'

'Do you mean you had passengers in?'

'And how! That college at the back of the Boulevard Barbès. You know where they did all that sewer work?' I nodded. 'They left a hump in the road. Of course, you can't see it in the cobbles. We went up like a rocket and came down with a hell of a bang.'

'You must have been pushing the needle a bit.'

He ignored my observation. Any driver would try to get a school job over and done with in the shortest time possible. It was essential if you wished to retain your eardrums and your sanity.

'Can you fix it?' He appeared a little anxious.

'What? Now?' I looked at my watch.

He nodded and glanced across to where Monsieur Fromme was working over the orders.

'And keep it quiet if you can. We don't want the boss to know do we? I've got another job at three.'

'You'll have to help me then.'

'Thanks Simon.'

'Whatever you do, don't switch the interior lights on. With the way those wires are tangled you'll blow a fuse.'

We set to work. Like any repair task in a coach of this age, it became more and more complex. Some of the plugs that were supposed to hold up the lining were missing. I searched in my box to find screws, bolts, bits of wire, anything that would do the job. Some of the lugs were broken. I could do nothing to alter those without a power drill and that would have alerted Monsieur Fromme.

At one point he came out of his office and stood looking around the garage as if searching for some kind of inspiration. We loafed in the coach, idly chatting, passing the time of day, casually supporting the loose ceiling with our heads and praying that he would not come across to us.

By half past two we had effected some kind of repair. It would be sufficient to hold until I would have the chance to do it properly. As Noel drove out of the garage, Madame Chan walked in. She was carrying a small suitcase and had changed into a gauzy summery dress with a faint pastel flower print on it. One of those shapeless confections that floated vaguely around the body. She caught me looking.

'I have my working clothes in my case. This will be more comfortable for a journey. It will be even hotter in Lyon.'

'I passed no comment.'

'That's true,' she admitted with a wry smile. 'You passed no comment.'

Monsieur Fromme came out. He looked at his watch and then at Madame Chan.

'Early. Good, good.' He handed an envelope to me. 'Here's the agency card. Don't lose it.' He watched whilst I tucked it into my wallet. 'And here is a float. That should cover the tolls on the autoroute, oh and your hotel and some meals. I'll need receipts.'

'Of course.'

He looked quickly across at Madame Chan.

'I presume you are provided for by the Ministry?'

'Yes, my hotel and meals will be no problem.'

'Good. Off you go then.'

I indicated the coach to Madame Chan.

'Laperche.' Monsieur Fromme looked me in the eyes. 'This group is important. I am relying on you. Don't let me down.'

'I can only do my best, monsieur.'

Madame Chan settled on the front passenger seat and I put her suitcase on the seat behind.

'There's no point putting it in the boot,' I explained as we nudged out into the street. 'You might want it on the journey.'

'Highly unlikely.'

'You can never tell with women.'

'I would believe that you could never tell. How far did Monsieur Fromme say it was?'

'About five hundred kilometres.'

'When do you think we will arrive?'

'In about six hours, I suppose.'

'Six hours.' She sighed heavily.

'Oh don't worry. All you have to do is sit there. I'll drive the coach, thank you.'

Her face clouded with irritation.

'Good,' she said briskly. 'Do you know the way?'

'Porte d'Orléans. Autoroute A6. Get off at Lyon. Not that difficult.'

'This is not the way to the Porte d'Orléans.'

'No, it is not. You are absolutely right. I am so glad you came along.'

'So where are we going then?'

'My flat. I have to feed my canary before I go away.'

She stopped talking and watched the hot, sweaty world of Paris as it drifted by the window. I drove to the Gare St. Lazare and hid the coach in the Cour d'Amsterdam. I knew that the time that the SNCF would need to decide that I had no right to be there would be less than the time that I intended to stay. I pulled the coach in as far under the shade of the awning as I could.

'I'll leave the doors open in case you want to stretch your legs.'

She looked around the dirty loading bays with their oil stained concrete and dented fenders.

'How long will you be?'

Her voice had lost some of its confidence.

'I don't have a canary.'

'I never thought for a moment that you had.'

'But whilst you were flitting about Paris getting into your fairy princess outfit, I was mending coaches. I now have to get my overnight things.'

'My fairy princess outfit?' She looked at her dress. 'So Monsieur Laperche does not like my dress?'

'It is not for me to like or dislike it.'

'I am glad you recognise that.'

'But I did not say that I did not like it.' I went down the steps into the yard. 'I shan't be long. I only live five minutes away.'

I decided against taking a shower. I threw some things into a soft bag and then, on a whim, pulled off my trousers and slipped into a pair of shorts. Comfortable for the journey? Two could play at that game. When I got back to the coach I could see that somebody was already in the coach talking to Madame Chan. Damn! Trust the SNCF to be awake on a day like today.

'I'm just going...' I began my excuse and then I saw the leather skirt.

'Sisi!' Monique greeted me with a big kiss. 'I knew it would be your coach.'

Madame Chan was sitting stock still on her seat as if she were watching an obscure play in a foreign language.

'What are you doing here Nikki?'

'Working. What about you?'

'The same.'

'In shorts? Who are you trying to kid?' She turned to Madame Chan. 'He's got nice legs hasn't he? You should see his bum!'

'Nikki!'

I pushed past her and dropped my bag on the seat with the suitcase. She looked at the bags.

'Are you going away then?'

'We're going to Lyon and you're going back to work.'

'Lyon! Oh take me with you Sisi. Take me with you. I'll be ever so good.' She hung onto my arm in a mock pleading manner. 'I'll cook your food and wash your clothes and rub your back... again.' She grinned at me.

'Nikki, will you just...'

She turned suddenly to Madame Chan and said, 'Oh, are you Sisi's girlfriend?' And before Madame Chan could react she added, 'Is he taking you away on a dirty weekend?'

'Nikki, that's enough!'

She pouted at me and then confided to Madame Chan, 'He's short tempered but he's a darling really. He saved my life once.'

'Really?' Madame Chan pursed her lips to display her uninterest.

'He leapt on my attacker, wrested the sabre from his hand and then kicked him down the métro steps. Bong! Just like that.'

'It wasn't a sabre and if I had known then how you could fight I would have sided with him.'

'Beast!' She swung her bag at my shoulder. 'Oops!' she said and scooped a naked breast back into the pink fluff of her bolero.

'Do try and stay in your clothes Nikki, there's a lady present.' I sat down at the wheel and waited. When Nikki was like this there was nothing to do but wait.

She turned to Madame Chan and curtseyed, nearly losing both breasts in the process.

'I like your dress,' she said. Madame Chan flinched as Nikki felt the cloth. 'I bet you keep cool in that.'

Madame Chan looked at Nikki's leather skirt.

'Yes,' she said.

'Yes,' Nikki repeated vaguely then she seemed suddenly to lose all her energy. She sagged onto a seat.

Madame Chan raised her eyebrows and studied the overhead luggage rack. Nikki's voice sounded very small.

'Take me away Sisi.'

'I can't take you to Lyon.' I looked purposefully at Madame Chan. 'I've got myself in enough trouble already by carrying unauthorised passengers.'

'Anywhere,' she pleaded.

'Nikki,' I said softly, 'I can't take you away from yourself. That is where you are trying to go.'

She looked down at the floor and nodded. I looked at her slumped shoulders. Madame Chan looked out of the window.

'All right.' She came up with a brave grin. 'Which way do you go out of Paris?'

'Porte d'Orléans.'

'Can you drop me near the Parc Montsouris? I want to see some real trees.'

'O.K.,' I sighed, 'but you get off with no fuss when I say so?'

'Promise.'

Madame Chan cleared her throat.

'Perhaps we should leave,' she suggested. 'It is getting late.'

'You heard what the boss said,' Nikki said.

We drove down the Boulevard Raspail, past the Hotel Lutétia, pressing on towards the faint blotch of green. The traffic was building up again after the lull at lunchtime. I stopped by the Cité Universitaire.

'Passengers alight here for the Parc Montsouris,' I called.

'Thanks Sisi.' Nikki leaned across and kissed my cheek.

I squeezed her arm.

'Are you O.K.?'

She nodded and looked towards the shaded haven of the trees.

'I just need to walk sometimes, for the pleasure of walking, not for work.'

'I understand.'

She jumped down to the pavement.

'Cheerio,' she called.

Madame Chan jumped and vaguely lifted a limp hand.

'Nikki!' She turned at my voice. 'Have you eaten all those haricot beans yet.'

She grinned at me.

'No, you bastard.' And she wiggled her bum at me and walked off.

7

Madame Chan did not talk and that suited me. The traffic for the first ten kilometres was heavy and progress was slow. As we passed the police HQ where I had abandoned my truck, I could feel my head sinking into my shoulders. It was a subconscious reflex. They could not see me from that distance and would not know who I was if they did. That all seemed so long ago. But I was back in coaches thanks to Monsieur de Mello and a spot of good luck.

I twiddled the knobs on the radio. The Merc had a superb Blaupunkt radio and PA system. I pressed a button and then cringed at the twanging of an electric guitar. Georges obviously liked FIP 514. I found France Musique and sat back to the tones of a piano. The music was so unlike the weather. Outside, the heat was cloying, the air sticky. Inside, the music was clear and cool.

The traffic began to thin out and I opened up. We curved through the edge of the forest of Fontainebleau with the needle sitting squarely on the hundred and there it stayed. We wafted along, floating on music and soft suspension. Monsieur Fromme was right. The V8 pushing the empty coach was hardly idling and did not recognise any inclines at all. I glanced across at my passenger, wondering whether I should try to make myself sociable but her head was back on the rest and her eyes closed. She was either asleep or maintaining a distance. I drove on.

As we came around Auxerre she suddenly sat up. 'Something wrong?' I asked, my eyes fixed on the road.
'Where are we?'
'Just going around Auxerre.'
'I must have been asleep.'

I turned down the volume on the radio.

'Chopin's Grande Polonaise,' I said. 'One of my favourite pieces.'

'Yes.' She sounded surprised. 'You can leave it on.'

'Thanks for the permission.'

She leaned forward and pressed her elbows on her knees.

'Monsieur Laperche,' she said, 'Don't you think it would be a good idea if we tried to get on with each other? We have to work together. It may not be our choice but we have a job to do.'

'It certainly was not my choice. Not for Maxim's, not for Orly, not for Lyon. I blame you for all this.'

'Maxim's was your own fault. You helped me out. You offered, spontaneously.'

'I really can't think why. I must have been mad.' I remembered her face, almost on the point of tears and the blustering, bullying minister. I recalled the way her hair swung when she ran and how her breasts moved in her shirt.

'You only have your good nature to blame for that,' she said.

'I don't have one. It certainly was not that. You don't know me.'

'No I don't know you Monsieur Laperche. I am still trying to decide whether I want to. You don't make it easy.'

'Simon.'

'Pardon?'

'Not "Monsieur Laperche". My name is Simon.'

'Simon,' she repeated, then with realisation, 'of course — Sisi.'

'No,' I said sharply, 'not Sisi. That is what Nikki calls me. It is reserved for her.'

'Ah yes, Nikki.'

'What do you mean, "Ah yes, Nikki"?'

'Nothing. You're very sensitive aren't you?'

'Just leave Nikki alone. That kid is alright. She's just having a hard time that's all.'

'Have you known her long?'

'Some years.'

'She told me she worked at the station. Is that how you met her?'

'Not the way you think. I've never been a client.'

'What do you mean, "a client"?'

'She does not work AT the station. She works the station.'

'I don't see the difference.'

I threw her a quick look and realised that she was serious. She did not know. She really did not know. Her innocence went to her credit.

'Some girls work the stations, some the pavements. I'll leave you to fathom it out.'

She thought for a few seconds then her lovely brown eyes opened wide and she stared at me.

'Do you mean that Nikki was ...a lady of easy virtue?'

'Not "was" — "is." And she is a prostitute. Her virtue does not come into the equation.' Her face coloured up. 'I suppose now you are going to say again that you don't like my friends.'

'Do you know many prostitutes?'

'Just the one. And when that one is Nikki, one is enough.'

'Yes I suppose so,' she observed absently. 'Was that true what she said about you saving her life?'

'Nikki has a vivid imagination. She also packs a hefty punch. Anyway she returned the favour two days ago. And that reminds me, I owe her an umbrella.'

'An umbrella?'

'She broke it on somebody.'

'How?'

'I'll spare you the details but he won't be wanting the services of any of Nikki's colleagues for a few weeks.'

'Oh,' she said. 'You like talking in riddles don't you?'

'I don't know what you mean.' I pointed at a road sign. 'Look, there is a service station in five kilometres and another in thirty nine. Do you want a coffee or... um... anything?'

'Shall we wait for the thirty nine? The traffic is running well at the moment.'

'Please yourself, I'm easy.'

'Then I shall drink a coffee with you with pleasure in thirty nine kilometres.'

She did not call me Simon, but then neither did she call me Monsieur Laperche.

Half an hour later we pulled in to the services.

'I shall have to put the coach in the lorry park. Shall I drop you here?'

'No, I'll come to the park with you. I would benefit from a walk.'

We parked up amongst the lorries. I locked the coach and we walked across the greasy tarmac towards the main services. Had I been on my own I would have gone to the drivers' café.

'Take care on this tarmac, it's slippery. You'll need to rub your soles in some dust when we get across.'

She looked down and picked her route carefully. A puff of breeze gently lifted the skirt of her dress and the driver of a St. Gobain tanker whistled. She hurriedly snatched down the cloth.

'I wish they wouldn't do that,' she said, her girlish embarrassment detectable in the short, staccato syllables.

'Quite natural. Pretty lady, nice ankles. What do you expect?'

'Would you have whistled?'

I grinned at her.

'Probably.'

I realised that this admission would put me back down to zero. I would have to stop telling the truth.

The self service was packed, hot and noisy. The windows had been propped open to gain the most benefit from the sparse breeze and the roaring of the traffic pervaded the building. And yet, amongst all that noise, we drank our coffee in silence.

'I'll see you back at the coach,' I said as I got up. 'You know where it is, don't you?'

She nodded.

The traffic leaving the car park was at a standstill. This was bad news. I walked up to the front of the line of simmering cars and found a Dutch registered Audi towing a caravan. The driver had started up the exit and then realised that he had missed the filling station. He had tried to turn across the verge and had now stranded himself and blocked the road. It did not bother me because the heavy vehicles used a different run. The man was tall and bald headed. He wore blue shorts and a tee shirt. His wife was heavy like a Dutchwoman, with a round face and red cheeks. She was tugging at the grab handles on the caravan. Half a dozen people were watching and giving the kind of advice that they do in such situations. I could see that he needed to uncouple the caravan.

I tapped the sweating woman on the arm and pointed to the drawbar. She turned and said something to me in Dutch. I shrugged my shoulders. She called to her husband. He looked at me and nodded. I held up the bar whilst he disconnected everything.

'Can't some of you give a hand instead of just gawping?' I shouted at the bystanders. They began to slope off. Together the three of us wriggled the caravan off the grass back onto the tarmac. Without its weight forcing down the back of the car, the Dutchman was able to drive off. We recoupled the caravan. Somebody in the queue began to blow his horn. I straightened up to go and give the musician a piece of my mind but then recalled the futile argument I had seen on my way to Le Bourget. I shook my head pityingly.

With what I took to be profuse thanks they climbed back into the car. They were still facing the wrong way. I stood before him and, making a wide arc with my arm, showed him where he could drive around the back of the station to come up to the pumps. As the queue began to move I thanked the occupants of each car for the assistance that they had not given. They looked blankly at me as they passed, not understanding; their senses bludgeoned by the heat.

I walked over grass baked dry like concrete to the lorry park. Madame Chan was standing by the coach talking to a lorry driver. She had one hand on the closed door and the other entwined in a bunch of her skirt, holding it near to her. I did not like the pose.

'Ah, here's my driver now,' she said loudly and her face brightened nervously.

The lorry driver turned towards me. He had tattoos on both forearms and weighed about one hundred and thirty kilos, only ten of which was muscle.

'What do you want?' I said sharply.

'Oh just passing the time of day with your charming friend,' he leered.

'Clear off!'

'No need to take offence,' he bristled. He did not like to lose face.

I pushed the point of my keys against my pocket.

'If I catch you within fifty metres of madame again I will give you a tattoo you won't want to show anybody. Now bugger off!'

He waddled away as quickly as his unhealthy legs could carry him. I caught Madame Chan looking at my shorts. She was supposed to have been looking at the shape in my pocket.

'Have you really got a knife?' she asked, trying to cover her confusion.

I laughed, pulled out the keys and unlocked the door. She climbed inside. She did have nice ankles.

'Do you have to be so... so aggressive?' She shook her head tensely as she said 'aggressive'.

I sat behind the wheel and stared at her.

'You like lecherous lorry drivers trying to pick you up like a common tart do you?'

She flinched. It did not make me feel any better.

'Whatever the situation,' she said, 'however you perceive it, you still do not need to be so rude to people.'

I put the Merc in gear.

'We'll be at Macon by about seven. We'll stop at the services there and get something to eat.' I pulled out onto the driveway. 'I know the way,' I added.

She crossed her arms, pinched her lips together and stared through the windscreen.

Ten kilometres before Macon everything stopped. We sat in silence, watching the line of stationary vehicles head of us. I could hear the distant 'pam-pom-pam' of an ambulance and looking in my mirror I could see the headlamps and flashing blue light as it weaved its way around the occasional vehicle which had pulled onto the hard shoulder for a break.

'Somebody must be hurt,' she said as the ambulance squeezed past us. It was the first thing she had said for an hour and three quarters.

I looked in my mirror again. I could see an orange light.

'I think they're going to try to cut them out. Here comes the fire truck.' She shivered at the thought. I stopped the engine. 'This is going to mess up our plans.'

'Is that all you can think about? Somewhere ahead, injured people are probably trapped in a crashed car and all you can say is that it will mess up our plans.'

'Madame Chan,' I said, 'why don't we just accept that we are never going to get on with each other and leave it at that, eh? God knows I've tried. Let's just leave it. I'll not bother you and you won't bother me.'

'Jocelyne,' she said.

'What?'

'Not Madame Chan — Jocelyne.'

The sun was shining through the glass in the door at a low angle and highlighting her hair. I had thought that it was dark brown but now I could see that it had many colours. And in amongst the palette of tints was some silver.

'Jocelyne Chan. Unusual combination. Why Chan?'

'See if you can work it out for yourself. It's not so difficult.'

'Married to a Monsieur Chan?' I suggested. She raised her eyebrows to show me how easy it had been. 'And Monsieur Chan is Chinese?'

'Yes, he's Chinese.'

She waited.

I waited.

Nothing moved ahead.

'What does Monsieur Chan do?'

'He used to be a businessman.'

'Used to..? Oh, I'm sorry. It was thoughtless of me.'

She looked at me with amazement and then burst out laughing.

'Oh Simon you are funny!'

'I'm glad you think so,' I retorted.

'Monsieur Chan used to be a businessman. I don't know what he is doing now. He is in China.'

'What is he doing in China?'

'I just told you, I don't know.'

'I mean, why is he in China? And don't say it is because he is Chinese.'

She looked at me thoughtfully and then smiled down at her knees.

'That is not the question you are asking, is it?'

'Now who is talking in riddles?'

'What you are trying to ask is, why am I not in China with my husband?'

'It had crossed my mind.'

'It's a long story,' she said. I indicated the stationary traffic ahead of us. 'Even longer than that,' she added.

'O.K.'

'What about Simon Laperche?'

'What about him?'

'Tell me why he is dangerous. As if I could not guess from his behaviour so far.'

'Who says he is dangerous?'

'And why must I be frightened of him?'

'I don't know what you are talking about.'

'And why did your friend at Orly call you, "the most despicable driver in Paris"?'

'You're wrong on two counts. He is not my friend and he called me, "the most detested driver in Paris".'

'Why?'

'Oh... it's a long story.'

'I see.'

And so we sat there.

Two people, both with long stories to tell and the time to tell them, and we said nothing.

After another ten minutes of inactivity I looked up at the clock above the windscreen.

'We are cutting it fine for a meal,' I said. 'We really

need to push on to Lyon as soon as this clears.'

'How far away are we?'

'About eighty kilometres, but it might just as well be eight hundred if we are not going anywhere.'

'Why the rush?'

'Do you have a hotel already booked then?'

'There will be room somewhere.'   She began to rummage in her bag. 'You don't happen to have any sweets or something to suck do you?'

I shook my head. 'There's a bottle of water in the locker in front of you.'

She tore the foil from the capuchon and flipped it off with her thumb. She looked around the coach, vaguely seeking inspiration.

'No glasses, I'm afraid. You'll have to drink straight from the bottle.'

'Well, look the other way then.'

'Why?'

'Because it is what a gentleman does when a lady has to drink from a bottle.'

'I'm not a gentleman. You already know that.'

'Please.'

I turned away and watched her reflection in the chrome strip above my side window. She gingerly put the bottle to her lips and gently tilted her head back. I studied the curve described from her nose, across her lips, over her chin and down her neck.

'How do I know when you've finished?' I asked.

'I've finished.'

'And very pretty it was too.' I pretended to polish up the chrome strip. 'Georges is good at housework.'

'You beast.'

'I told you I was no gentleman.'

'Who is Georges?'

'Coach driver. This is his coach.'

'Why is he not driving it?'

'He wanted to but Monsieur Fromme decided that your group had to have the best. In coaches, that is. The reason I am driving it is because your revolting Minister of Commerce and Industry insisted on the same driver as before. How he knew which coach company it was I have no idea. He seemed so self centred I am surprised he had time to notice it at all. Perhaps I did him an injustice.'

'Ah... that was my fault. I copied down the name on the back of your coach as you drove away.'

'I said all along that it was your fault.'

A movement caught my eye. About two hundred metres ahead, a plume of blue smoke suddenly belched from the vertical exhaust stack of a long-nosed Scania. 'I think we are moving again. How hungry are you?'

'Hungry.'

'We do need to crack on a bit now.'

She nodded bravely. It made me feel like the MC at the Spanish Inquisition. I pushed home the fuel tap and started the engine. The coach body began to rumble again to the vibration of the motor.

We slowly built up speed as the queue began to stretch out. The ambulance had gone but the firemen and police were still standing around a tangled knot of a dismembered Citroen. I did not look at my passenger but I felt her shudder.

'It's twenty to eight now,' I said to distract her. 'It will probably take us another hour to get to a hotel. Do you know Lyon?'

'Not really. I've been through it on the train.'

'I've been past it on the autoroute. This is going to be a voyage of discovery for both of us then.'

She looked at me strangely.

'It certainly seems that way.'

Suddenly I remembered the sandwiches. I pulled the bag from the pouch hanging beside me and swapped it left hand to right over the wheel. I waved the bag at her.

'Sandwich,' I said. 'If you're hungry.'

'Oh I couldn't.'

'I'm not stopping to eat and I haven't brought my ear plugs.'

'Ear plugs?'

'To blot out the rumbling of your stomach.'

'It was not rumbling.'

'It was, I could hear it from here.'

'It was not!'

I waved the bag at her. 'Do you want me to drive the next eighty kilometres with one hand on the wheel?'

She took the bag and pulled out one of the baguettes, it was about forty centimetres long. She looked at it, eyes wide with astonishment.

'Sorry,' I grinned at her discomfort. 'It was made for a hungry coach driver. The barman didn't know I would have genteel company.'

'Apparently. What is in it?'

'Ham in one. Rillettes in the other.'

'With gherkins?'

'With gherkins.'

'Can I have the ham please? I don't like gherkins.'

'Help yourself.'

She handed me back the bag. I put it on the dash so that I could help myself. The corner of a paper napkin poked from the bag. I tugged at it.

'Here, spread this on your lap. We don't want to spoil that nice dress of yours.'

'I thought you didn't like it.'

'I believe you made it clear that it was not my prerogative to either like or dislike your wardrobe.'

'Oh that was such a long time ago.' She caught me looking at her handling the sandwich. 'And a gentleman does not stare at a lady whilst she eats.'

'You know that I'm not a gentleman.'

'Well you probably don't know it, but you are, in spite of yourself.'

Whilst she was occupied with trying to assuage her obvious hunger and still retain some dignity I pushed the speed up to one hundred and twenty — twenty kph above the legal limit for the coach. It was a risk but I got away with it. By half past eight we were running along the old route nationale through the suburbs of Lyon. At a large crossroads by an old tram depot I saw a service station. I checked the fuel gauge and decided that it would be a good strategy to fill up now. Another fifteen minutes would not make much difference to our timetable tonight.

Madame Chan sat patiently whilst I pumped two hundred litres of diesel into the tank.

I hung up the hose and screwed the filler cap back on then I jumped up into the coach and pulled Monsieur Fromme's envelope from my wallet.

'It takes a bit longer than filling up a Volkswagen,' she observed.

'Yes, sorry about that. The garages on the autoroute have high speed pumps.'

'No matter.'

As I waited for the till receipt to print out I noticed a display of sweets. I pulled a bag of mints from the rack and dropped them on the counter. I slipped the agency card across. Monsieur Fromme would not notice the extra one franc thirty.

'You can put those on the card as well can't you?' I said to the cashier.

'What card?' he said, his finger poised above the keys on the register.

'Agency card,' I said, pushing it into his view.

'I don't do agency.'

'What do you mean, you don't do agency? Every garage does agency.'

'Not all the independents. And I don't.'

'You don't do agency?' I did not want to believe my ears. I had just pumped two hundred litres of his fuel into the tanks.

'You heard me. Cash only.'

'This is ridiculous. Get the manager.'

He folded his arms across his chest and leaned heavily on the counter. He spoke deliberately at me.

'I am the manager. I am the owner of the business. I am the title holder of the freehold. I do not do agency because if I did, I would have to pay one and a half percent of my turnover in commission to the agency. One and a half percent is three fifths of my profit margin on fuel.'

He straightened up, pressed the key on the register and ripped off the receipt. I took back the card and studied it for a second as if it would prove him wrong, but I knew exactly where I stood. I pulled out the float that

Monsieur Fromme had given me and counted out the money, thinking as I did so, 'that is my hotel room, that is my breakfast, that is my lunch'.

'Do you still want the mints?'

What the hell, I thought. She would never know what they had cost me.

'Everything alright?' she asked as I climbed back up the steps. 'You're looking a bit thoughtful.'

'Yes, I was just wondering where we should go to look for a hotel,' I lied. 'The airport is on the other side of town. I suppose they are arriving at Bron aren't they? I don't think Satolas is operational yet is it?'

'I don't know. I have to phone Knopf for the final details when I get to the hotel.'

I did not like the sound of that. I pulled out onto the avenue and made for the city centre.

'I thought you knew. Could you not have phoned from the services?' Her inactivity irritated me. I had just driven five hundred kilometres and she had not even bothered to find out where we were supposed to be meeting this group.

'I tried. I could not get through.' She looked hurt again.

'All right, never mind. Have a mint,' I said and tossed the bag into her lap. She jumped.

'Thank you.' She unwrapped a sweet and sucked on it thoughtfully. 'Do you want one?'

'I don't eat sweets.'

'Oh,' she said, looking at the bag and then at me. 'You bought them for me then?'

'I thought they would keep you quiet.'

'They won't,' she smiled.

I sat outside the hotel whilst she went in to check on rooms. I was gambling that I could ask her to cover my room on her allowance and get Fromme to pay her back or take it off the invoice or something. I dared not admit that I was bankrupt. I had only enough money left to cover the tolls on the autoroute.

Two minutes later she came out.

'Full up,' she said brightly. 'But there are another two around the corner.'

'Oh good.'

At half past nine I pulled the coach under some trees on a small square.

'This is as far as we go,' I said. 'It's not a taxi. I do not intend to drive a twelve metre coach around the streets of Lyon all night. We've tried nine hotels and none have room.' I switched off the motor and pulled on the parking brake. 'I said we should have got here earlier.' The accusation was unfair and I knew it.

'Well if you had not spent all afternoon conducting your friends on a guided tour of Paris, perhaps we would have been here earlier,' she blazed back at me.

'I told you to leave Nikki alone. She needed a break.'

'And I suppose you had to give it to her did you?'

'Yes, I did.' I snapped back. 'Nobody else would. And why do you keep coming back to Nikki?'

'Oh, no reason,' she said quickly and then added a little sadly, 'We're at it again aren't we?'

'You started it.' She opened her mouth to speak and then shut it. 'Good,' I said. 'What you need to do is to phone Knopf and find out where we are supposed to be and when. Can you contact him at this time?'

'Oh yes, there will be a duty officer.'

'Why was there not a duty officer to answer the phone earlier on then?'

'It was the Minister's office I was ringing. There is no duty officer during working hours.'

'You seem to know a lot about this. Do you do these groups often?'

'Yes.'

I thought of the blustering minister.

'Is that why they are so rude to you?'

'Yes. It doesn't explain why you are so rude to me though, does it?'

She looked defiantly up at me. At that moment, I did not want to think why I was so rude to her.

She pointed at an illuminated sign.

'One more hotel. The Majestic Palace, five stars. Come on, we'll phone from there.'

The Majestic Palace was colonnades of marble, potted palms and sparkling mirrors. I stood outside the cubicle under the frowning eye of the concierge and picked bread crust crumbs from the hairs on my legs. I watched Madame Chan scribble in her notebook and then she folded back the door and stepped out into the glittering light.

'What's the matter?' she asked.

'I was just thinking that you looked right in a place like this.' I laughed awkwardly and showed her my handful of crumbs. 'And I am a disgrace.'

'Well just try to behave for a minute and I'll see if they have any rooms. Keep with me.'

'So when are they arriving?'

'They are on their way now.'

'What?'

'It does take fourteen hours, don't forget.' She turned to the reception clerk. 'Have you any rooms for tonight?' He looked down at his screen. He was shaking his head.

'We are absolutely full madame. It's the Silk Fair. All the city is full.'

'Brilliant,' I muttered.

'Oh, one moment madame.' He studied the screen and then picked up a phone and made a short conversation which seemed to consist entirely of abbreviations and numbers. 'Yes!' he said, pleased with himself, 'We have a no-show. Monsieur and Madame...?

'No, just Madame Chan.'

He shot me a glance.

'But it is a double room.'

Madame Chan did not look anywhere near me.

'I'll take it,' she said. 'Have you another room?'

He shrugged his shoulders helplessly.

'It's the only one we have. We are now full.'

'That's alright,' I said bravely. 'I'll find somewhere. I'll go and get your case.'

I walked back to the coach wondering if I had the guts to ask Madame Chan if I could share her room. I knew I did not. I picked up her case and walked back to the hotel. Madame Chan was leaning on the counter, writing on a sheet of paper. I put the case by her feet. Only glancing momentarily at her legs as I did so.

'There you are madame,' the clerk said, 'room three two seven, on the third floor. The lifts are over there.' His hand poised above the bell. 'Would you like the porter for your case?'

'No, I can manage thank you.' She turned to me and held out the paper. 'That's the ETA nine thirty, and they are not arriving at Bron or Satolas. What's the matter?'

'I was just asking myself how many more hundred kilometres you might want me to drive before breakfast tomorrow morning.' I allowed my disgust to show. 'Which airport are they landing at then?'

She moved away from the counter and handed me the paper. She edged closer to me. I could smell the sweet odour of her fatigue.

'St. Maurice,' she said quietly. I had never heard of it. 'It's a military base about ten kilometres out on the road to Bourg-en-Bresse. The Minister has arranged it. The air traffic control will be handled by the military. For obvious reasons, we need to be discreet.'

'Not something I'm good at.'

'Try,' she said and lifted her case.

'I'll pick you up at eight thirty, outside the hotel.'

'Thank you,' she said. She laid her hand lightly on my forearm. 'I'm sorry about this, Simon.'

I shrugged. What a brave man I was.

I decided that the coach would cause no problem under the trees where I had parked it. It would be in nobody's way before half past eight tomorrow morning. I pulled down all the blinds at the back and unpacked my small bag. I hung my trousers and clean shirt over the backs of seats to let any creases fall out. For a moment I stood, undecided as to whether I should exploit the cloakroom facilities of the Majestic Palace but eventually confined my toilet to rinsing my mouth with bottled water and rubbing some on my face. I stretched out on the long back seat and waited for sleep to come. Across the square I could see some lighted windows of the hotel, some even on the third floor. I was weary beyond measure.

8

The sun awoke me a little after five in the morning. The garbage lorry then took up the baton just when I ran the danger of relapsing into slumber. By six o' clock the square was playing host to delivery vans with steel roller shutters and whining tail lifts. The street sweeper growled past and then the motor bikes started. I gave in. I sat up and rubbed my hands briskly over my face. The stubble scraped my palms. Where was I going to shave? I tried to imagine the bathroom of room three two seven. Rather like a starving man conjures up in his mind the most extravagant meals, after about five minutes I had endowed Madame Chan's bathroom with golden taps and marble basins. And then I thought, why not? She said we needed to try to work together.

I dressed in my trousers and shirt, straightened my hair, threw my toilet things into my grip and walked over to the hotel. I strode boldly through the entrance hall.

'Monsieur?' the clerk addressed me.

I stared stonily at him and entered the waiting lift. The carpet in the third floor corridor was plush and decorated with a monogram. I tapped lightly on the door of room three two seven. I looked at my watch. It was about six forty. I waited. My heart was thumping and I did not know why. I tapped again, a little louder.

'*Oui?*' came from behind the door.

I took a deep breath. 'Jocelyne, it's me, Simon.'

'Just one moment.' I waited. The door opened a few centimetres. 'What's the matter? Is there a problem?' She wore a towel wrapped around her shoulders and her hair was in a tangle of wet disarray. She pulled at it as she spoke.

'Um... it's a bit of a cheek but can I use your bathroom to shave in?'

She looked me in the eyes. They were dark and expressionless.

'Yes, it is a bit of a cheek. But not unexpected from you.'

'O.K. Never mind. Sorry I asked. I'll risk it in the cloakroom downstairs.'

'I didn't say "no".' She opened the door a little wider and inspected me. I resisted the temptation to inspect her. I had a vague impression of a nightdress floating around somewhere below the towel. 'Where did you spend the night then?'

'In the Mercedes Suite of the Hotel Fromme.'

'Does that account for your bad humour?'

'No, I'm always a ray of sunshine like this in the mornings, didn't you know?'

A door opened further up the corridor. She quickly stepped back and opened her door. 'Come in,' she hissed. I slipped in.

As I had expected, the room was enormous. A double aspect set of windows gave onto the square — I could see the tops of the trees. I walked across and looked sideways down through the net curtains.

'Well the coach is still there anyway.'

I sensed an immobility behind me. I turned. She was standing barefooted with her arms crossed in front of her and her head on one side. Her lips were pursed in an amused smile.

'Did you just come in to enjoy a different view of your coach?'

'No... no. Sorry. Have you er...?' I gazed around the room. The giant bed was rumpled and her dress was draped across the back of a chair. The case I had carried back from the coach was lying open on the stand. I could see a small hairdrier on top of her folded clothes. I had no idea where the bathroom was.

She suddenly opened her eyes wide in realisation and said, 'You are embarrassed aren't you?'

'Please may I use your bathroom to have a shave and

freshen up and please will you show me where it is?'

'You ARE embarrassed.' Her eyes were sparkling now. She looked ravishing. 'The third door along the wardrobe is actually the bathroom. It took me ten minutes to find it.'

'Thank you.'

'You can have a shower or whatever you like. I have finished,' she called after me.

I was right about the marble but wrong about the taps. They were chrome and porcelain. I stripped off my clothes and hung them carefully on the back of the door. I caught sight of my naked body in the mirror. The purple and yellow bruises on my chest almost matched the marble. I lathered and shaved and without bothering to wipe off the soap, clambered directly into the shower. That was a mistake. Had I tried to wipe off the soap before taking a shower, I would have noticed that the bathroom was devoid of towels. When I climbed out a few minutes later, tingling with health and cleanliness, I realised my situation. I cleared my throat.

'Madame Chan?' I thought a formal approach would be most likely to have success. I heard the hairdrier die. 'Madame Chan?' I half called.

'Yes Monsieur Laperche?' her voice came from close to the door.

'It would appear that there are no towels in here.'

I heard a sort of scuffling noise.

'Really?' It sounded to me as if she were laughing.

'Yes, really.'

'And what do you expect me to do about it?'

Now that caught me out. I had not thought the conversation through before initiating it.

'Have you a towel you could lend me please?'

'Are you naked?'

'Yes.'

'Close your eyes then.'

'Close MY eyes?'

'Yes.'

'Why?'

'To spare your blushes. You will never know whether

I look at you or not.' The logic was unbeatable. 'Ready?'

'Yes.'

The door opened a hand's width and a large towel was thrust in.

'I knew you would cheat,' she said and closed the door again.

When I came out, some minutes later, Madame Chan was fully dressed and her case packed. She was wearing the light linen suit that I had first seen her in and was looking at a large scale IGN map. A Michelin map lay folded on the bed.

'I've ordered breakfast in my room so we can share it,' she said.

'Now that is a good idea. I appreciate that.'

'Here is the camp.' She placed an elegant finger on the road and I spent a little more time than necessary in studying the location.

'Where did you conjure the maps from?' I said. She waved her finger at her attaché case. 'And how do we get into this camp then? There will be barriers and a guard house and all kinds of paraphernalia.'

'I don't think we will have a problem. Knopf will have informed them we are coming. They will know it is us. How many Paris registered coaches do you think they are expecting this morning?' She looked up at the knock on the door.

'I'll slip into the bathroom,' I said. I pulled the door closed and waited whilst the room service waiter recounted the family tree of every egg in the omelette and gave a travelogue devoted to the provenance of the coffee beans. At last the door closed.

'I thought he would never go,' she said. 'Would you like some breakfast? I'm starving.'

'Yes, so am I.'

She moved the tray to the desk and we started making inroads into the food. The phone on the desk rang and she picked it up. I continued eating.

'Yes, this is Madame Chan.' She listened and then waved to me to pass her the pad and pencil. I handed them across. She acknowledged me with a quick flip of her eyebrows. 'Yes,' she said as she wrote. 'And you have booked this have you? Well, we will try. Yes I understand that. No, I don't foresee a problem there, I'll speak to him.' I stopped eating. I had a feeling that decisions affecting me were being made without my accord. Yes, I will ring tonight. The number you have given me. Au revoir Monsieur.' She replaced the receiver, thoughtfully.

'I've got a feeling you want to tell me something.'

'Yes,' she admitted. 'It's a good job you're sitting down. You're stuck with me for another day I'm afraid.'

I had mixed feelings about that but let nothing show.

'Oh yes?'

'We are booked in tonight at the Grand Hotel de la Seignerie at Arnay le Duc.' She looked down at her pad. 'They will do a buffet meal for whenever we arrive. Afternoon visit is a stroll in the famous Arbor Walk, dinner at seven thirty. It's all been reserved for us. We go on to Paris tomorrow morning.'

'But I'm expected back in Paris this evening,' I protested. 'That is what I was booked for.'

She became defensive.

'I am sure Monsieur Fromme will be delighted to charge the Ministry for another day's hire. There must be other drivers who can cover for your work.'

I thought back to her telephone call.

'Was that the, "I don't foresee a problem I'll speak to him" part of your conversation?'

She started to blush.

'I did not think there would be a problem. It's only another day.'

'In my life, Madame Chan. Another day in my life. And tomorrow happens to be my day off. I choose what I do on my day off, not you.'

She pushed the phone across to me.

'You had better phone Monsieur Fromme and tell him to send another coach then.'

'I shall have to phone him anyway,' I muttered. She knew she had beaten me.

Noel answered the phone.

'Simon? That poxy roof lining fell on me again yesterday,' he complained.

'I expect you were driving down a flight of stairs,' I retorted. 'Is Monsieur Fromme in yet?'

'Any minute. Hey what's the matter? Have you bent Georges' coach? Have you?' he asked gleefully. 'A stove-in front, or perhaps a nice long scrape down the side?' Before I could deal with his exuberance there was a muffling sound and he suddenly said, 'No Monsieur, it's Laperche, he wants to speak to you.'

'Fromme.'

'It's Laperche.'

'I know. Where are you?'

'I'm in the hotel in Lyon. We'll be picking the group up in just over an hour.'

'What's the problem?' His voice was guarded. I was certain that he he had overheard some of Noel's outrageous speculations.

'There's no problem Monsieur Fromme. In fact I think it's probably good news. The Minister has asked to have the coach for an extra day. I have agreed on your behalf.' I avoided Madame Chan's eyes. 'I presume that is alright?'

'Another day? Any extra mileage?'

'Not really. We are booked in overnight at...' Madame Chan turned the pad around so that I could read it. 'Grand Hotel de la Seignerie.'

'La Seignerie?' Monsieur Fromme confirmed. 'Near Arnay le Duc? You've landed on your feet there my boy.'

'Yes, Arnay le Duc, that's the one.' I leaned across to Madame Chan and said quietly, 'Can you pass me the map?' She held up the IGN map. 'No,' I said, 'The one on the bed.' She passed it to me.

'Is that Madame Chan with you?' Fromme said.

'Yes,' I replied, glancing across at her, 'Do you wish to speak to her.'

I did not hear his reply because I was dumbfounded by the sight of Madame Chan bringing both hands to cover her face in a demonstration of shame. I stared at her. What had I done wrong now? Fromme was still speaking.

'...and in any case you've got the agency card haven't you?'

'Oh yes, the agency card,' I said, distractedly.

'That's OK then, Laperche. We'll expect you some time tomorrow evening then.'

I put down the phone and looked at Madame Chan's bowed head.

'Now what's the matter?' I asked, testily.

She raised her head and looked over her fingers at me. Her eyes were glistening.

'You really do not know do you?'

And I didn't.

I did not bring the coach to the hotel, we walked across the square.

'I shall have to put your case in the boot now, but I will put it in the small front locker just here, with mine.'

She nodded silently and got on the coach. I let my breath out in a noisy rush and looked about me theatrically for support but there was only two shapes sitting in a dark coloured Peugeot across the square. I shivered involuntarily. The last time I had seen two people in a dark Peugeot they had beaten me up. I slammed the locker and got into the coach.

'Are you going to use the mike?' I asked.

'Probably. At some stage.'

'Because if you use it from the front seat, the plug pulls out of the socket.'

'No I shall sit in the guide seat,' she explained. 'I was only sitting up here to wait for you to get in.'

I stepped past her. She pulled the guide seat out from under the dash and sat down. Whilst I started the engine and checked the dials she unfolded a map in front of her.

'Where did you get the city plan from?' I asked as we drew away.

'From the hotel concierge.'

'You think of everything don't you?'

'Somebody has to.'

'Meaning?'

'Follow that red truck.'

I did.

And so did the Peugeot.

Madame Chan gave excellent directions. They were crisp, precise and accurate. She gave them at just the right moment, not so early that I would forget them and not too late for me to act. I could find no fault in her performance but I could find no merit in her conversation.

I took solace in the landscape. The Lyonnaise ladies take full advantage of the sun to air their extensive wardrobes and the pavements were awash with colour. The girls hurrying to the offices or shops were pretty to look at, distracting to the mind and easy on the senses. They looked somehow... uncomplicated.

We waited at some lights and I idly watched an olive skinned girl cross the road before us. She had black hair hanging in a plait down below her waist. It bounced from one buttock to the other as she walked.

'It must be fatiguing to wear hair so long in this heat,' Madame Chan said, looking at me sideways from the guide seat. I readjusted my glance from the girl's buttocks back to the lights.

She directed me through the city as though she had lived there all her life. I was grudgingly impressed.

'Which way is the Rhone flowing?' she asked. 'I can't see from down here.'

I looked over the parapet to my right where a black barge was buffeting against the current. I jerked my thumb backwards.

'That way.'

'Good. We are going in the right direction then. This should take us to the N83.'

Even as she said it, the road sign appeared.

'Bravo,' I said.

She made a small mocking curtsey with her head. I settled down to some easy driving in an unhurried line of traffic all going my way. At the head of the line was a milk tanker and the traffic in the opposite direction was constant and so we remained in line — the milk tanker, four cars, a flatbed lorry, another car and us. I glanced in the mirror.

And a dark Peugeot with two men in. Just a coincidence that they were travelling on the same road but it rattled me nevertheless. I had not understood the undercurrent of the brutal attack that I had been subjected to. If I could have convinced myself that I had been a target taken at random, somehow that would have reassured me, but I could not. I had seen the nod of confirmation that the one assailant had given to the other. He had known whom he was attacking. I could feel my spine going cold. I stole another glance in the mirror. They were still there. I tried to identify faces but the distance was too great.

Perhaps if I slowed down I could force them to overtake? If they slowed down with me that would prove they were following me. Even as I thought it, I realised that it would prove nothing. Nobody could overtake me with the constant stream of traffic running in the opposite direction.

I shot a quick glance at Madame Chan. She was looking far ahead for the first evidence of the St Maurice military base. She had noticed nothing untoward. I thought of the probable consequences to my employment if I got involved in a brawl. I would lose my job with Fromme and that would be me finished. I would never get another chance. My critics would make sure of that as they rubbed their hands with vindication.

The car was still there. Why were they picking on me? I could find no answer. I did not know who 'they' were. We topped a gentle rise and a military camp came into view before us on our left. Rows of huts, acres of concrete and tarmac, lines of parked olive green, a couple of radar scanners and some tail fins jutting above hangars. The road soon began to run alongside a tall chain link fence, topped with three strands of barbed wire.

'That looks like the camp,' she said.

'Or somebody with a big garden who has trouble keeping his giraffes at home.' My nervous attempt at humour made me look stupid. She threw me a look that one would use for a particularly silly child. 'All right,' I said, 'It's the camp then.'

Keeping an eye on my mirror, I swung the Merc off the main road onto the alley leading to the guard house.

The dark Peugeot swished on without faltering. A wave of relief flowed over me, quickly followed by a surge of anger directed at myself and my stupid behaviour. I pulled up to the pole barrier. The camp reminded me of my military service. A subaltern came out of the hut towards us.

'You had better let me do this,' I suggested to Madame Chan. 'I've got inside information. I've been on the other end a few times.'

I could tell by her pressed lips and raised eyebrows exactly what she thought of my proposal.

'Can I help you sir?' the subaltern said.

That was a new approach. In my day we just used to shout 'Where are you going?'

'Hello mate. We've come to pick up a Chinese group. They'll be landing in about...' I glanced at the clock. 'Fifteen minutes. Just pop the pole up would you?'

'Can I see your authorisation sir?'

I sighed dramatically.

'Look, this is a special group from...'

'Shut up!' she snapped.

I shut. She got up and leaned across me and held a card wallet open to the window. Her torso was centimetres from my face. I froze in my position, not daring to speak, breathe or look.

'Could you just glance at this please?' she asked the soldier pleasantly.

I moved my head a fraction and saw his eyes open as they focused on the card.

'Yes ma'am,' he jumped and waved to his colleague to lift the barrier.

'Thank you so much,' she said and smiled sweetly. 'Where do we go to meet an arriving flight?'

'First right ma'am and park at the end by the Mirage. It's a plane,' he added apologetically. 'On display.'

She sat down and motioned me forwards. I nodded to the soldier as I passed. His eyes did not flicker. I swept around the back of the Mirage and pulled up outside a single storey building. It had been built in concrete slabs and then painted cream. The metal framed windows opened outwards and they were all open.

'So what was all that about?' I asked.

'I told you... I asked you to try to be discreet and the first occasion which presents itself, you start to blab your mouth off.'

'He was military. They're supposed to be on our side aren't they?'

'You were not being discreet. He does not need to know.'

But I knew what had really upset me, and I suppose I was still shaken by the appearance of that Peugeot because, being the fool that I was, I told her.

'I've never seen you smile at me like that.'

She looked hard at me for a second and then her gaze drifted away to fix on the listless flag drooping in front of the building.

'No,' she said, 'you haven't.'

I decided to be a coach driver. It was her job to find the passengers and their baggage, get them to the coach, talk to them, sort out their problems, tuck them into bed and wipe their noses. She could dictate when we should leave and when we should stop and where we should go. All I needed to do was drive the coach and that was easy. You merely tread on a few pedals, wiggle a wheel and try not to hit anything.

I followed Madame Chan into the low building. The base had a small passenger handling area which was presumably used for the military flights. The walls were cream. The floor was dark red linoleum. Olive green steel and canvas chairs had been arranged in lines to serve the needs of those who waited. I could even smell army-cooking vegetables.

Without so much as a backward glance she walked confidently up to the first officer she saw, explained what she wanted and he whisked her away. I slouched to a chair and picked up a discarded newspaper.

One forest fire had been brought under control, the other was still burning. The rector of the Sorbonne had addressed the student rally and had been pelted with eggs. The air traffic controllers' strike had brought the airports of France to a standstill but had hindered the escape of a wanted terrorist, see front page. I turned to the front page.

'Terrorist caught at Orly.' I grunted. So it had not been an exercise at all, it had been for real. I wondered if they had already caught him when they had told us to move our coaches. Reading between the lines it seemed to me that they must have worked on a tip off. I could hardly credit the claim that an airport policeman had spontaneously recognised the terrorist. Surely terrorists disguise themselves? I examined the blurred photograph of a handcuffed man with no shoes being pushed into the back of a police van. Siggi Hanaps was his name. I had never heard of him. He was the operational chief of a Baader Meinhof action cell. Now I had heard of them. If they kept true to form, their next move would be to bomb and shoot their way into the police station and free Siggi Hanaps before the machinations of justice could secure him.

Well, we do see life! I thought. I rolled up the paper and stuck it under my arm. It might amuse Madame Chan to know that she had shared Orly airport not only with the most detested coach driver in Paris but also the most wanted terrorist in Europe, and at the same time.

I tried to get a drink from the machine by the wall but it would only take tokens of some sort. I crossed to a cream-painted hatchway through which I could see a man in shirt sleeves. He was pounding furiously at a typewriter fed with three of flimsy and two of carbon. Not the person to ask. A large woman in dungarees waddled down the corridor towards me. She had wrapped a scarf around her hair and the cold butt of a *gitane* poked from the corner of her mouth. There seemed to be more civilians in this place than military.

'Where can I get a token for the drinks machine, love?'

She looked at me and then at the machine.

'What do you want a token for?'

I checked the machine again. I was right.

'It doesn't take coins,' I said. 'Only tokens. Where can I get one?

She waddled over to the machine and inspected it. She read the notice engraved on the steel plate which clearly explained the need for a token and warned that coins would be rejected.

'No you don't need a token. What do you want to drink?'

I thought the question a little premature. I was not convinced that the machine would deliver my desires, however, to please her and since I had nothing else to do, I said, 'black coffee'.

'Black coffee,' she repeated. She bent and peered at the buttons. 'Black coffee,' she said, and prodded one. A light came on. She thumped the front of the machine with her fist and a cup slid down the chute and began to fill up. 'Black coffee,' she said and shook her head. 'Never needed tokens for that machine,' she muttered to herself and waddled away.

I watched her depart and wondered if all the machinery on the camp worked in the same fashion. It could make landing an aeroplane exciting. I took my cup outside and inspected the dilapidated Mirage perched on the concrete plinth. It had been painted to spruce it up but the result was to make it look like a faded prostitute. I grinned when I thought how shocked Madame Chan had been to discover what Monique did for a living. My gaze fixed on the fighter. I did not want Nikki to end up like that.

Trucks and people began to agitate and I could hear the rumbling of an approaching aeroplane. I shaded my eyes with the newspaper and peered down the runway. Without being able to distinguish the markings I knew that this had to be China Airways. I knew little about planes but even I could tell that this was not the latest model. The pilot landed without fuss and followed the jeep down the taxiway as if arriving on a military airfield was something that he did every day. Perhaps it was.

I opened my coach. It was hot. I started the engine and put the ventilators on 'boost'. I should have pulled down the blinds on the sunny side as soon as I had parked — it would have kept out some of the heat. My angry resolve to 'only be a coach driver' was making me even less than that. I sat on the front seat, put my feet up on the dash, folded my arms and waited.

I had not bothered to imagine what thirty seven Chinese businessmen would look like. My knowledge of China and the Chinese was restricted to whatever I had seen on television or read in the occasional newspaper. The Chinese, I knew, men and women alike, dressed in funny suits that buttoned up to the collar and they waved a little red book whenever they could. So when I saw Madame Chan leading the group out towards the coach, I thought she had made a mistake. They were all dressed in Western style business suits and the only publication I could see was a *Paris Match* that one of them had managed to acquire.

I took my feet from the dashboard, but not before I had made sure that she had seen them, and then came down the steps to open the luggage compartments. A Chinese man, about thirty years old, was speaking to her in a slow, exact French of unusual tempo. He wore a miniature Chinese flag on his lapel and he was making a speech of tortuous civility whose central theme was a declaration of his disappointment at being welcomed by a woman. Madame Chan nodded and smiled and thanked him warmly and entreated him to enter the coach. I wanted to punch his face.

With much smiling and grinning they clambered on board. At closer quarters I could see that their suits, although in the Western style, were of identical cloth and cut. It made the group look like a national sports team.

A camouflaged tractor towed out to the coach a trailer load of identical grey canvas bags. The driver looked at the bags and then looked at the men.

'It must be a really stimulating country,' he observed sarcastically. 'I can't wait to go there.'

'I would not be able to cope with the excitement,' I said. I began to stack the bags in the lockers. I knew better than to offend his sensitivity by suggesting that he help me.

'Now that's nicer to look at,' he said.

Madame Chan walked up and proffered a bundle of cardboard tags.

'These are all the baggage checks. Can we be sure that we have all the bags?'

I groaned inwardly. I should have let her check before loading. I looked at the tarmac and whistled softly.

'I took every bit of baggage from the hold myself,' the tractor driver declared. 'I brought every piece here.'

'Good,' she said.

He saluted and drove away. I just hoped that he was telling the truth.

'I think we can go when you have loaded those,' she said brightly.

I pushed the final bag into the locker and slammed the door. She stood aside to let me get behind the wheel and then she tugged out the guide seat. She took the microphone from its hook. I leaned across, switched on the Blaupunkt and selected the PA system.

'We can go when you are ready,' she said and gently scratched the mike with her finger nail as she adjusted the volume. Only comedians blow into a mike.

I nodded and started the engine. She began to speak to the group. I stared at her.

'What's the matter?' she hissed from the side of her mouth.

'You're speaking Chinese!'

'Mandarin, yes. Of course. What did you think I was here for? Just so that you would have somebody to be rude to?'

I shut my mouth and moved the lever into gear. When she spoke Mandarin she sounded a different person.

I waved at the subaltern at the gate and still got no response. Madame Chan managed to get a salute from him without having to pause in her commentary.

'You can find your way back into Lyon and out to the motorway can you?' she asked, 'or do you need me to give some directions?'

'I can manage,' I replied but she heard me catch my breath.

'What's the matter?'

'Nothing. Bit of indigestion,' I said as I watched a dark Peugeot slip into line behind us.

I tried to convince myself that it was a different car. But I failed. I could see two faces but not distinguish them. I slowed down, they slowed down. I speeded up, they kept with me but once again, that proved nothing — the traffic was such that they had no choice. I wondered if I should try to outrun them but I knew it was pointless trying. What were they going to do? What were they waiting for?

By the time we re-entered the outskirts of the city, the Peugeot had dropped two cars back but that was no bother to them. They would not lose sight of me. A twelve metre coach is not easy to hide.

'I might need some help here please,' I said to Madame Chan during a pause. 'I can't remember how many rivers we have to cross.'

She nodded and said something into the microphone. Then she swivelled around on the seat and pulled out her city plan. She quickly found our location and began to direct me. I turned left, the Peugeot followed. We forked right, so did it. It could just be coincidence couldn't it? I needed to know. We approached a large junction where two tree-lined avenues met at right angles.

'Straight across the lights,' she said.

The lights were green. I slowed down. She looked up at me.

'Straight across,' she repeated.

I dawdled up to the orange then slammed my foot on the floor as the lights turned red.

'It's red!' she shrieked and grabbed the dash as the Merc leapt forward. It was a wide junction and I had already checked that all the crossing traffic was stationary. They would have to be impossibly quick off the mark to hit us. The group were utterly unaware of the drama as we roared across. I ignored Madame Chan's upturned white face as I grimly watched the Peugeot swerve out of line, roar pass the central island on the wrong side, and in a chorus of protesting horns, slalom through the traffic to catch us.

'What are you playing at?' she said through gritted teeth.

'Sorry, I must have been day-dreaming.'

'Well for Heaven's sake, wake up!'

I had woken up. My mind was working at top speed. I had now positively identified the problem. I was definitely being followed, but I had not found the solution and I could not see one. I was at their mercy. They could follow me for as long as they liked. I could not get away. They were now driving close behind me. I wondered whether they thought that I had deliberately tried to lose them or whether I was just a reckless driver. Probably the latter.

'At the end, this avenue splits into two streets by an old market. We take the left road.'

I nodded. Concise and confident directions, as always. As we approached the old shuttered market I looked at the two streets in turn and knew that I would take the street on the right, not the left. They were both cobbled, lined on both sides with parked cars, but fifty metres down the right hand street was a small crossroads. And in the middle sat one of the old circular cast iron stands for a traffic cop. I indicated left and then veered right at the last minute.

'I said left!'

'Shut up, I'm busy.'

The Peugeot's tyres squealed on the cobbles as it followed my change of direction. I accelerated quickly. I needed them to believe that I now knew I was being followed and was trying to escape. They took the bait. The Merc thundered down the street with the Peugeot accelerating hard behind to catch up.

'Oh God!' Madame Chan saw the iron island and gripped the dash before her.

'Don't worry, don't worry! Plenty of room for us,' I assured her as the wheels passed either side and the murderous mound of metal disappeared underneath us.

The driver of the Peugeot must have lived a split second of terror as the island had suddenly materialised before him. He had no chance to brake. There was a tremendous bang behind us and the car leapt a metre into the air in a cloud of steam and white smoke. The stand would have ripped out all the front suspension, the sump and the exhaust.

'What was that?' Madame Chan jumped and leaned

forwards to look in my side mirror. The Chinese were already up and gawping through the back window.

Slewed athwart the street behind us was the steaming wreck of a dark saloon, sagging on splayed out wheels. A man began to climb out and then the street turned, blotting him out of sight. I eased back my speed. She looked accusingly at me.

'You did that on purpose!'

'The idiot wasn't looking where he was going. Very careless.' I was shaking but managed not to show it.

'You did it on purpose,' she repeated.

'Now you know why they said I was dangerous, don't you?' I looked harshly at her. 'The important thing is that I inadvertently took the wrong street. Sorry. Are you able to get me back in the right direction?'

She stared open mouthed and her hand crept across to the plan.

9

'Explain it to me again, but slowly,' I said.

We were cruising sweetly up the autoroute at a steady ninety kph. The sun was shining, the sky was blue, the Chinese Trade Delegation was snoozing gently behind me and nobody suspicious was following us. Even Madame Chan had softened a little. I could almost think I was enjoying myself.

She pulled a face and tried again.

'Don't you remember your *Histoire/Géo* at school?'

'School? I'm an old man. You might be still young enough to remember school but I'm not.'

'They got on the plane at 19.30 Paris time last night.'

'When we were about where we are now but going the other way.'

'Don't try to complicate it.'

'I'm not. I'm trying to understand it.'

'Pekin is ten hours ahead of Paris. So 19.30 last night in Lyon was 05.30 this morning in Pekin.'

'Yes?' I said guardedly.

'They flew westwards for fourteen hours. If you add fourteen to 19.30 you get 09.30 this morning. Don't you?'

'If you say so.'

'But the time in Pekin when they left was 05.30. So you add fourteen to that and you get 19.30.'

'So when they arrived this morning their bodies were telling them that it was half past seven in the evening?'

'Exactly.' She sat back, relieved. It had been a hard struggle.

'The man with the badge in his lapel is the leader?'

'Monsieur Wong? He's not exactly the leader. The delegation is supposed to be autonomous. He is a sort of Commissaire.' I looked blankly at her. 'He's in the Party. He is there to ensure that they behave themselves. And that everybody gets back on the plane at the end of the tour.'

'I don't like his manners.'

'His French is exquisitely polite.'

'And downright insulting. I didn't like what he said to you.'

She glanced up at me and smiled wryly.

'It would have sounded worse in Mandarin.'

'I wouldn't know.' I was still struggling with the time difference and trying to calculate what repercussions it would have on the job we had before us. 'So... when we get to the hotel, they will want to go to bed?'

'Probably.'

'So will I.'

A look of concern crossed her face.

'Is it very tiring, driving a coach all day long?'

I laughed.

'No, it's a rest cure. But I didn't sleep much last night that's all. The back seat is not a four poster and Lyon is a very noisy city.'

'I'm sorry.'

'It's not your fault.'

'I could see no other... acceptable solution,' she said awkwardly.

'Nor could I,' I assured her. She looked at me and then nodded shortly. 'You won't be very popular,' I added, 'dragging them around the gardens this afternoon if they all want to go to bed.'

'No, but that is why I have to do it. To acclimatise them gently to the time change. Unless you want to start work at four thirty tomorrow morning?'

'I'll ring you if I do.'

'Don't bother.'

'What is this hotel like? Monsieur Fromme seemed to know it.'

'It's well known for the Arbor Walk. I've never stayed at the chateau itself.'

'Chateau?'

'Yes, the hotel is a converted chateau. It used to belong to one of the minor princes in the Orléans family. They lost it, of course,'

'Of course,' I said, trying to pretend that I knew why and how they lost it.

'The chateau and its estate passed through various hands until a paper merchant called Jussieu bought it about one hundred and fifty years ago. You've heard of 'Papiers Toutblancs'?' I nodded. 'Well it all started there. The chateau came with hundreds of hectares of forest. Jussieu built a mill on the river and started pulping wood. He had fourteen children, nine were sons and he set them all to work. One son, Darnand, went around the world collecting tree seeds and the Arbor Walk, a century later, is what his collection grew into.'

'And you can say all that in Chinese, can you?'

'In Mandarin, yes, if I have to.'

'Quite a little brainbox aren't you?'

'Sorry. I thought you were interested. I might have known you were making fun of me.'

'And you called ME "sensitive"!'

'Yes well I was obviously wrong. You are insensitive.'

The pomp and splendour of the Grand Hotel de la Seignerie drew gasps of admiration and outbursts of excited chatter from the Chinese. Even I had to admit that it was a little awe inspiring to drive Georges' Mercedes up the two kilometre tree-lined alley leading to the chateau. The men were like schoolboys as they crossed from one side of the coach to the other, pointing things out. They stared at the deer and the deer stared back. But what drew a round of spontaneous applause was the bright green and yellow ride-on mower which was spewing a spray of fine grass cuttings out in a peacock's tail behind it. That really did set them chattering. I had to stop the coach so that they could have their photographs taken standing in front of it. The old man in the straw hat who had been driving it grinned a toothless grin for them and then they all trooped back onto the coach.

When we reached the top of the drive, the carriage sweep before the chateau was the size of a football field. As I steered around it, Madame Chan explained that this was a feature introduced to ensure that the staff got ample warning of any arrival. I remembered not to mention how clever she was.

Four liveried porters descended the stone perron steps towards us followed by a concierge in a magnificent uniform. I sat there in my short sleeved shirt and did not envy him his position at all. Madame Chan walked off with the group towards the vast entrance portico which was surmounted by an indistinguishable animal. I knew nothing about chateaux or architecture and this one looked to me very similar to the several of the lesser known smaller chateaux of the Loire valley that I had been subjected to when driving for Papa Coursamel. It was constructed of a yellowish stone and the roof was laid with slate. The first floor was a gallery of identical high windows which stretched the length of the facade. The floor above was a similar gallery of smaller windows. And so on.

Inside, the high ceilings provided a welcome cool and the tiled floors a confusing echo. Madame Chan's heels smacked out like pistol shots whilst the group's footfalls provided rumbling cannon. I stood at the back, holding her bag and mine in one hand, whilst she worked down the rooming list and paired off the guests. As each enormous key was unhooked from the board a porter led the guests off to their rooms. We were all on the first floor overlooking the front alley.

'There is your key,' Madame Chan handed me half a kilo of mild steel. 'Shall I take my bag?' I handed it to her. 'The buffet lunch is in the Salle Darnand through the double doors there. Come down as soon as you are ready.'

I touched my forelock.

'Yes Ma'am.'

She gave a sigh of exasperation and walked off towards the broad curving staircase whose polished marble reflected the light from the gallery above. The concierge beckoned me. I walked over.

'There is a parking place for the coach round at the

side, by the workshops.' He smartly smacked the bell and a lad hurried over from the porter's alcove. 'Gilles will show you.'

I backed the coach up under some trees alongside a low building which must have been a later appendage. It was brick built with stone quoins and its wide doorway had obviously been designed to facilitate the entry and exit of wheeled machinery.

'You wouldn't have a tap and a hose in there would you?' I asked the lad.

'There's one over in that corner.' He pointed to a corrugated tin shelter. 'What do you want to do?' he asked as he lit a covert cigarette.

'Wash the coach.'

'It doesn't look very dirty.'

I shrugged.

'Must keep the customers happy. Where is the drain?'

'It all runs back to that gully.' He pointed to some stinging nettles. I thanked him and he dawdled back in the direction of the front door, his cigarette cupped in his hand.

Once installed in my room, certain difficulties became apparent to me. I had only brought clothes for an overnight stay. I now had to sleep two nights away from home. If the Minister stretched the tour any further I would have to add to my wardrobe. That consideration reminded me of my finances. I had barely enough money to cover the autoroute tolls. This room did not come cheap. The standard rule in tourism was that the driver and guide were not charged for their accommodation. I prayed that the Grand Hotel de la Seignerie were aware of that maxim.

I glanced in the mirror and tidied myself up as much as I could. I left the enormous key on the inside of my pastel blue door and closed it behind me. I could not be bothered with locking it and dragging that piece of ironmongery around with me. In the corridor I met a chambermaid pushing a linen basket on wheels. On a sudden inspiration I asked her if she could launder my shirt for me for tomorrow. She said she could do it for tonight.

She followed me back to my room and took the clothes I handed her, assuring me that they would be ready this evening. I told her that if they were not, I would come down to breakfast naked and tell everybody that it was her fault. She listened seriously to me and then assured me that I had nothing to worry about. I don't think she really understood. She sounded Jugoslav.

The hubbub emanating from the Salle Darnand indicated that the Chinese had grasped Madame Chan's instructions perfectly. The room had been arranged as a sitting buffet. Down the long side were set the serving tables displaying the dishes. This suited the Chinese because they were able to point to whatever they wanted and the attending waiter would add it to their plate and pass the plate along to the next table and thus they progressed until either the plate was full or their courage failed.

I hovered by the potted plants at the entrance and watched Madame Chan as she moved from table to table, ensuring the comfort of individuals and seemingly answering three questions at a time. The maitre d' saw me and came over.

'With the group sir?'

'Yes and no. The driver.'

'Ah,' he said, understandingly, 'there just happens to be a small table behind this screen. Would that suit?'

'Admirably,' I smiled.

'Shall I make you a selection of cold meats and salads sir and bring them over?'

'That would be very kind. Thank you.'

'My pleasure sir.'

I lounged at the table, gazed dreamily out at the park and decided that this kind of life suited me.

The Chinese were still going strong when I put down my coffee cup and slipped unobtrusively out of the dining room. I saw the lad, Gilles, in the hall and asked him if there was a staff door that I could use whilst I cleaned my coach. I did not think they would like me wandering back and forth through the front entrance dressed in my shorts and tee shirt. He took me through a back corridor and pointed to the door below the iron fire escape.

'That comes out opposite the workshop,' he said and then added smugly, 'It's where I go for a quiet smoke.'

It is astonishing how much litter and disarray even a well behaved group can bring to a coach. I took my cleaning materials from the front locker and set to work. I had fashioned myself a short-handled broom by the simple process of sawing a length from a standard broom. There is no space in a coach to wield a full size broom.

I started at the rear, brushing the seat squabs with a hand brush, re-arranging the antimacassars and then sweeping along the floor with the broom. I continued up to the front and then swept all the rubbish down the steps and out into a plastic bucket. I crossed back to the foot of the fire escape and emptied the bucket into the hotel waste bin.

I closed the coach door and then assembled the next piece of equipment in my arsenal. This was a soft bristled broom whose handle I could extend by screwing on an extra section. This enabled me to clean from the roofline to the road in one movement. I uncoiled the hose and drenched one side of the coach. Taking my bottle of liquid soap, I doused the soft bristles and before the water could run off or evaporate, I brushed the soap onto the windows and bodywork, leaving it looking as if it were enjoying a giant shampoo. I rinsed with the hose to remove the suds and then, replacing the broom head with a rubber blade, I cleaned the water from the glass, leaving it sparkling.

Despite the various shields that I had incorporated into the handles of my tools to prevent the water from running down onto me, I always ended up wet and grubby after washing a coach. I defy any driver to be otherwise. It was inescapable.

The physical exertion did me good. Sitting in a coach, turning a wheel and bouncing up and down on a countersprung seat is not exercise. The bending, reaching, crouching and stretching required to clean the hectares of glass and metal that made up the Mercedes, set my metabolism going and left me glowing with a physical and mental contentment. It was also a useful opportunity to take stock of situations.

I knew that my continued employment rested on a thread and mishandling this group could easily snap it. I hoped fervently that the two mystery thugs in the Peugeot had been dissuaded from any further attempts and had lost track of me. I could see no way that they could find me. I had been very discreet. Well, perhaps not quite as discreet as Madame Chan had wanted me to be. But their disappearance still left questions as to who they were, what were they doing and why? I found it unsettling to know that I was a target but to not know why.

I sluiced down the shaded side of the coach and soaped it. A steady breeze had sprung up now and I found it most welcome — it took the edge from the heat. Looking around, I could see that the park was still exploited for its timber. Some areas had been felled, others replanted. The crests of the distant hills were crowned with the regular points of conifers, mathematically aligned to give the greatest yield per hectare. Nearer, a plantation of young eucalyptus rippled blue-grey as the breeze chased through its foliage and out across a vast meadow of waving yellow grass which stretched as far as the river.

I was cleaning the windscreen, my feet on the fender footrests and one hand on the grab on the middle upright of the windscreen, when I caught the reflection of Madame Chan approaching with one of the group. I left a portion of glass dry so that I could watch her. She had changed into flat soled shoes ready for the afternoon stroll.

'In your working clothes, I see,' she said, eyeing my now grubby shorts and sodden teeshirt.

I jumped down to the ground and grinned.

'Not as smart as your working clothes,' I said.

She pretended not to hear but introduced the man who was with her. 'This is Monsieur Tan Lee.' I rubbed my hand on the back of my shorts and shook hands with him. He nodded and smiled. 'Monsieur Tan Lee would like to look at your engine.'

'My engine?'

She took a deep breath. I watched her blouse fill and then loosen.

'Monsieur Tan Lee would like to see the engine of your coach. He makes motor engines in his factory.'

'OK,' I agreed and smiled at him encouragingly. 'It's at the rear. What kind of engines does he make?'

'Tractor engines.'

'Well, he might find this a bit different.'

I propped up the engine cover and we gathered under its shade and gazed at the complex assembly that is a modern V8 diesel engine. Monsieur Tan Lee made sucking noises on his teeth and little whistles. He pointed and said something to Madame Chan. She said,

'What is that he is pointing at?'

'This?' I asked. He nodded. 'It's an injector.'

'Ah,' she said. 'You will have to explain to me what it does. I have no idea what the Mandarin equivalent is.'

'It squirts the fuel into the cylinders.'

She translated and he nodded and pointed to another part of the motor. Madame Chan translated again and so forth. Just when I thought he was satisfied he asked if I would start it up.

'I will,' I said to Madame Chan, 'but I want you both in front of the coach where I can see you.'

'Why?'

'The last thing I want to see is bits of Madame Chan flying off into the countryside.' She blushed. 'Or Monsieur Tan Lee, of course,' I added quickly.

At length he was satiated and went happily back to the hotel to change his clothes for the stroll in the Arbour Walk. Madame Chan watched me collect up my brooms, brushes and bucket and stow them in the locker.

'Sorry,' I explained, 'you caught me in the middle of my housework.'

She shaded her eyes and looked the coach over.

'It's sparkling.'

'Georges would hound me out of the garage if I brought it back dirty.'

She idly traced a pattern in the gravel with her shoe.

'Are you coming on the walk with us?'

'Where is this Arbour Walk?'

'It's to the right of those trees.' She pointed across to the eucalyptus plantation. 'You can't see it from here.' She squinted at the sun. I watched the way that her nose wrinkled when she did that. 'At least it will be shady there.'

'I don't think I will.'

I looked at her.

She looked at me.

'Why didn't you come down to lunch?' she said.

'I did. It was excellent.'

'I didn't see you.'

'No, I kept out of the way.'

'I thought that we...' she faltered and then smiled grimly. 'I suppose thirty seven Monsieur Tan Lees are a bit frightening.'

'It's not the Chinese that frighten me,' I said.

They went for their walk. I sat on the step of the Merc and watched them depart. The group's casual clothes appeared to be trousers and polo shirts spun in bright cottons topped by grey peaked caps. They wandered away from the hotel in a disordered crocodile with Madame Chan answering questions and pointing out sights. Twelve of the older members of the group had decided to skip the walk and go straight to bed, thus frustrating Madame Chan's attempt at acclimatising them to the time change. I just prayed that they would not wake up and start bouncing around at four o'clock tomorrow morning.

I sat for a while, enjoying the breeze and then I decided to do some exploring by myself. I had already noticed that from behind the workshop ran one of those deeply rutted tracks that could only have been made by a heavy tractor hauling logs. I walked up the hard crusted mud and eventually found a footpath winding from it at a tangent. The trees here were deciduous and cast a filtered and welcome shade. Some distance away to my right a chain saw started up so I edged away and after a few minutes came across a small glade where the sun dappled through the thinning branches onto a carpet of grass.

I sat down. I was soon lying on my back gazing up the perspective of the trees as they appeared to lean their swaying tops together. I closed my eyes and let the sunlight play over my eyelids, producing beige patterns the same colour as Madame Chan's linen suit. The swishing of the wind in the leaves soothed away my anxieties. Before me was the prospect of a light dinner in a quiet corner of the dining room and then a real bed. Tomorrow would be a straightforward drive into Paris. Even the Minister could not complicate that.

My mind drifted to Madame Chan. She was a bit of an enigma. An attractive lady but prickly. And she had a Monsieur Chan in China, but we did not know why. Perhaps he had found her too prickly as well. As well as whom?

I changed the angle of my reflections. I thought about the soldier at the barrier this morning. How he had almost jumped to attention for Madame Chan. What had she shown him? Just her I.D. card I had supposed. I grinned salaciously to myself. Perhaps it had a good photo on it. Now what would Madame Chan look like without...?

Concentrate. Concentrate on something else. The sunlight. The sunlight shining through the coach window yesterday on the autoroute and glinting on the silver in her hair. Silver? But she could only be twenty eight or nine. You don't go grey at that age.

The wanderings of my mind were interrupted by the sound of a car engine revving hard. It came nearer. I sat up. Some forestry workers bucketed along the track below me in a red four wheel drive pick up truck. It was obvious from the way they were driving that they did not pay for the maintenance or the tyres. A chainsaw and other odds and ends bounced about in the open back and looked to be in constant danger of being pitched out. That would take some explaining to the foreman.

Their intrusion broke the spell and I stood up to walk back, choosing a different path to vary my return route. Perhaps I would walk out to meet the group coming back. I looked down at my wrinkled shorts and creased tee shirt. Perhaps not. Funny that I should have thought of going to meet them. It was not as if I was particularly involved with the group. They were just passengers. It is difficult to get to know somebody when you don't speak the same language. Unlike Madame Chan.

I came to the edge of the stand and looked across. I could see the coloured shirts of the Chinese as they picked their way up through the young eucalyptus trees. The full significance of the plume of smoke did not strike me immediately. I could see the forestry workers and I could see the group, which was hidden from them. And the group was ambling gently up towards the fireline that the two men were laying. I watched the men extend the line and with a strange feeling of detached concern realised that the group were downwind and walking towards it. I shouted and waved my arms. With a spurt of flame, another ten metres of eucalyptus caught fire.

I began to run. I stopped yelling, I needed all my breath. Down through the edge of my stand I charged, ignoring the brambles tearing at my bare legs. The smoke was now rising rapidly. As I vaulted over the fence at the corner of the field I saw that what had looked from a distance to be a meadow now revealed itself to be a crop of a feathery grass growing to nearly two metres height. It stretched for hectares down to the river. If that caught fire, it would be a death trap. The coloured shirts had begun to group and were looking at the pall of smoke rising before them. I shouted and ran towards them, searching as I did so for any glimpse of beige linen. Why had she not worn something brighter?

I was about three hundred metres away and they still could not hear me but now I could hear a crackling and popping as the trees passed the flames along. In an anguish of frustration I watched as the group began to hurry away to the left, in a direction which would trap them in a thicker belt of murderous tinder dry eucalyptus. They could not see that the fire was already burning on the other side of the ridge that they were making for. They needed to come towards me. I began to wheeze as the first wafts of smoke played around me. In white-eyed fear, four deer suddenly crashed past me and down the slope. Why didn't the Chinese do the same?

I took a risk and stopped. I cupped my hands around my mouth and shouted as loudly as I could. I saw faces turn as they struggled up the slope. I waved my arms. They stopped climbing. I ran towards them and then swore as they began to climb again. I yelled again and again, waving my arms until I got their attention. They gathered into a group and watched me. I could not count how many. I could not see beige. Some began to trickle down towards me. I shouted and waved my arms to hurry them up. The breeze had caught hold of the fire now and it was roaring in a cauldron of red. With a sudden whooshing sound it seared over the crest of the ridge they had been making for, turning the trees instantly to flaming skeletons as the foliage shot skywards in a cloud of burning embers. They now saw their danger and scattered pell mell down the slope towards me.

The first ones to reach me jabbered and pointed.

'Where is Madame Chan?' I shouted at them. More arrived, their faces running with sweat. I tried to count them. How many were we supposed to have? Subtract twelve from thirty seven or was it thirty eight? More shirts and peaked caps mingled around me.

'For Christ's sake,' I shouted above the roaring, 'has anybody seen Madame Chan?' I counted twenty then a sudden swerve in the wind brought a cloud of smoke and embers down amongst us and we reeled about choking and smacking the red hot leaves from our clothing. We needed to move. I recognised the tractor engine manufacturer.

'Tan Lee! Tan Lee!' I shouted. I grabbed him and shook him. He grinned at me faintly. I pointed to the corner of the field and shouted at him until I was certain that he was looking at the same point as me and then I pushed him off and shoved the others after him, counting as I did so. Twenty three and no beige. I felt sick.

All kinds of creatures were rushing by, heedless of the danger of a human compared with fire. Visibility was now about ten metres and I was continuously batting at embers which lodged on me. I set off up the slope into the rolling smoke, and was immediately bowled into the undergrowth by a stag which snorted past. I pulled myself up.

'Jocelyne,' I yelled into the roar, 'Jocelyne! Madame Chan!' It was pointless, nobody could make themselves heard above that noise. 'Jocelyne!' I yelled again and choked as I inhaled a lung full of smoke. As I coughed I heard a cry. It came from further over to my left.

'Jocelyne!' My voice was a bark. 'Jocelyne!'

I heard the cry again and stumbled and ran blindly through the smoke.

'Simon!'

I could see red, I could see green and I could see beige. Her hair was astray and her clothes smeared with dirt and soot.

'Oh thank Christ I've found you!' I hugged her quickly and then said, 'I've got twenty three down at the bottom. Is that the lot with these two?' She coughed and nodded. 'Right! Follow me! Grab a Chinky and run!'

I caught hold of the hand of the man in the red shirt and dragged him with me, jumping over the small patches of burning undergrowth where the embers had been blown ahead of the main conflagration. I looked behind. Madame Chan was leaping like a gazelle with a startled green shirted Chinese businessman welded to her wrist. The noise was deafening. One minute a tree would be leaning in the searing breeze and the next it would suddenly explode in flame alongside us. Just when I was certain that I had lost my way we stumbled into an area of better visibility and I caught a glimpse of coloured shirts.

'This way,' I shouted and veered left.

We arrived gasping and panting at the bottom of the slope by the corner of the field of giant grass. The group were chattering excitedly amongst themselves and greeted our arrival with a burst of applause. I realised that if I lived to be a hundred I would never understand the Chinese.

'Listen,' I shouted at Madame Chan. 'We need to go up there. I know it is into the wind but I also know that the fire has not got across onto the back of this ridge. I saw it all start.'

She nodded.

'Simon,' she gasped. 'We must count again. There's got to be twenty five.' Always the professional.

'Get them into a line.'

She shouted at them but it had little effect. Another bank of smoked rolled down across us and high on the top of the ridge a tree trunk crashed to the ground in a bouffon of red sparks. I shoved and pushed them until we had got some order and then we counted. Twenty four.

Merde.

'Count again!' she insisted. 'Both separately.' Then she shouted something at them which made them stand stock still in shock.

'Twenty five!' I shouted.

'Same here.'

'Come on! This way.'

I pushed them towards the slope, yelling hard at them, harrying them upwards. I caught a flash of red on top of the slope. The pick up truck. Help at last. Then I stopped dead as the entire ridge erupted in a sheet of flame and the truck disappeared behind the smoke. I could not believe what I had seen.

'Back!' I yelled. 'Back.'

They thought I was spurring them on. They were not looking upwards. Almost weeping in desperation I pelted after them. I grabbed the first one I came to and spun him around. I did the same with the second.

'Chan!' I yelled at Madame Chan. 'Chan!' It had not occurred to me how common the name was in China. The men who turned saw me gesticulating at the wave of flame creeping down the hill towards them and saw two of their compatriots already charging back down the hill. They also turned, yelling to the others.

Even from thirty metres I could clearly see the horror on Madame Chan's face as the rolling wave of flame advanced down the hill towards her. She shrieked at the few remaining climbers. They stopped. As soon as they saw the flames they turned and pelted back down the slope. They staggered back to the corner of the field. They were all in. Eyes staring, gasping, coughing, choking. Some bent double, holding their sides, panting, their chests heaving. Madame Chan staggered in with the last three.

'Count,' she gasped.

I counted. They were not moving now. They were transfixed by the roaring and crackling of the advancing fire. They waited patiently, looking at me for orders.

'Twenty five, you twenty six, me twenty seven.'

'Which way? Into the grass?'

'That's a death trap. There is hectares of it and the flame would shoot even faster through there.' I gazed about wildly. 'We'd be roasted alive.'

'We will anyway, Simon. Simon!' her voice was desperate. It tugged at my heart.

'Quick!' I said. 'Has anybody got any matches? Cigarette lighter?'

'What?'

'Just get something.'

She shouted at the group and there was a frenzy of excitement. A man hurried forward with a flip top petrol lighter. I yanked out a frond of the grass.

'Stand back!' I shouted. They could not stand very far back. The hot draft gusting from the wall of crackling flame a hundred metres away was already searing our skins. I lit the end of the frond and thrust it into the base of the grass before me. The fire caught. I tugged it out and ran along the edge of the field, repeating the movement. The Chinese stared at me with strangely fatalistic eyes.

'Simon! What are you...?' the rest of Madame Chan's query was drowned by a frightening roar as the feathery seedheads of the grass ignited and the flames immediately leapt five metres into the air.

'Don't worry, don't worry!' I shouted, with much more conviction than I felt. 'Don't you see? The grass will burn quicker than the trees. It will give us a fire break. Get together. Get them together.' I instructed Madame Chan.

She began to badger them into a group. Their eyes switched nervously between the fire advancing upon us and the fire which was supposedly advancing from us. I licked my lips. They were cracked and dirty. A sudden gust of breeze blew a roaring tongue of flame through the undergrowth and the advancing fire was suddenly ten metres nearer. I looked to the grass. The flame was already distant, scorching through the crop at about thirty kph, leaving a charred pincushion of black stumps behind it. I stamped into them and the skeletons crumbled into ash.

'Get them to do the same as me,' I told Madame Chan. They needed no second bidding. We kicked and stamped into the field. But I had forgotten that our new fire would create even more draught. With a terrifying roar another twenty metres of eucalyptus exploded into flame.

'Quick!' I shouted. 'Do this!' I began to kick down to a patch of clear earth.

Madame Chan shouted at them to copy me. Her voice was almost drowned in the roar of the conflagration. I glanced back and saw a towering, leaping spiral of heat driven flame flaring towards us. No time for orders. I ran amongst them pushing them face downwards to the into the earth.

'Get down, it's going over us!'

But Madame Chan remained standing, yelling instructions at the top of her voice. Frightened faces, roaring flame, a noise like an approaching train. The men dropped to the ground. I swept Madame Chan's legs away with my foot, threw her to the hot earth and fell across her as a dragon's breath rolled over us scorching the back of my leg. The roaring went on and on, the air got hotter and hotter until I thought I would burst into flame and then suddenly everything seemed to stop. The noise dropped. The flame had passed. Behind us I could hear the gentle cracking and popping of wood burning. Somewhere a man was sobbing. My head was on Madame Chan's shoulder. I discreetly nuzzled her hair aside and kissed the back of her neck. She did not feel it.

She wriggled.

'Will you get off me?' she said irritably.

I rolled onto my back and winced as an ember burned through my tee shirt. I was back on familiar ground.

10

The fire caused a sensation. The fuss created was such that I was able to smuggle the group into the hotel through my private service door and see them to their rooms. According to Madame Chan, it would be very upsetting for the dignity of the group to be seen in public in such a dirty and ragged state. I supposed it would not please the Minister either.

We were all very shaken but unwounded. Most of us had scratches and bruises and two of the men had suffered slightly singed hair when the fire had rolled over us but far from being upset about it, they laughed and displayed it proudly to the others.

Once we had settled the group down, I went to my room, tore off my shorts and tee shirt and scrubbed myself clean in the shower. On my bed my freshly laundered clothes were awaiting me. I wrapped myself loosely in the towel robe and stretched out alongside them. I gazed vaguely up at the plaster escutcheon on the ceiling and had a good think. I did not like what I dredged up. The pall of smoke was now clearing but the odour of burning hung over everywhere. It even pervaded the rooms by the open windows.

I dressed in my pressed slacks and clean shirt and went down to the dining room. Some of the other guests were already dining and the short lived forest fire was the main source of conversation. I paused at the door and pretended to read the carte whilst I glanced nervously at the twinkling chandeliers and the slightly formal dress of the guests. I could not see any of our group. I was on the point of turning back when the maitre d' noticed me.

'Good evening sir.' He immediately put me at my ease. 'Your usual table?'

One or two of the guests looked up at this and I stifled a smile. I inclined my head in what I hoped was an elegant acquiescence.

'That would be lovely,' I said.

The maitre d' winked imperceptibly. He was enjoying the game as much as I was.

'Please follow me sir.'

He led me around a screen formed by a mound of enormous dark green foliage.

'Good evening,' Madame Chan said. She smiled at the maitre d'. 'Thank you Charles,' she said. Her hair was groomed, her face was delicately made up and she wore her fairy princess dress. She looked like a million francs.

The maitre d' smiled warmly and drew back the chair for me. I gave him a look to condemn his treachery but he continued to smile. Madame Chan said,

'Do sit down, Simon, we've got things to talk about.'

'We certainly have,' I agreed and took the carte which the maitre d' offered me. 'The first thing is, where is the group?'

'Safely tucked up in bed.'

'With no dinner?'

'For those that wanted it I had some light snacks sent up to their rooms. All they really wanted to do was to go to bed and get some sleep. It's been a long day for them.'

'Yes... You could say that. It's not every day you nearly get roasted alive in a forest fire. And whilst we are on the subject, that was the stupidest thing I ever saw anybody do — standing up in front of that flame and shouting out instructions in Chinese.'

'Mandarin,' she corrected.

'It was also the bravest.'

'Hmm,' she said, and looked into her plate. 'I can recommend the smoked salmon.'

'I don't think I want anything more smoked tonight.'

She caught my eye and we laughed.

'I've had a doctor to check over the party, just to

make sure there were no injuries,' she said.

'That's not very clever. Not exactly discreet. It will be all around the district by now.'

She looked at me evenly.

'I doubt it,' she said. 'It was Docteur St Claire de Genève. He is staying in the hotel at the moment.'

'St Claire de Genève? The President's doctor?' She nodded. 'Do you know him then?'

'We have met.'

'Oh,' I said. 'That's alright then.' I was out of my depth. I looked across the table at her. 'I said yesterday that you looked right in this sort of place. You do. But then, I expect you have been in them a few times.'

'Not very often.'

'I feel like a fish out of water.'

'You don't look like one, Simon, so don't act like one. Order your dinner.'

I ordered a salade de tomates followed by a grilled trout. I never have been a big eater. And my conversation is not much either.

We sat in a cosy salon and ordered coffee. Down by the river we could see the lights of the fire trucks pumping up water to douse the remnants of the blaze. When the waiter came, Madame Chan asked for a telephone. He brought one and plugged it in to the wall behind her.

'I have to check with Monsieur Knopf and confirm the arrangements for tomorrow.'

'Are you going to mention the fire?'

'I don't really see how I can avoid it. It was on the television news. No mention was made that we were here, of course, but Knopf knows we are here.'

I thought, 'and so does somebody else'.

Whilst she asked for the number, I poured the coffee. I looked out at the darkness and the pinpoints of light flickering across the fields where the firemen were still working. The fire had been a close run thing. If it had not been for the river, it would still be raging across the countryside like the one that was out of control in Provence.

155

Madame Chan listened to Knopf's instructions, writing occasionally in her notebook then she covered the mouthpiece and whispered across to me, 'The Minister is coming on the line for some reason.' I shrugged. She paid attention to the phone again. 'Yes, this is Madame Chan. Certainly, Monsieur le Ministre, I understand Monsieur le Ministre.' I realised that she was taking orders from the big oaf himself. Suddenly she stiffened and her knuckles went white as she gripped the receiver.

'Yes, monsieur, we did go for a walk. As suggested by Monsieur Knopf. No, we went to the Arbour Walk. I have not seen the television report but we did see the fire.' She glanced quickly across at me. 'No, I do not believe that we were in danger at any time.' She suddenly bit her lip and went very red. From where I was sitting I could hear the Minister shouting. She swallowed hard once or twice and her eyes began to water. The raving eventually stopped and she looked at the silent receiver. She placed it carefully on the cradle and then whispered, 'Yes, Monsieur le Ministre.' Her hand was shaking.

I waited. She picked up her handbag and stood up.

'I'll be back in a minute,' she said and walked over towards the ladies' cloakroom.

I sipped at my coffee. Then I called the waiter over and got him to remove the telephone. I had decided that she had used it enough for one evening. I did not want to witness another scene such as that.

Madame Chan came back and sat down.

'Well, we've got the details for tomorrow,' she said brightly. 'Quite straightforward. We pick up on their already planned programme and get them to Paris for the press reception at the Palais de Chaillot.

She put her hand to her coffee cup but it rattled on the saucer so she left it where it was.

'Oh dear,' she said, putting on a brave smile, 'I must be a little overwrought. The Minister was upset.'

'You don't say?'

She sat back, folded her hands in her lap and took one or two deep breaths. 'I've never really been able to cope with people shouting at me,' she said.

I tried rapidly to recall whether I had ever shouted at her.

'What was upsetting the Minister?'

'The Chinese Ambassador in Paris.' I looked puzzled. She continued, 'He has registered an official protest over the danger that the trade delegation had been placed in. A reckless disregard for the safety of the honoured citizens of the People's Republic of China as guests of the French Minister of Commerce and Industry.'

'Well what does he know about it?' I exclaimed.

'Monsieur Wong has already phoned in his report from the hotel.'

'Monsieur Wong? That commissionaire fellow?'

'Commissaire,' she said absently.

'I didn't like him from the beginning. You know, I can take an instant dislike to some people.'

She looked at me.

'Oh, I believe you,' she said vehemently.

'What a bastard.'

'Please don't use language like that. In any case, he is doing his job. That is what he is there for — the security of the group. It was stupid of me to take them off the Walk and attempt a short cut. I ignored the notices about the logging operations. I thought nobody was working in our part of the forest.'

'Yes but, all the same,' I protested, 'it's hardly your fault if a forest catches fire.'

'We should have stayed on the Walk. The Walk was untouched. It must have been upwind of the outbreak. We would have been safe there and had a grandstand view.'

'Yes, we were rather close to the action.'

'Closer than I would have liked. I was terrified.'

'So was I'

'You were terrified?' She sounded surprised. 'You didn't look it.'

'Well neither did you. Standing there in the middle of a raging inferno and calmly ordering me to count the bloody group.'

'We had to know that everybody was with us. It's our responsibility.'

'Whose? I am just the coach driver.'

'My responsibility,' she sighed. 'And my fault.'

'What do you mean, 'your fault'?'

She smiled sadly at me.

'Somebody's head will have to roll, won't it?'

'Yes but you're doing a damn good job! You really are good — the way you look after the group, sort out their rooms, answer their questions and I've never had a guide to give me such clear directions as you do.'

'Even if you don't follow them,' she said. 'What exactly was going on this morning with you and that car?'

'Oh, it's a long story.'

'We've been here before haven't we?' she observed quietly. 'And we are still no further.' She turned sideways and lifted her legs onto the couch. The skirt of her dress swept in a fan to the carpet.

'Well I am comfortable. And I like stories.' She looked at me with expectation.

I looked at her and swallowed. The light from the wall lamp was highlighting the silver strands in her hair and casting interesting shadows below her breasts. She had no idea of the effect she was creating.

'Erm... which story do you want?'

'The one that you say is a long story every time I happen to ask you something that you do not want to tell me. Let's try, "Simon Laperche, the most hated driver in Paris", to start with.'

'Oh you don't want to hear...'

'Simon! I want to hear. It is not for you to decide what I want to hear and what I don't.'

'All right. Don't blame me if you hate me even more after the story.'

'Are you worried by what I might think of you?'

'Not in the slightest,' I lied.

'Good. Then that is OK then, isn't it? Start.'

I filled my cheeks with air and puffed it out.

'Before I got this job with Autocars Fromme,' I said, 'I worked for a man called André Coursamel. He owned a coach company out at Bobigny. It wasn't a big company. We had about eight or nine coaches. I don't know how old he was — getting on for seventy at least. He had been in coaches for so long that everybody called him "Papa Coursamel". He was very popular. If anybody had a problem, Papa Coursamel would help. If you needed a driver to replace one going sick, Papa Coursamel would lend you one. If your coach broke a back axle in the Champs Elysées he would send out his tow truck and mechanic. He was a likeable man, always ready to pass the time of day with you.

'I started driving for him just over four years ago. It wasn't exactly demanding work. The usual stuff: schools, factories, outings.' I stopped and swept my gaze around the sumptuous salon. My eyes came to rest on Madame Chan. 'Not in your class at all,' I laughed a little awkwardly.

'Carry on,' she instructed.

'The one thing that I aspired to was.... This will sound so mundane as to be pathetic but it is the way you get to feel in a garage. We had a Saviem E7. It was our top coach and we used to supply Cityscope on an occasional basis. You know Cityscope?'

'The excursion coach people? City tours and that?'

'Yes, that's right. They could never know exactly how many coaches they needed each day. It depended on how many tourists turned up and bought a tour ticket. Cityscope would book what they thought was the required number of coaches from their contracted garages but they would often throw in a booking for Coursamel or other small companies because if it transpired that the coach was not needed — not enough tourists — it could be sent back to the garage and they only paid a waiting fee. With a coach from their contracted garages, they would have to pay for a half day's hire. So my ambition was to get on the E7 and do a day excursion around Paris.'

'And did you manage it?'

I glanced at her to make sure that she was not laughing at me. She was not.

'Occasionally. Most of the time I was doing the schools and factories. That was when it all happened.' I stopped for a few seconds. I could see the open swinging door, the ambulance, the accusing faces. 'The coach I generally drove was an old Fiat with a Van Hool body. Coursamel had bought it secondhand from a garage near Lille. They had bought it secondhand in Belgium. It had been well used, the seats were faded, the floor covering was worn through in places but it was ideal for what he wanted.

'As I was driving out of the yard one day, the emergency door at the rear of the coach swung open. The Fiat had jack-knife passenger doors at the front but alongside the rear bench was a large swinging door which was intended only for emergency use. You could not use it in normal service because it had no steps to it. You would have to jump about a metre to the ground but you would not worry about that in a real emergency of course. So I drove back into the yard, found an odd length of cord and tied it up. When I got back I told Papa Coursamel and put it on a repair docket. I could probably have fiddled about with the latch myself but the mechanic was paid to do that sort of thing.

'A few days later I took the coach out again and the door was still not repaired. I told Papa Coursamel. He said he would get it fixed and I thought no more about it. Not my responsibility. I was just a coach driver. The next day one of Papa Coursamel's old mates phoned up with some sob story about needing a coach and driver to do a school. Coursamel was no businessman. It did not occur to him that what the other companies were regularly doing was negotiating contracts, picking out the lucrative bits for themselves and then farming the messy bits out to mugs like Coursamel. The client paid the contract price, the coach company paid Coursamel an adjusted price and kept the difference.

'He sent me out in the Fiat. When I arrived at the school, it was not one that I had done before, they were four teachers and seventy two children to go a kilometre down the road to the sports ground and back.'

'Seventy two!'

'And four teachers.'

'In one coach?'

'That is what the company had promised the school.

What they had told Papa Coursamel I don't know.'

'How many seats had you got?'

'The Fiat was a fifty three seater, sixty five with the straps.'

'Straps?'

'Strapontins. The fold down seats in the aisle.'

'What did you do?'

'Well, you know me for a pig-headed fool don't you? I took them. I told them to double up where they could, sat one teacher on the guide seat and another on the step and crammed the overflow onto the back seat. What the hell, we were only going one kilometre down the road. Nothing could happen in one kilometre could it?'

'But it did,' she said, her hand moving to her lips, parted in anxiety.

'I turned the first corner, I wasn't even going fast. The kids on the back seat were messing about as kids do. The emergency door fell open and out went two children. Just like that. Straight into the path of a car. Bang.'

'Poor children. What happened to them?'

I gazed at the heavy drape and tried to blot out images of little skewed bodies on tarmac, wild hysterical children, screaming teachers, white-faced car driver staring horror struck through the windscreen with a foot still cramped on the brake pedal.

'The girl was lucky, if you could call it that. She will never be the ballet dancer she had hoped to be but at nine years old you have time to readjust to life in a wheelchair. The lad does not know whether he has been lucky or not. His head was the first thing to hit the road. They have to feed him, dress him, put him to bed. And he can't even say his own name.'

I looked at the drapes again but the image still stayed.

'And that is why you are the most despised coach driver in Paris? It's not fair. It wasn't you fault.'

I held up my hand to stop her.

'It's not finished. I warned you that it was a long story. There had to be an enquiry of course. I was initially charged with dangerous driving but they realised that the charge would not stick so they concocted a catch-all charge encompassing unroadworthy vehicles and carriage of unauthorised passengers.'

'What happened then?' she asked.

'I pleaded guilty to overloading my coach. I could not do otherwise. It is the driver's responsibility to know how many passengers he has on board and I clearly knew that I was over the limit.'

'But you had no choice!'

'I should have left some behind.'

'But you were trying to help!'

'And that has always got me into trouble hasn't it?' I looked pointedly at her. She had the grace to fiddle with the hem of her dress. 'But when it came to the state of the coach, I decided to make a stand. I had no axe to grind with Papa Coursamel but the enquiry could not escape the deduction that he had sent me out in a faulty coach. He knew it was faulty. They called him in. They put me on the witness stand. Yes, I had notified the boss that the door was faulty, yes that is the repair docket. No, I discovered on a subsequent drive that the door had not been repaired and yes I did bring this to the attention of Monsieur Coursamel. Yes he did assure me that it would be fixed.

'The trouble with Papa Coursamel was that he was a bumbler. He bumbled along doing things but never really got to grips with what was really needed. For a start, the door should have had an alarm fitted which would sound by the driver as soon as it had been opened. It did not. The first that I knew that I was sowing children along the highway was when I heard the screech of brakes and looked in my mirror.'

She shuddered.

'Needless to say, the authorities went through Papa Coursamel's with a fine tooth comb. The old man almost went white overnight. Two of his coaches were condemned on the spot. His customers left him in droves. The press really went to town. Crippled children, callous coach operators, unfit vehicles — it had everything they needed. They got transcripts of the enquiry and misquoted me. I was the driver who had put the knife into Papa Coursamel.'

'But that's no reason for all this...'

I put up my hand again to stop her.

'I've not got to the punch line yet.'

'There's more?'

'You asked for the story,' I said, 'and you're getting it. Papa Coursamel had a little fishing chalet in some village in the Somme. You know the kind of thing — a single storey two roomed affair with a pond and some poplars. He would go up there and have a quiet weekend. I think he liked to get away from Madame Coursamel sometimes. He had aged. He looked dogged when I saw him at the enquiry. Staring at me from under those shaggy eyebrows and wondering why I was doing all this to him. Bringing his life's work to his knees. So he went off fishing. But he did not take a rod, he took his shotgun and blew his head off.

'You have, sitting before you, the man who crippled two children and killed the most loved coach operator in Paris.'

'Rubbish!' she snapped. I jumped. She swung her legs to the floor to face me. 'You don't believe that anymore than I do.'

A waiter casually drifted in at the sound of her explosion. A discreet check that all was well. I called him over.

'I'm think I'm going to have a cognac,' I announced scandalously. 'What will you have?'

'Oh why not?' she said. 'A port and ice please.' She turned to me and repeated, 'You don't believe that do you?'

'It's not what I believe that is important. It's what they believe.'

'Who are "they"?'

'Everybody! The Press, the drivers, the employers. I got a suspended licence for twelve months. They made it clear that when I got it back there would be no job for me in coaches.'

'Are coaches important to you?'

'Oh I don't know. I don't care anymore.'

'That wasn't very convincing, Simon. Coaches were obviously important enough to you for you to try and succeed in getting a job with Autocars Fromme.'

We watched the waiter slide gracefully into the salon with our tray of drinks. The oil paintings on the walls stared down upon us in their heavy browns and cracked canvas as he placed the glasses on the table between us. He glanced around the room and noted that we were now the only occupants.

'Should you require me further, Madame, Monsieur, there is a bell on the wall. Otherwise I shall leave you in peace.'

'Thank you,' I acknowledged and then turned to Madame Chan. 'I just had an incredible stroke of luck with Monsieur Fromme. Somebody who had never met me before backed his hunch and gave me a recommendation.'

'He must have been influential for Monsieur Fromme to have taken any notice of him.'

'You are not the only person who knows important people.' I felt quite smug. 'He is important in our little world and he did me a good turn for which I shall never be able to repay him. More credit to him.' I took a sip from my cognac and my heart nearly stopped.

'What's the matter?' she asked quickly. 'Is the cognac bad?'

'No, it's fine, fine.'

I had just noticed the bar slip under the glass. I did not have that much money to my name.

'You looked as if you had seen a ghost.'

I shook my head easily but she had caught the line of my glance. She leaned gracefully forwards and scooped up the bill and her glass.

'I think the Minister can treat us to this,' she said as she delved in her handbag and took out her pen. 'Medicinal purposes, treatment for shock.' She signed the bill.

'Shock? You mean his telephone call?'

She pulled a sour face at me.

'No, I did not mean the telephone call. I meant the little incident in the burning forest.'

'Oh that!' I said. 'I had almost forgotten it.'

She deftly changed the subject.

'Tell me about the car this morning.'

I looked into my glass and swirled the amber liquid around. It was the finest I had ever tasted.

'Oh just a bit of careless driving.'

'On whose part?' she asked tartly. 'Come on, Simon, I want to know the truth. You caused that car to crash on purpose.'

'Maybe I did,' I said defiantly. 'Should be no bother to you. They weren't your friends were they?'

'Not that I know of.' She peered hard at me. Her brown eyes were unsettling dark beads, catching a glint from the light. 'Were they your friends?'

I thought of the car at the Place de l'Europe, the shoe swinging at my head, the relentless thudding of the heavy fists as they slammed into my chest.

'No,' I admitted slowly, 'they were not my friends.'

'So?'

'So what?'

'So you haven't finished the long story you were telling me.' She swung her legs back up onto the couch. I tried not to watch. 'Go on. I'm waiting.'

I looked at her in silence, hoping she would give up. I might just as well have tried to outstare the Mona Lisa.

'All right.' I gave in. 'A couple of days ago I was jumped on by a couple of thugs by the Place de l'Europe. It's near the...'

'I know where it is.'

'Yes, of course. Of course you do. Well, they er... they beat me up.'

'Why?'

'I've no idea. They didn't try to rob me. I don't know how much they intended to hurt me but they laid into me pretty well.'

'Were you hurt? You look alright to me.'

'Oh I'm alright. But you should have seen the other fellows.'

'But why did they do it? I don't understand.'

'Neither do I.'

'And was this the incident you referred to when you said that your friend Monique had saved you?' I grinned at her. 'What are you laughing at?'

'I was just trying to imagine you doing what Nikki did — screaming down the sidewalk and deploying her umbrella as a broadsword and then a lance.'

She fiddled uncomfortably with the hem of her dress again. Then she glanced up. 'How do you know that I would not have done the same?'

'You might have an umbrella like Nikki's but I doubt that you have her vocabulary.'

'I think I would agree with that supposition,' she said stiffly. 'But what has all this to do with the car?'

'Ah, well, these two thugs were driving a dark coloured Peugeot.'

'Like the one this morning?'

'Exactly.'

'Simon, it's probably one of the commonest cars in France. You can't go around pushing them all off the road just because one such car was linked to an unexplained attack on you!'

'They were following me.'

She gave a sigh of exasperation.

'They were behind you,' she explained. 'It's not the same thing.'

'You remember when we got in the coach this morning at the hotel? They were already waiting for us across the square. I didn't say anything — you were acting your usual tetchy self.'

'My usual tetchy self? Was this just after you had told Monsieur Fromme that we were both in the same hotel room, sitting on the same bed, by any chance?' The anger flashed in her eyes.

'Oh.' I suddenly realised what I had done.

'Is that all you can say — "Oh"? It will be all around the garage by now. "Simon Laperche has bedded the guide — again!"' Her eyes began to water. 'Why don't you ever think before you speak?'

'They won't think that.' I tried to sound reassuring. 'Monsieur Fromme knows I'm not like that.' She glowered at me. 'Anyway,' I added, 'I haven't.'

She banged down her glass and stood up.

'And not likely to either!'

She snatched up her handbag and strode out, her dress foaming around her legs as if she were wading in a mountain stream.

Now how was I going to convince her about the fire?

11

How was I going to tell her the truth about the fire? I lay in my bed with my head propped on my folded arms and stared at the early morning sunlight making dappling patterns on the powder blue ceiling. Did I know the truth and would she believe me if I told her? It was depressing to admit that the answer to both questions was probably 'no'.

What I did know was that the fire had not been accidental. I had seen the men in the red pick up truck laying a fireline upwind of the group. I should have realised at the time that genuine forestry workers would have had more sense than to light any fire with the dry spell we had sweltered under these last few weeks.

And then, when we had led the group out of the line of the advancing flames and were making our way up to the safety of the other ridge, the fire had suddenly broken out above us. I had seen the roof of a vehicle glinting red amongst the foliage a moment before the flame. There was no doubt in my mind that it was the same truck that I had watched earlier. The truck that had charged recklessly through the wood. I remembered seeing their power saw bouncing on the cargo platform. And now, as I lay thinking it over, I recalled the image of the ten litre cans of petrol which had been strapped to the headgate. The fuel for the saw. That was how they had produced the second wall of instant flame to thunder down upon us, cutting off our only retreat.

They had sandwiched us between an impenetrable curtain of roaring flame and hectares of inflammable grass. They had given us the choice — stand still and be roasted alive or run into the grass and be roasted fleeing.

I suddenly felt very cold. They had meant to kill us. And this conclusion did not advance my reasoning one jot. I did not know who 'they' were nor why they were doing what they were doing. I was sure of only one thing — the game had passed into a higher league. There was a world of difference between the uncoordinated bruising meted out by the two thugs in the Peugeot and this cold blooded attempt to wipe out nearly thirty people.

I lay there and wondered. How do I get myself into such situations? Hanging by frantic fingernails onto my last chance of rehabilitation into the only business that I enjoy and I find myself cavorting around the countryside being nursemaid to a bunch of Chinese VIPs; subjected to every mad whim of a megalomaniac minister; harangued by a neurotic guide whose charm disables me and pursued by an unidentified enemy whose intentions now reveal themselves to be simply our total destruction.

It would really help me to have at least one other person on my side. I was not convinced that I had sketched the full picture nor was I confident that I possessed all the resources necessary to handle any extensions to its perspective. I needed assistance. And instead of asking for it each time, I upset her. Would it help if I told her I thought she was the sexiest woman I had met? No, probably not. And it wouldn't be true would it?

Would it?

Merde.

I kicked the thin sheet from the bed and got up. It was five fifteen in the morning and I knew I would sleep no more. I showered and then stood looking out of the window at the parkland. On a whim, I dressed and went out. I paused in the corridor, having no plan in mind. I wondered which room was Madame Chan's. I had not even noted the number and she had not told me. That was unprofessional. The driver and guide should always know where to find each other. She would know where I was, of course, because she held the rooming list and had handed me my key. I gave a sardonic grunt as I thought of her on the previous evening snapping, 'and not likely to either' when I had pointed out that I had not bedded the guide.

As I dawdled down the panelled passageway, I wondered whether I should get her number from Reception and present myself at her door and apologise for my remark. It might do some good. Then my mind conjured up an image of the pyrotechnics that would result if I knocked on her hotel door at half past five in the morning and that dissuaded me.

I slipped outside through my service door and stood with my back against the wall, feeling the rising strength of the sun on my face and breathing the morning air. It still had a tang of old bonfire about it. I could hear the buzzing of a mobylette as it weaved towards the hotel along the lane which ran through the estate farm. The bike rattled across the yard and slithered to a shaky halt on the loose gravel. The engine popped a few times and then died. The rider pulled off his helmet and nodded to me.

'You're up early,' Gilles said.

'So are you.'

'Not early enough.' He grimaced at the clock above the workshop. 'Five minutes late.' He delved in his pocket and pulled out a packet of American cigarettes. 'Still got time for a smoke though.' He lit up and threw the match onto the gravel.

'Good job gravel is not inflammable,' I observed.

He looked at the smoking match and laughed.

'I bet you got a good view of the fire yesterday.'

'Fairly good.'

'Bit of fun, wasn't it, eh? Better than the fourteenth of July.'

'An interesting opinion,' I said. 'But I don't think that whoever owned the timber and the grass would agree with you.'

'It was only young timber. I bet the boss is livid about the grass though. It was some special giant type of alfalfa. They were growing it for paper.' He drew on his cigarette and blew the smoke down his nostrils just like he had seen them do on the movies. 'They reckon it was kids.'

'Oh yes?'

'They stole one of the foresters' trucks. They ask for it, really. They park them in the wood where they are going to be working for the day and then walk away and leave the keys in the ignition. I've often thought about borrowing one for a ride. You know, bit of a laugh.' He sucked his cigarette again and screwed up his eyes to make himself look mean. 'But who wants to rattle about in a truck?' He laughed. 'If they had Jaguars I might have been interested. Or an Alpine Gordini at a pinch.'

I smirked with him.

It's called empathy.

He flicked his stub against the brick wall where it exploded in a spray of orange sparks and he began to wheel his bike off towards the workshop. The sun had not yet broken through the foliage onto the coach. The Merc was covered with a skim of fine condensation, dulling the sheen of the green paintwork and giving an imitation frost to the windows that I had cleaned the previous afternoon. I knew that once the sun reached them, then the humidity would evaporate without marking the glass. I crossed the yard to the coach and began a leisurely tour of inspection. It was my insurance. When I returned the coach to the garage, Georges' tour of inspection would be painstaking.

The bodywork was unmarked still. Underneath? Well, I was certain that the Merc had ample ground clearance to have straddled the road island yesterday with no damage. The scuff mark on the front bumper where I had crushed the wire paper basket at Orly Ouest was well camouflaged. I was hoping that he would not notice it once it was covered with a few millimetres of dust. I rounded the front of the coach and was startled to see a figure crouched on the ground. It wore one of those thin all-in-one suits which is black skin tight material and zip fasteners. For a moment I thought it was Gilles because it was obviously a motorbike rider. My hesitation was my downfall.

'What the...?'

In one lithe movement the rider rose and jabbed up a leg. I instinctively thrust out my arm to protect myself and the impact smacked my forearm into my face and threw me bodily against the coach.

'Oh not again!' I thought and tried to cover my head with my hands as I slid, stunned to the ground.

I waited for the follow up but the figure was gone. Leaping into the woodland like a ballet dancer. I felt blood trickling warm down my face.

'Are you all right?' Gilles suddenly stuck his head around the front of the coach. He was dressed in his hotel uniform. He frowned at me as I lifted my hand dismissively but made no attempt to stand up. 'Blimey you're not are you? What happened? he asked and then looked around as a powerful motorbike burst into life nearby and accelerated away behind the cover of the trees. He stood with his mouth open, staring in the direction of the rapidly departing motorbike. He snapped his attention back to me. 'Can you get up?' he asked.

'Wha..?' I mumbled. My head was buzzing. I could not make sense of what was happening.

'Look, you just stay there OK? I'll get help. You just stay there.'

He ran off towards the hotel, his feet kicking up the gravel in little spurts. I lay, slumped, my head spinning and my eyes not focusing. To pass the time I gazed down towards my legs and tried to concentrate on the blur that was my knees. With a bit of effort I made them into one image. Now try the feet. Two pairs of shoes, no, three. And all different. This was getting worse. I recognise those ankles.

'Simon, what's the matter? What happened?' I looked into her worried face and grinned stupidly. 'Just hold still whilst I clean this blood away.'

'What shall I do Miss?' Gilles asked anxiously. 'I just found him there. I thought you ought to know.'

She wiped carefully at my face and said almost to herself, 'I think it's only a nosebleed.' She held a finger before my face. 'Look at this Simon!' I managed to focus on it quite easily. She appeared relieved.

'Just stunned,' I managed to mutter.

'Say again,' she put her ear near to my lips. I could smell her. She was straight from her bed.

'Just stunned. Nothing broken.'

'Good.' She turned to Gilles. 'What's your name?'

'Gilles, Miss.'

'Right Gilles. We are going to try to get him inside.'

They stood me up and with a swimming head, I staggered between them up to the first floor landing. I felt that history was repeating itself.

'In here,' Madame Chan said and we swayed into her room. She propped up her pillows and flicked the counterpane over the bed. 'We'll put him on here till he gets his breath back.' I was not out of breath but I thought it sensible not to argue.

I felt a lot better once I got my legs up onto the bed. Madame Chan looked at me and shook her head as if admonishing a schoolboy.

'You are a mess Simon, look at you.'

'Rather look at you,' I mumbled.

She blushed. Gilles smirked.

'You know where Docteur St Claire de Genève has his suite?' she said to him.

'Yes miss.'

'Go to him. Tell him that Madame Chan presents her apologies but asks if he could oblige her by examining one of her group who has had a slight accident.'

He went.

She sat on the bed and tried not to look concerned. She did not succeed. I found comfort in her failure.

I felt that I was recovering swiftly. My vision was drifting back into focus and the buzzing in my ears was now only one bee not a swarm.

Docteur St Claire de Genève did not look like a doctor and certainly not a presidential physician. He was a man of about sixty years, roughly my size, neat and slim with a roundish face and thinning hair. He looked very ordinary, particularly with the legs of his striped pyjamas visible below his dressing gown. It was only then that I noticed that Madame Chan was wearing the hotel dressing gown over her nightdress. I had made a bit of a nuisance of myself with my early morning perambulations.

'Good morning Madame Chan,' he shook hands genially with her. 'What have we here then?' he turned to me.

'It's very good of you to come so quickly doctor.'

'Oh delighted to help, delighted.' He waved his hand at Gilles who stepped forward and handed him a sports bag. 'Thank you,' He took the bag. 'I am sure that you have other duties to occupy you now,' he said in dismissing him. His voice suddenly became stern. 'And I am sure you know how to keep your mouth shut.'

Gilles opened his eyes wide and nodded.

'So what happened to you then, young man?' the doctor addressed me as soon as the door had closed.

'I took a knock on the chest and head.' My voice was getting stronger now. 'I think it stunned me, that's all.'

'Ah ha.' His grey eyes met mine for an instant. He took some swabs from his bag and cleaned up my face properly. 'Just pinch your fingers across your nose there,' he instructed me. 'Does it hurt?'

'Not really.'

'Keep pinching. It will stop the nose bleed. You are the driver for Madame Chan's group?' I nodded slightly. His eyes met mine again and held them. 'I heard about your exploits yesterday. You almost certainly saved everyone from being burned alive.' I flicked my eyes across to Madame Chan. She turned away and studied something invisible but very interesting on the opposite wall.

'Exaggeration,' I said shortly.

'Hmph!' he said. He felt around my scalp. 'You've got a nice bruise coming up. You could put a cold pack on it but it's not necessary.'

'Oh, not more frozen beans, please!'

'Quite,' he said. 'Let's get this shirt off and have a look at you. You won't be able to wear it with all that blood on it anyway.'

He unbuttoned my shirt and pulled it open. I heard Madame Chan gasp. Her curiosity had got the better of her and now she was staring at the sight of my chest. I had forgotten about my technicolour bruises. Docteur St Claire de Genève looked at me and then sucked on his teeth.

'I see you've been in the wars young man. When did this happen?'

'A couple of days ago.'

He nodded confirmation to himself.

'How did it happen?'

'I had a disagreement with somebody.'

He traced a finger around the bruises.

'Fists,' he grunted. 'Not very skilled fists.'

'Even unskilled ones hurt.'

'And this?' he asked, pressing firmly on my rib cage. I yelped in pain. He continued, 'and of course you did not go to the hospital?'

'Not worth bothering them for that.'

'He's as stubborn as a mule!' Madame Chan snapped.

The doctor raised his eyebrows and looked at her.

'A mule with a couple of cracked ribs,' he said.

'Oh,' I said, 'is that why it hurts when I laugh?'

'You idiot!' she said.

The doctor grinned.

'She's probably right, you know.' Madame Chan had folded her arms and was scowling down at me. 'I wouldn't argue with her anyway,' he added.

'Oh I never do,' I assured him.

'So how did you get the bump on your head this morning then? Same disagreement?'

Madame Chan looked puzzled now.

'My attacker didn't wait to explain,' I said.

'Ah,' he said. 'Just lie still whilst I check your pulse rate and blood pressure. It's what they always expect doctors to do.'

'What about my cracked ribs?'

'There is nothing you or I can do about those. They will heal on their own. It will take a few weeks though. I suppose you could try not to laugh.'

'That won't be a problem,' I said, and pulled a face at Madame Chan. 'Ouch, that hurt my nose.'

'Serves you right.' She sat down sharply on a chair and sighed in exasperation. She nodded at my bruises. 'You should have seen the other fellows!' she mimicked. 'Ha!' She looked sharply at me and caught me peering at where her dressing gown was gaping open. She snatched it around her. 'Oh, you infuriate me, Simon Laperche!'

The doctor turned slowly to her, eyebrows raised.

'I'm sorry doctor. I didn't sleep well.'

'It's hardly surprising with what you went through yesterday,' he observed. He packed his things back into his bag. 'Just rest there for an hour and I am certain that everything will come back to normal. You have not sustained any additional injury. Not vomited have you?'

'No.'

'Fine. When are you leaving?'

I looked at Madame Chan.

'After breakfast,' she said. 'But will he be fit to drive? We can wait.'

'Oh I'm sure he will be all right. He's quite tough.'

'Ha! He thinks he is.'

'Pop in and see me before you go and I'll give him a final look over.'

'Thank you doctor. It's very kind of you. I'm sorry to have called you out so early.'

'I told you yesterday that you could call on me whenever you needed.'

'Yes but...'

'But you didn't think that I meant it? That's a little hurtful.' But he smiled at her.

She shut the door behind him and then turned to look at me.

'Just like a child!'

'I wouldn't want you for a mother.'

'So now I'm stuck with you on my bed.' She put on a disgusted voice that did not quite ring true. 'You're obviously feeling better.'

'Oh I can go to my room now the doctor has gone.' I made to get up. She was at me in a flash, her hand on my chest.

'You stay right where you are like the doctor ordered. I want you to get better. I need you to get better.'

'Well perhaps if you stopped punching me in the chest it might help.'

She snatched back her hand as if she had burned it.

'Oh sorry, sorry,' she said.

'No harm done. I'll just stay here for a while. I've got some thinking to do.'

'Yes,' she said absently. 'I must get dressed.' She realised what she had said and blushed.

'I'll shut my eyes,' I volunteered majestically.

'Don't worry,' she said, 'I'll shut the door.'

She lifted her case from the rack and swirled into the bathroom. After a short delay she reappeared, properly made up and wearing her dress.

'I ruined my suit yesterday.' She looked down at her dress and gave a little self conscious smile. 'My "fairy princess" dress. I know you don't like it but it is the only thing I've got left.'

'You know nothing of the sort,' I contradicted her. 'I liked it the first moment I saw it.' She stared in surprise. 'But you made it perfectly clear that your wardrobe should be no concern of mine so I was not able to tell you how ravishing you looked.'

'Yes, I did say that.' She frowned at me. 'But only because I thought you disapproved.'

'You've forgotten your hairband.'

'What?'

'Your hairband. The pastel coloured one that matches your dress. You were wearing it last night.'

'Do you think I should wear it?'

'I'm sure you do not care what I think.' I gazed vaguely around the room and whistled softly under my breath. 'Would you do something for me please?'

'Possibly.'

'Could you go to my room and get my other shirt? It's in my bag. I can't go down to breakfast like this.'

She nodded. 'Have you got your key?'

'It's in the door. The door's not locked.'

She shook her head disbelievingly.

'You are a case, Simon.'

I lay back and tried to relax but every time I closed my eyes I saw the foot lunging at my throat. I turned my head to look at Madame Chan's alarm clock on the bedside table. Ten minutes to seven. Breakfast would be served from seven and now I began to feel hungry. I took that to be a good sign.

As if disturbed by my attention, the alarm clock suddenly set off a tinny ringing. I picked it up, turned it around and flipped the button to silence the bell. On the inside of the leather case was a clear plastic window designed to contain a photograph. I studied the minute colour photograph of a baby. A very young baby. I heard the key turning in the lock and put the clock back quickly on the table.

'Found it,' she said and closed the door behind her. 'Thanks.'

I took it from her.

She imitated the tone of my earlier declaration and said, 'I'll close my eyes whilst you get dressed.'

'So will I.'

I laughed and then winced.

'You told the doctor that you were not going to laugh,' she accused me.

'I didn't know then that you were so entertaining. In any case, I never tell the truth to doctors.' I swung my feet to the floor. 'I think I'll get up.'

'The doctor...'

'Shh!' I stopped her. 'I need breakfast. Look. I haven't fallen over. My nose is not dripping blood. And I'm wearing a clean shirt.'

She gave a resigned sigh.

'Come on then.'

I could tell from the noise in the breakfast room that the Chinese Trade Delegation was well advanced into its breakfast. The other guests were exchanging amused but discreet glances with one another as the Oriental visitors prodded and poked at the unfamiliar food and passed comments, explanatory or otherwise, to their companions.

I found myself an unoccupied table and ordered croissants, bread and a pot of coffee. Monsieur Tan Lee, the engine manufacturer, caught my eye and waved a greeting. I smiled and nodded back. He nudged his neighbour who then inspected me through thick lenses. Madame Chan moved from one table to another, exchanging pleasantries and giving help. They seemed in high spirits. I had a feeling that a good proportion of the conversation was represented by the walking group recounting its adventures to the early to bed people. What an amazing race! They appeared completely untouched by the near disaster of the previous afternoon. But then, they probably did not realise the risk they had run, nor were they aware of the malevolent intent. And neither was Madame Chan.

As she passed my table for the third time I grabbed her wrist. She turned and threw a scandalised look at me.

'Sit down and eat some breakfast,' I ordered.

'But they want to know...'

'Sit down, I said.' I pulled her back to my table.

'I am here to help the group.'

'They know where their mouths are. You will be no good to anybody if you don't eat.'

'Am I to eat single handed?'

'What?'

'You're still holding my hand.'

'Sorry.' I released it quickly.

She sat down and the waiter took her order.

'I need to talk to you,' I said, 'something important.'

'Yes?' She did not wait for her order but helped herself to some coffee from my jug.

'But you've got to tell me the truth.'

She stopped pouring and looked at me.

'Do you think I don't tell you the truth?'

'Up to now it hasn't mattered.'

'I see.' Her voice was clipped. 'And now it does?'

'And now it does.'

'May I ask why?'

I ignored the question.

'Who do you work for?' I asked. 'You're not just a guide are you? What exactly is your job?'

'Oh well, if you are worried that I am falling down on my job description...' Her voice tailed away as she saw my expression.

'I'm not joking Jocelyne. I don't get paid to be kicked in the face by kung fu experts; I am a coach driver. What are you?'

She stared at me, shocked by my abruptness. She cleared her throat.

'I am what is called a "Ministerial Welcome Hostess". This is my job.'

'Who are you employed by?'

'Simon, what is this? What's the matter with you? Is it the bump on the head?'

'Yesterday morning at the St Maurice military airfield, what did you show the guard that made him jump a metre in the air and obey orders?'

'Oh that?' She delved in her handbag and pulled out her card wallet. 'It's just a facilitation card we are given.'

She flipped the wallet open onto the table. The card bore her name and photograph and the title, *carte de facilité ministèrielle.*

'What does that mean?' I pointed to the words *mandat présidentiel* which were printed in black underneath the diagonal tricolour stripes which ran across one corner of the card.

'Oh that's nothing really.' She dismissed it. 'The entire card is a monumental bluff. We are issued with them exactly for situations such as yesterday morning. They don't actually mean anything but they have to look as if we have some authority.'

'And do you have any authority?'

She looked me straight in the eyes.

'None whatsoever.'

'So who do you work for? I mean, who pays you?'

She pulled a croissant apart.

'Yes, you are obviously feeling better,' she mused.

'Well?' I insisted.

'The Guild of Ministerial Welcome Hostesses is run in theory on behalf of the President — thus the "mandat présidentiel". For practical purposes we are employed by the Protocol Section of the Ministry of Foreign Affairs and our services are charged to whichever ministry uses us.'

'And your job?'

'Exactly what I am doing now. Trying to smile sweetly through adversity for the greater benefit and understanding of mankind.'

I switched my tack and pointed at her bag.

'Do you carry a gun?'

She gazed at me, her lips parted in incredulity.

'I think I'll get the doctor to examine you again.'

I grabbed her hand as it lay on the table cloth.

'Jocelyne, I must know that when I ask you for help, you will help me and not work against me.'

She wriggled her hand out from under mine.

'Are you going to ask me for help? Are we likely to be enemies then? What exactly did happen out at the coach?'

'I was checking around the outside of the coach and I surprised a person crouching by the front wheel. Before I could do anything they kicked me in the face and ran away.'

'One of your friends from the car?'

'No.'

'How do you know?'

'I know.' I did not want to say how I knew.

'How can you be certain?'

'Because the two men who jumped on me at St Lazare were exactly that.'

'What?'

'Men.'

'You mean...?' Her lovely brown eyes opened wide and an amused smile began to creep across her face. I waited to see if it would make her nose crinkle.

'Yes, today's thug was a woman.' Her freckled nose crinkled. 'Oh I'm glad you find it so funny,' I snapped irritably, 'I might point out that if her kick had connected correctly you would now be looking for another driver and Monsieur Fromme would be packing up chattels for my next of kin.'

That wiped the smile from her face. Now was the moment or never to convince her about the fire.

'Bonjour Madame Chan.'

Monsieur Wong was standing stiffly erect by our table. Madame Chan stood up.

'Good morning Monsieur Wong. What can I do for you?' she asked.

He fixed his gaze at a point two metres up the

opposite wall and said, 'I have to communicate my country's great displeasure at the peril in which the esteemed Trade Delegation of the Chinese Peoples' Republic was placed and inform you that I have been requested to submit a full report to our representative upon arrival in Paris.'

'I thank you for your communication Monsieur Wong and assure you that I will help in any way that I can to assist you in compiling your report.'

'It will not be necessary.' He bowed and walked away.

'Don't say a word,' she said to me sternly as she sat down. 'Certainly not anything in consort with your expression.'

'How can you just stand there and take that?' I exclaimed. 'I would have thrown him through the window.'

'Yes, I could believe that. Diplomacy is not high on your list of achievements and Oriental politeness is difficult to understand for many Westerners.' She took out her notebook. 'We have lunch booked for twelve thirty at Fontainebleau — the Gril du Roy. Do you know it?'

'Where in Fontainebleau is it?' For my last visit to the town I had been driving a coach load of tourists with a multilingual guide in the jump seat rattling like the machine gun at Sedan.

'In the rue Grande. I don't know the restaurant.'

'The rue Grande. That's the big one that runs back into town from the Palace isn't it? There is a newish grill type restaurant about half way down on the left. It might be that one.'

She nodded absently.

'Well, we'll see when we get there. After lunch it is a gentle drive into Paris and then to a champagne reception at the Palais de Chaillot for four o'clock.'

'I don't like champagne.'

'I don't think you're invited.'

'Well they're not sleeping at the Palais de Chaillot are they? Are you going to unload the baggage from the coach and send me off home to bed or will you keep me waiting outside until you lot have finished carousing and then ask me to drive you to some obscure hotel up a narrow one way street on the other side of Paris?'

'Good point,' she said. 'I'll phone when we get to Fontainebleau.'

'Well I do have a brain.'

'I never doubted it. You just excel at hiding the proof. Fontainebleau is about two hundred kilometres from here. Leave about nine thirty?'

'I would be happier at nine. It will take fifteen or twenty minutes to get to the autoroute but once on it, there should be no problem.'

'Departure nine o'clock then?' I nodded. 'Baggage down for eight forty five?' I nodded again. 'Good, well that gives us forty five minutes. I'll tell the group.' She stood up, gulped down her coffee and put the cup on the table. 'You must go and get a clean bill of health from the doctor.'

The doctor gave me a quick examination and then, grinning like a schoolboy, he handed me two aspirins for my headache.

'The ironic humour of the situation does not escape me,' he observed, his eyes twinkling with mischief. 'I have before me a man who single-handedly leads a group out of the jaws of certain death one day and suffers a violent assault the next and I behave like a caricature of a doctor. I give him two aspirins.' He shrugged and handed me a glass of water. 'Go on, swallow them.' I did.

'Doctor, how long have you known Madame Chan?'

He folded his arms across his chest and studied me. He seemed amused.

'If I said, "some years" it would be as accurate as I could make it.'

'Tell me, does she...?'

He wagged his finger from side to side.

'Oh no!' he laughed. 'What you want to know about Madame Chan, you have to find out for yourself.' He zipped up his bag. 'And I wish you luck,' he added.

I went to collect the coach. I took a deep breath and did a complete circuit of the vehicle. When I reached the scuff marks in the gravel where I had fallen I shuddered involuntarily. Why had she been hiding there? And why leap up and attack me? It made no sense to me. Perhaps she had not been hiding. Perhaps I had interrupted her doing something. I looked to where she had been crouching. As near as I could remember, it was just forward of the front wheel. Had she been tampering with the coach? I hated to imagine the effect of a wheel flying off at one hundred kph on the autoroute. I squatted and examined the wheel nuts but quickly realised that there was no way that she could have loosened them. She did not have any tools and the nuts had been hammered on with a pneumatic spanner. She could not cut the brake pipes — her arms would not have been long enough.

It was a mystery to me. And I was in no manner calmed by the recognition that I had immediately assumed that she had been trying to sabotage us in some way or another. Everything to do with this job was a mystery — the group, the guide, the aggression.

I tried to concentrate on the task at hand and reassured myself with the thought that, by this afternoon, I would have finished. No more Chinese. No more nastiness. Oh, and no more Madame Chan.

I drove the coach around to the carriage sweep, cut the motor and opened the luggage lockers. Gilles was one of the boys who brought the bags out to the coach. When I had stowed everything away I found him on the far side of the coach, a cigarette hidden in his hand. He grinned guiltily.

'You alright now?' he asked.

'Yes.'

'Gave me a fright. Finding you like that. Somebody knock you down?'

'You didn't see anybody?'

He shook his head.

'No. We both heard the motorbike though didn't we?' I agreed with him. 'One of the farm-hands came into the staff kitchen earlier. He said he nearly got run over. A bike tearing down the lane. Must have been the same one.'

I said nothing. He looked at me, speculatively. 'The quack said I should keep my mouth shut.'

'I think that is a wise idea. Did he say you should give up smoking as well?'

Gilles grinned, dropped his cigarette into the gravel and smoothed it over with his foot.

'Nah, I already knew that.'

12

It was exactly nine o'clock when I released the brake and the Merc scrunched its way around the carriage sweep to the drive. Madame Chan sat on the guide seat, her dress pulled up into her lap, and spoke on the microphone. I guided the coach along the cross-country roads leading to the motorway to the sound of her soft voice expectorating shards of Chinese. Had I been unable to see her face I would not have known that she was European. She sounded perfect.

We slipped onto the autoroute at about twenty past nine. It was Saturday morning and the Paris bound traffic was fairly light. I gently coaxed the coach up to its maximum permitted speed. If I could keep to this limit we would be in Fontainebleau forty minutes early and it would give us the option of spending some of those minutes beforehand for a coffee stop en route.

'Another lovely day,' Madame Chan said as she slid the microphone back into its socket.

'Finished with the mike?'

'Yes thanks. I think they will have a rest now until lunchtime. This motorway is not particularly interesting.'

With one hand on the wheel, I leaned across, turned down the volume and selected the radio button. I slowly edged the volume back up to see what music was available. The Blaupunkt had a superb FM receiver but all I managed to capture was hissing and bleeping.

'That's the trouble with FM — outside of Paris or Lyon there is nothing to pick up.' I fiddled with it some more but all I was getting was a radio beacon. We were probably near another military airfield. I switched it off.

'If we had been in Germany that radio would have been picking up stations right across the band,' I said. 'The Germans have been broadcasting in FM since the war. They had to — we would not allocate them enough long or medium wavelengths in case they started up propaganda. FM only travels about fifty kilometres.' I laughed ironically. 'The result now, of course, is that the best FM radio receivers are Blaupunkt and Grundig.'

'Have you been to Germany then?'

'Once or twice. You?'

'Once or twice.' She reached up and tugged the sun visor down. 'It's going to be another hot day.'

'Yes.'

I drove. And as I drove I thought. When had all this affair started? Monsieur Fromme had told me about the group on Tuesday. The two men in the Peugeot had attacked me on my way home that same evening. Was there a connexion there? Thursday, we had turned up at Orly Ouest and found no flight. Then we had driven to Lyon. Nothing amiss that day — apart from the unpleasantness with the driver Monceau and our being moved out by the CRS who had just caught that terrorist chap. By no stretch of the imagination could I link either occurrence to our present situation.

Friday morning, Lyon. I get up bright and early, well, perhaps not all that bright, and discover that the two men in the Peugeot are back. Where had they been on Thursday? I had not noticed them tailing me down the autoroute. But then, when I thought about the various prickly interchanges I had had with Madame Chan, I realised that I would probably not have noticed anyway. She was a distraction. I glanced across at her. The sun was filtering through the bodice of her dress, suggesting delicious shapes. Yes she was a distraction.

I returned to my problem. So on Friday morning I put the two men in the Peugeot out of action, there was no doubt about that. On Friday afternoon, two men had stolen the pick up truck and set fire to the eucalyptus plantation in an attempt to wipe out the group. And Madame Chan.

I glanced across again. She caught my eye and smiled. I looked ahead.

How had the two men from the Peugeot caught us up so quickly? Their car had been demolished. They must have moved pretty smartly. Or were there two lots of men? I found no answer to that.

Nothing much happens Friday night, apart from the firemen dousing the flames and Madame Chan telling me that I was not likely to bed her. Did I want to? Concentrate! Saturday morning, when one could suppose that the coach driver would be asleep, I catch a woman hanging around the coach. 'Catch' is not quite accurate. She disables me and escapes, probably on a motorbike. If I suppose that she is connected with the two men who set fire to the wood, then whatever I had stopped her from doing, would probably have been something intended to bring about another nasty end for us.

I still did not know who 'they' were but I was now certain of their intentions. And I did not like them.

'You are looking perplexed, Simon. Is something troubling you?'

She had a lovely smile. It was probably the smile which threw me.

'Who is the baby on your alarm clock?' I asked.

'My alarm clock?'

I was as surprised by my question as she was.

'There is a photo of a baby on the case of your alarm clock. I saw it this morning. Your baby?'

She stared at the motorway ahead.

'My daughter, Sylvie.' Her voice was a whisper. She continued to stare ahead.

'How old is she? She looks very young on the photo.'

'She was three months old on that photo.'

'How old is she now?'

She did not reply. I thought she had not heard me. I glanced across and noticed the tear rolling down her cheek.

'She did not get any older.' She fumbled in her bag and pulled out a handkerchief.

'Oh. I'm sorry.'

'It's the only photo I have of her.'

Merde. Why don't I keep my mouth shut? Change the subject.

'So how is it that you speak such good Chinese?' I asked brightly.

'Mandarin.' She blew her nose. 'And how do you know it is so good?'

'It sounds good to me. I don't speak Chin... Mandarin but I've heard the others speak it and you sound just like them.'

'I lived in China for five years.'

'I've lived in France for thirty two years but my French is atrocious.'

She smiled secretly as if she had just discovered an unexpected treasure.

'Thirty two?' she said. 'I would have thought you were older.'

'Oh, thank you,' I said sarcastically. 'I bet you're a wow at parties. "Hello, nice to meet you. You look old".'

She laughed.

'I rarely go to parties, except when I am working and that does not count.'

'Why did you go to China?'

'Oh, it's a long story.'

I pointed through the windscreen.

'So is the autoroute,' I said. She gazed ahead, saying nothing. 'Well?' She shrugged and turned to look down the coach. I checked in the mirror. Heads were nodding, eyes were closing.

'Well?' I repeated.

She looked up at me and for a moment I saw in her face the insecurity of a little girl.

'I studied languages at university. I think I probably wanted to get a job as a personal assistant to somebody important who would fly me around the globe. You know what teenage girls are like.'

'I used to, but as you know, I am so old now that I cannot remember.'

'I was a typical teenager.'

'I find that hard to believe.'

'Well I was.'

'What other languages do you speak?'

'Spanish, German, a bit of Italian. Oh and English of course.'

'Of course,' I agreed blithely. I could not imagine the power of brain needed to master so many different idioms. 'No Russian?' I was being facetious.

'Not much.' She was serious. 'I would not claim to be proficient in Russian.'

'No, that's not a claim that I would make either, but then, I am known for my modesty.'

She looked down at her lap.

'You're making fun of me again.'

'I've never made fun of you.' I was surprised.

'Yes you have. It's not very pleasant.'

'I'm not making fun. It's... it's a defence,' I said.

Now it was her turn to be surprised.

'A defence? Against what? What could you possibly be frightened of?' She stopped as if recalling something. 'It's not the Chinese you're frightened of, you said yesterday. You're surely not frightened of me?'

'I am a coach driver. I mix with men who talk about cylinder heads and sex in the same sentence. The most mentally challenging feat of the day is trying to remember which way to put the key in the ignition. When I meet somebody like you who can get her brain to work in three or four languages I don't quite know how to react. I apologise if you thought I was making fun of you. I wasn't. I respect you too much.'

'Apology accepted.' She flicked her hair back. I noticed that she had decided to wear the hair band after all. She saw me looking and smiled. 'You were right, it matches the dress.'

I glanced down and she deftly smoothed the skirt back over her knees. Pity. I liked the golden skin of her thighs.

'We shall be at the services at Auxerre soon,' I said. 'We can stop for half an hour if you wish. We are making good time.'

'Good idea,' she said and reached for the mike. 'I could do with a coffee.'

There were only about two dozen cars scattered about the parking lot so I pulled up to the front of the restaurant block and parked across a line of empty bays. Madame Chan made it emphatically clear to the group that they should be back to the coach in thirty minutes and they clambered down to the warm tarmac.

'I'll meet you in the café in five minutes,' I called down to her. I quickly checked the change in my pocket. 'I'll buy you a coffee.'

She waved and walked off. I watched her go. I liked the way she walked. I worked up the aisle to the back of the coach, pulling antimacassars straight and picking up scraps of litter. They were a tidy group, all in all. I moved back down to the front, pulling down the blinds on the sunny side as I did so.

I closed the doors and made my way over to the toilets. I combed my hair and studied my face in the mirror. No trace was evident of my nose bleed — the doctor had done well. I felt my spirits perking up a little. My headache had dissipated and we were nearly home.

Madame Chan was already sitting in a shady part of the café verandah. She waved and mouthed 'coffee' at me. I paused to watch her lips close slowly over her white teeth before picking up a tray. Some of the Chinese had filtered in to the café and were watching what I was doing before deciding what they would do. I got the coffee, carried the tray over and sat down.

'I think they are enjoying the experience.' I nodded over my shoulder at the few from the group who were gesticulating at the counter.

She looked over her cup, her eyebrows high.

'Yes, it will be good for them.'

'So,' I said, 'You were telling me why you went to China.'

'Was I?'

'Yes.'

She sat back and inspected me.

'You don't give in easily, do you?'

'On the contrary,' I grinned, 'I give in very easily but you have never tried me.' She looked puzzled. 'China,' I said quickly, before I could make more of a fool of myself. 'I studied languages at university.'

'We've done that bit.'

'There were various programmes for students to study abroad. I had been dabbling with Mandarin.'

'How do you "dabble" with Mandarin for heaven's sake?'

'I had been studying it in my spare time. It intrigued me. You know how it is.'

I had no idea how it was. What spare time do you have if you are already learning three languages? She continued.

'One of the extended programmes was an eighteen month place at Pekin University for students of Mandarin. I applied and got it.'

'How old were you?'

'Why do you want to know? Is it important?'

'Just curious. I thought you might be older than you look.'

'I was twenty.' She tilted her head to look at me. 'And am I older than I look?'

I glanced at the strands of silver in her hair.

'I can't say. I don't know how old you are.' I brought her back to the story. 'So you went to Pekin for eighteen months?' She nodded. 'But you stayed five years?' She nodded and picked up her cup. Why did you stay five years? Was the language more difficult than you had thought or was there another reason?'

She sipped thoughtfully, looking over the cup at me.

'I think you know the answer to that.'

'Monsieur Chan?'

'Monsieur Chan.'

'The Monsieur Chan who is still in China?'

'The very same.'

'Why is he still in China?'

'I left him.'

'Ah.'

'What do you mean, "ah"?'

What did I mean? It frightened me to work it out.

'Why did you leave him?'

She stared out of the window. A lad was languidly hosing a bush in a pot. The water seemed to evaporate before soaking the soil.

'We had a disagreement.'

Her eyes settled vaguely on the boy.

'Must have been a big one.'

'The biggest.'

I nodded, not understanding a thing. Why would any husband want to cheat on Madame Chan? She was gorgeous.

'And I was too young to get married, really,' she said suddenly. 'I met him at the university. His father was the manager of a rice starch factory. It was an important family. He was studying agronomics of some sort.' She shrugged and smiled thinly at me. 'It was love at first sight and all that rubbish.'

'Some people believe in love at first sight.'

'But not Simon Laperche?'

'So you got married? Where? In Pekin?'

'Yes, in Pekin and then out in the village.'

'Did you have any other children?'

She shook her head and began fiddling with a lump of sugar.

'No. I disgraced myself enough with Sylvie.' I waited, not daring to speak. She was thrumming with tension. 'Every Chinese husband wants a son. The firstborn child must be a son. I gave a daughter. It was an insult.'

'But, for heaven's sake, that was not your fault. Nobody can decide the sex of the child.'

'Considerations such as that are irrelevant in China. I should have given him a son and heir but I gave him a daughter.' She smiled, and I noticed minute crow's feet at the corners of her sad eyes. 'For three months I had a daughter.'

I had to ask. She had gone too far for me not to.

'How did it happen? Sylvie? Was it disease?'

She looked into my face. Measuring me up. She held the sugar lump over her cup. 'Sylvie fell down a well,' she said.

The cube rattled into the empty cup.

I felt my heart beating in the back of my throat. I swallowed, staring at the cup and seeing a helpless baby plummeting downwards into dark water.

'Oh God, that's awful. That's terrible. Oh the poor thing. Oh Jocelyne, I am...' I stopped. She was looking at me. Expecting the question that was forming in my mind.

'Go on,' she said. 'Ask.' She was quite calm.

'I was just... it... I mean, how did she fall? Surely a three month old baby can't climb or even crawl?'

'We were in the village. In the family house. I was told that I had to accompany my husband to the family shrine for a dynastic ceremony. I was told I could not take Sylvie. I had to leave her with the grandmother. When we came back, I was told that she had fallen down the well.'

'But, how?' I still could not grasp it.

'She was a firstborn daughter, Simon. A disgrace. Firstborn daughters do that in China. They fall down wells.' Her voice was toneless.

The whole world seemed to go silent as I stared at her face and read the tragic acceptance written upon it.

'But that's murder!' I breathed. The horror had robbed my voice of any force. 'It's just murder.'

Her eyes drifted back to the lad watering the shrubs.

'Yes,' she said. 'But even if I had been able to prove it, where would it have got me?'

'It's medieval.' I looked around at the dribs and drabs of the group in the café. 'But how can you bear to speak to these people? How can...?'

'Stop it, Simon! You're sounding like a racial bigot and I don't believe you are one. It was one man who caused my daughter to be murdered. He happened to be Chinese. You can't condemn the whole race on the actions of one man. You can't judge Germans by Hitler.'

'Hitler was an Austrian, anyway.'

Her face broke into a smile of relief. She laughed.

'That's more like the Simon I've come to know

and...' She stopped, blushing in confusion. She stood up. 'Come on, we must open the coach.'

I followed her, my mind working overtime.

A few of the group were already waiting at the coach. I opened the doors, started the engine and switched on the ventilation. Thankfully, the blinds had managed to keep most of the sun from penetrating the interior. Madame Chan counted the group onto the coach, pausing every now and then as she was proudly shown the various purchases that they had made at the shop.

She stood up on the step and counted again.

'One short,' she said. I groaned. 'It's your tractor engine friend, Monsieur Tan Lee.'

'He's not my friend if he makes us late,' I growled. 'Just a minute,' I said. 'Tractors.'

'Yes?' she said.

I pointed across to where the lorries were parked up for the weekend. I could see the cabs of two blue Volvos.

'Transports Issidore of Beauvais.' I said as I got out of my seat.

'You're not making sense, Simon.'

I casually put my hands on her waist as I squeezed past her. I felt her stiffen.

'Massey Ferguson have got a big factory at Beauvais. If those lorries are carrying anything to do with tractors, that is where we will find him. I just hope he has not started unbolting anything,' I muttered as I skipped down the steps.

I found Monsieur Tan Lee gawping at a double stack of bright red tractors. When he saw me he smiled and pointed at them. I pointed at my watch. He began to inspect it with interest. I took his arm and hurried him towards the coach. I had seen tractors before. But now I had seen something else.

I delivered him safely to Madame Chan and the group clapped him as he took his seat. I was not sure if it was in felicitation or derision. We started off, down the slip road and back onto the autoroute.

'Are we all right for time?' Madame Chan asked.

I glanced up at the clock.

'Yes, the traffic is still light.' I glanced in the mirror. The motorbike was joining the autoroute behind us. It had been parked on the far side of the trucks in a position where it could see the exit slip road. It was a powerful Japanese bike. The rider wore black. It looked like a woman.

Merde.

Madame Chan took out the microphone and I automatically leaned across and switched it on. She turned the volume up gently and the speakers gave out the bleeping and hissing on the FM radio which I had selected earlier.

'I can do it,' she said. 'You drive.'

She prodded her finger at one of the range of buttons and began to speak on the microphone. At one point she must have said something funny because they all laughed good naturedly. I glanced in the mirror at their Oriental faces enjoying the humour. All I could see was a baby hurtling down into darkness. I had to admire her resilience. What a woman! She was fantastic.

But the bike was still there. About two hundred metres back. It did not need to keep close because it could see me easily from that distance and would catch me if it needed to. Was I becoming paranoid? Madame Chan had finished speaking and the group was settling down again. In their ignorance they were comfortable and happy. When the next junction came up, on an impulse I indicated and joined the exit road. Madame Chan glanced up at me.

'Simon, where are you going?'

The bike joined the slip road behind us.

'If you lean forward you can see in my side mirror.'

'Why should I want to?' she asked, but did so.

'Watch the motorbike. It's been following us since the services.'

'Oh not again Simon, please,' she pleaded. 'I thought you had got over all that. Why are we coming off the autoroute?'

'We're not,' I said. 'We're going straight back on again. Straight down the other slip road and if that motorbike is following us, it will have to do the same.'

We reached the roundabout, the bike slowed behind us so as not to catch up. As soon as the road was clear I accelerated across and down the road opposite to rejoin the autoroute.

'Satisfied?' Madame Chan asked as the motorbike ignored us and continued onto the roundabout. 'If you are going to leave the autoroute every time you see a motorbike we will never get there.'

Was I getting jumpy?

When we got to Fontainebleau the sun was beating mercilessly onto the rue Grande, casting thick black shadows under the shop awnings and archways. I idled the coach down the street on tickover as we searched for the restaurant where Knopf had made the reservation. A few desultory tourists wandered aimlessly along the sidewalks, stopping to inspect the postcard displays and souvenirs. One shop caught my eye and I noted it mentally.

'Fifty metres down on the left,' Madame Chan said.

'On the left?'

'Yes, Simon, you were correct. It's halfway down on the left, like you said.'

'Just a guess. I've never been here before in my life.' She opened her mouth to argue but I stopped her. 'And where do you want me to park?' I said, indicating the stationery cars which were sweltering on both sides of the street.

'Well, I suppose you could drop us here and go and park elsewhere?' she suggested tentatively.

'I've got a better idea,' I said and pulled the coach to the kerb ten metres short of the restaurant. 'I'll park on the bus stop.'

'You'll get a ticket.'

'On a Saturday? Do you think the mayor of Fontainebleau pays his traffic wardens overtime to work on Saturdays? Don't be daft.' I cut the motor. 'Anyway, if I do get a ticket, I'll give it to Knopf.' I opened the doors and she reached for the mike. 'Whilst you do that I'll just pop up the road. I've got a spot of shopping to do. I shan't be long.'

She raised her eyebrows in enquiry but I just grinned and added nothing so she stood up and folded the seat to allow me past. She continued talking in Mandarin as she lifted the microphone flex for me to duck under. It did not leave me much room to pass.

By the time that I returned to the coach, she had assembled the group on the sidewalk and was leading them off to the restaurant. I put my purchase inside, locked the door and followed them. I knew that I had done something that at least one person would appreciate. I had spent the remaining few francs of Monsieur Fromme's float and was now the proud possessor of a clear plastic umbrella.

The Gril du Roy was one of those traditional French restaurants that can spring up overnight, complete with stag's heads, ceiling beams and a vast hunting lodge fireplace. Knopf must have put the fear of God into the manager because he nearly scraped his chest along the tiled floor with his sycophancy.

He showed us into a mock banqueting room where a chandelier of entwined antlers hung on chains over a long table which had been set with high backed carved wooden chairs. They looked mightily uncomfortable to my practised eye. And I was not convinced of the ferocity of the wild boar which figured as the main course.

Towards the end of the meal, as the Chinese men grappled with the intricacies of France's secret weapon — crème caramel served on a warm plate — Madame Chan came over to my little table in the corner.

'Do you never eat with the group?'

'It's not traditional,' I said. 'Besides which, the driver usually comes last and has to leave early to open the coach so he needs to be at a table near the door.'

'On his own.'

I shrugged. 'You could have joined me.'

'One day, Simon Laperche, I might just do that. However, I'm going to phone Monsieur Knopf just to check that the arrangements still stand.'

'I'll come with you.'

'There's no need.'

'If I spend my life doing needless things, at least let me do them in pleasant company.'

The telephone was in a dark wood kiosk which had been let into the wall of the corridor. She propped the door open with her foot and spoke to me as she dialled.

'You really do not need to assist.'

'Just pass me the extension piece.' She unhooked the extra receiver and stretched the flex to its fullest extent over her shoulder. 'When I hear the arrangements I might need to exercise my power of veto.'

'You'll do no such thing!' she declared in horror. She turned to the phone. A voice said,

'Commerce and Industry.'

'Monsieur Van der Leeuven's office please.'

There was a pause, then, 'Knopf.'

'This is Madame Chan. We are at Fontainebleau at the Gril du Roy.'

'Is everything alright?'

'Yes. Monsieur Van der Leeuven asked me to check the final arrangements.'

'One moment.'

There was a scuffling noise and a few clicks and the minister himself came on the line.

'Chan?' he said.

'Madame Chan!' I corrected. He could not hear me because mine was only an earpiece. Madame Chan elbowed me brutally in the chest. My cough moved the hair on her neck. She shook her head irritably.

'Yes Monsieur le Ministre. We are at Fontainebleau with the delegation.'

'Who is that with you?'

She leaned backwards and purposefully stood on my foot.

'Just the coach driver.'

'I'll speak to him in a minute.'

I made a face in the mirror and she leaned more weight onto her foot and then removed it.

The minister continued,

'The press reception is at the Palais de Chaillot, West Wing. You know the layout, I presume?'

She made a grimacing shrug and shook her head.

'Yes, Monsieur le Ministre,' she lied.

I snorted down a laugh and got the elbow in the chest again.

'Good. You need to be there by four. A quarter to, would be better. You've got the driver nearby?'

'Yes Monsieur le Ministre.'

'Is it that pig-headed one we met at Orly?'

Madame Chan stiffened. I held my breath. Being called 'pigheaded' was no problem to me; Madame Chan's angry buttocks pressing into me, were.

'It's the same one.' Her voice was short. There was no 'Monsieur le Ministre.'

'Put him on.'

We swapped apparatus. The flex on the handset was shorter. I edged into the cabin, trying to ignore her perfume, her freckles, the warmth of her body where it touched mine. She held the earpiece under her hair and half turned from me.

'Laperche,' I said into the phone.

'Monsieur Van der Leeuven, the Minister of Commerce and Industry,' the pompous voice announced.

'What can I do for you?' I tried to sound pleasant. I probably did not succeed.

'Your route has been arranged with the ORTF. You must approach the Palais de Chaillot from the Eiffel Tower.'

So the route that a coach driver takes is now chosen by the French television company, I thought. Never mind the traffic, never mind the passengers, just get the right camera angle for the Minister.

'Over the Pont d'Iéna?' I said, just to show Madame Chan that I also knew Paris without a map.

'Yes. Along the river.'

'The Quai d'Orsay is still closed,' I said. 'They've had the surface up for a month. I shall have to go onto the voies sur berges.' This was a one way lane which had been constructed for two kilometres along the left bank of the Seine. It dropped to the river level and ran along the old wharf line, under a couple of bridges and then swooped up to the quay level again. It was a useful bypass in the rush hour and now, at the slack period of summer, it was being used for the diverted traffic from the road works.

'Can you get off the voies sur berges to get across the Pont d'Iéna?'

'Yes. No problem. The traffic goes that way in any case.' I could see Madame Chan frowning. I raised my eyebrows to show her what I thought of his knowledge of the real world. Then I dropped my bombshell. 'Now what about the security of the delegation?' Madame Chan hunched her shoulders as if expecting a blow. There was a deafening silence from the phone. 'Because I am worried for their safety.'

'You are worried for their safety?' he thundered when he had found his breath. 'You are worried for their safety!' Madame Chan put her head back against the wall of the cabin, shut her eyes and sighed heavily. 'Your job is to drive the coach. Do you think that I do not know how to ensure the security of...? It... I... How dare you!' He stopped to draw breath. He was beside himself with outrage. 'It is irrelevant what you think. You are just a coach driver. You do as I say. The group is quite safe with my arrangements. It's when irresponsible idiots wander off the beaten path into forest fires that problems arise. There will be an enquiry about that, never you fear. Now get to your job. Get the delegation here by the agreed route on the agreed time and I'll deal with your insolence then.'

The line went dead.

'He's not a very nice man is he?' I said as I replaced the receiver.

Madame Chan's face was drawn and pale. Listlessly, she handed me the earpiece.

'Did you have to do that, Simon?' she asked sadly. 'Did you have to do that?

'I didn't like the way he spoke to you.'

She shook her head.

'It doesn't bother me. He thinks he is important. I have to concur with his opinion if I wish to keep my job. It's called, "getting along with people". You should try it sometime. You would be amazed at the result.'

She pushed past me into the corridor.

A waft of perfume and she was gone.

I was on my own.

13

Whilst we had been eating, the shadow of the buildings had crept onto the coach. It was cool and so was Madame Chan. Somehow the light had gone out of her. Had I really put her job in jeopardy? She obviously thought so but rather than show anger; disappointment was her reaction. As if I had failed her. This intrigued me. Why should she have expected anything different of me?

The restaurant manager stood on the doorstep, bowing and scraping as the Chinese clambered heavily to their places in the coach. The large portions of wild boar were taking their toll.

'A present for you,' I said to Madame Chan.

She turned, surprised. I handed her the parking ticket. She looked at me blankly.

'Go on, say it,' I prompted, expecting a triumphant, "I told you so".'

She looked at the ticket and sighed.

'Oh Simon!' she said. The sorrow in her voice caught at my throat.

The last member of the group climbed the steps and I followed. Madame Chan picked the plastic umbrella from the floor and looked at it curiously.

'Yours?'

'Another present to another girl. You should not expect to have everything.'

I took it from her and stowed it in my door pocket.

'For your girlfriend, Nikki.'

She looked at me for confirmation.

I started the motor.

'For my friend, Nikki, who happens to be a girl. Not

the same thing. I don't get girlfriends. They don't like the way I talk to their bosses.' I could feel her questioning eyes on me as I nudged the coach out into the street. 'I presume we are all here?' I asked in a conversational tone. 'I don't want to lose anybody now; not after all we have been through together.'

'We are all here.'

Just before we rejoined the autoroute I saw a service station which displayed the agency card sign. Our fuel reserve was adequate and we were nearly home but for some reason, I decided to top up the tank. Perhaps I expected the Minister to demand that I drive to Norway or maybe I just wanted to prove that the confounded card worked.

'It won't take long,' I assured her. 'They have high speed pumps here.'

She looked at the clock.

'I think we are all right for time,' she said.

I stopped at the HGV pump but walked over to the cashier first. He assured me that they did agency. I did not want a repeat of Lyon. I filled the tank and went back to pay. He handled my custom with indifference. He was trying to watch the tennis on the television which was mounted on a bracket above the door. No problems with the card. I signed the chit and as I slipped the card back into my wallet I saw two things. One was the business card that the President of the Coach Operators' Federation, Monsieur de Mello had given me and the other, was a motorbike. The motorbike. I had no doubt of that. I could see that the rider was a woman. She was parked fifty metres down on the other side of the road and facing in the opposite direction. Clever. She could appear uninterested whilst secretly watching us in the mirror. She would have no difficulty turning her motorbike in the street to follow us.

I froze. My mind racing through possibilities. Should I go and challenge her? No, she would just ride away. Were the others with her somewhere? In another Peugeot? A pick up truck? What were they planning? Who could I turn to for help? Madame Chan thought I was mad. The Minister considered me an insolent upstart.

'Anything else you wanted?' The cashier spoke without moving his eyes from the screen.

My eyes were focused on my wallet. Raoul de Mello. 'Where's your telephone?'

He pointed. It took twenty centime coins. That was about all I had. I dialled the number on the card. The voice answered. I began talking immediately but it continued unabated its measured tone. I should have expected that Raoul de Mello would have had an answering machine on his private phone. It wanted a message. The words tumbled out of me in a panic of desperation.

'This is Simon Laperche. I changed the wheel on your Rolls. You got me a job. I'm doing it now. I've got a Chinese Trade Delegation at Fontainebleau to take to the Palais de Chaillot. Somebody is trying to wipe it out. They have made one attempt and are still following me. I don't know who they are. I've tried warning Van de Leeuven — he thinks I'm insolent. I've tried telling the guide — she thinks I'm deranged. Before it all goes nastily wrong I just need somebody, somebody to know that I tried. I did try.'

The phone cut off. I placed the receiver carefully on the cradle. As I let my breath out, my sigh sounded uncomfortably like a sob. I left the pay office. The cashier did not acknowledge my thanks. I recognised bitterly that I was transparent to everybody.

I was in no mood for dissent when I slammed back into my driving seat.

'What is the matter?' Madame Chan started. 'You look like thunder.'

'Go to the back of the coach and look through the rear window. There's a motorbike parked...'

'Oh not that, Simon!'

'Shut up! Do as I say. The rider is the woman who kicked me in the face this morning. She's pointing in the opposite direction so that we don't notice her. See if she turns to follow us. Then make up your mind about me.'

I started the motor and engaged gear. I waited. Madame Chan looked at me. I could not read her expression.

'Jocelyne, if you have ever wanted to please me,

though God knows I can't think why you should have, do this for me please.'

She compressed her lips into a line. Silently she stood up and made her way down the coach, exchanging remarks with the men as she did so. Professional to the end. I hoped it was not to be the end. I let in the clutch and drew gently out into the avenue and turned towards Paris and the autoroute. The motorbike was hidden from me. I drove mechanically, dividing my glance between the view of the road ahead and that of Madame Chan, kneeling on the back seat. Eventually she stood up and made her way back down the coach, stopping again to answer questions or inspect things proffered to her.

She pulled out the guide seat and sat down.

'Well?' I said.

Her mouth was still set grimly.

'She is behind us.'

It was irrational but I felt relief.

'Now listen to me Jocelyne. I've got some serious talking to do.'

'Are you sure it is the same woman?'

'She was the one we saw first at the service station at Auxerre.'

'It can't be. When you came off the autoroute and went straight back on again, she turned off.'

'She turned onto the roundabout. We both saw her disappearing off at a tangent but we could not follow where she went. She simply did a complete circuit of the round-about and joined the autoroute thirty seconds behind us. She knew we could not get away from her. All we succeeded in doing was announcing to her that we suspected we were being followed.' I glanced in my side mirror as the road curved towards the autoroute junction. The bike was about a hundred metres back. She would not lose us now.

'But who is she? What does she want?'

'That is what I have not been able to work out. I need you to help me.'

'Me?'

'You have got a brain. I'm just a coach driver.'

'You already knew something at breakfast didn't

you? Is this what you meant when you said that you had to know that I would work with you and not against you?'

'I think this group is in considerable danger. And whether we like it or not, we are caught up in it.'

'What sort of danger?'

'The worst.'

'But...?'

'Just listen. I am going to tell you some things that you are going to find hard to believe. If you don't believe them, then you are not with me. I shall be on my own.' I paused whilst I negotiated access to the autoroute. The bike followed. 'Right, first. Jocelyne, I like you a lot and I think you look really sexy in that dress.' She stared open mouthed. 'Do you believe that?' I asked. She continued to stare. 'Do you believe me?' I insisted.

She lowered her head and I could see the colour filling her cheeks.

'Do you?' I asked.

Her head began to nod.

'Yes,' she whispered. She looked up at me. 'Yes, I believe you Simon.'

'Oh thank God for that,' I sighed. 'That was the difficult one. If you can believe that in spite of the evidence, then the next bit you will find easy but even more unpalatable.' I took a deep breath. 'The fire was not an accident. It was a deliberate attempt to kill you all.'

'What?' She started in her seat. 'But they said it was youngsters.'

'I saw it all happen. I was taking a walk on the opposite ridge. I saw the stolen pick up truck go by. But I didn't know it was stolen at that time. I saw you coming down the slope with the group. I decided to walk over and meet you. I saw them drive upwind and set fire to the plantation so that you would be driven down into the field of alfalfa.'

'Is that why you came down?'

'Of course. From my position I could see what neither you nor they could see — that there remained an escape route if you took it quickly enough.'

'But we weren't quick enough.'

'They were quicker. They drove over to the ridge and laid a fire trail along the top. They had ten litre cans of petrol to do it with. That cut off our escape. We should have been burned alive.'

She shuddered.

'That's horrible! Are you sure, Simon? I can't believe it.'

'You don't want to believe it. Do you believe that I think you're sexy in that dress?'

'Don't start that again.'

'Well do you?'

'I said I did.'

'But do you believe it because you want to or because you think it's true?'

'Because... both.'

'Surely it is more difficult for you to believe that, than what I have told you about the fire. The truth is that you do not want to believe what I have told you about the fire.' She nodded slowly. 'I have no reason to lie to you about either.'

'You might be mistaken.' She looked up with the ghost of a smile hovering around her lips. 'About the fire.'

'I am not. Nor about you.' I looked in the mirror. 'And the bike is following us down the autoroute.'

'We should stop and tell the police,' she said suddenly. 'They'll help us.'

'Tell them what? Do you think that the bike will hang around to be identified? It will hide around the corner and after we have made a fool of ourselves, it will pick us up again. I can't outrun it in a coach. That bike can probably do two hundred kph.'

'We could tell the Minister.'

'One of us had already tried that line and look where it got us.'

'Well you weren't very diplomatic were you?'

'At least I wasn't a sycophantic toady. 'Yes Monsieur le Ministre. No Monsieur le Ministre."

'I was not a toady! It's called "respect".'

'I can't respect a man who talks to you the way he does.'

'You're not exactly silver tongued yourself!'

'Well I...'

'Just be quiet and let me think,' she snapped.

I drove. The bike followed.

She thought.

'Intelligence! That's what we need,' she announced.

'One of us does,' I agreed.

She ignored me. 'One of the group was showing me a small pair of binoculars. I'll borrow them and take a look at the bike. It might tell us something.'

'That's a good idea. I'll slow up a bit when you are in position. That might bring her closer.'

Whilst Madame Chan negotiated a loan of the binoculars I gently increased the speed of the coach, hoping that I could calculate my variations so that I was slowing down by the time that the motorbike was accelerating. I waited till Madame Chan was settled in her kneeling position on the rear seat and then I began to ease the speed down. I tried to ignore the wriggling contours of her bottom as she braced herself on the squab.

After a short time she pushed herself from the seat and made her way down the aisle to the front. She sat down. Some of the men were beginning to take an interest — looking behind and then forward at us.

'She's got a radio,' Madame Chan said. 'It's clipped to a shoulder harness. It is one of the latest type with a small, stubby black aerial. I saw her speak into it.'

'Well that tells us that she is not acting alone — but then we did not doubt that did we? I suppose the other two are around somewhere.' To our right lay Viry Chatillon and the road was beginning its sweep around Orly airport. 'The others can't be far away because that radio would only carry a few kilometres in this terrain.'

'What are we going to do, Simon? What can we do?'

'Whatever we do, we must try not to panic the group. You are pretty good at giving orders in Mandarin. You certainly got them lying down quickly enough when the fire came.'

'I used the vocabulary I picked up in the village paddy fields. I would blush to translate it.'

I looked at her in astonishment. This woman amazed me.

'Your language won't make me blush. If it works quickly when we need it, then use it. It could easily be a matter of life and death.'

'Simon?'

'Yes Jocelyne?'

'I'm frightened.'

I gave what I hoped was a confidently reassuring smile.

'You've got big bad Simon, the most hated coach driver in Paris to look after you. You'll be alright.'

'I wasn't frightened for me,' she said.

The Saturday afternoon traffic was beginning to leave Paris. It swished by on the other lane, churning on the hot tarmac and drumming on the concrete stretches. As we began the descent towards Paris, Madame Chan pulled out the mike. This was the first distant view of the Eiffel Tower that the group would get. I tried not to reflect that it might be the last one. The bike was still there. She had run a little closer now that the exits were more frequent. I had toyed with the idea of slipping down an exit at the last minute without indicating but I knew that it would not work. The bike had the advantage over us on everything except ice and wet cobbles — neither of which we had the remotest chance of finding today.

We came to the end of the autoroute and drove into Paris proper. Paris of wide avenues and heavy leafed trees. Newspaper kiosks and terrace cafes.

That an attack was coming, I could not doubt. The group had been shadowed since it landed. One attempt had already been made to annihilate it in a most gruesome manner. I had possibly foiled another this morning. Or had I? Had I interrupted her before she had achieved what she had wanted to or had she already done it? And then the obvious truth came to me. They would always find the group because they knew the coach. The coach would be the target. I needed to get the group off the coach without the enemy knowing. How could I do it? Where should I start? 'Intelligence' Jocelyne had said. Well, we could deny them intelligence.

'Jocelyne!' She jumped. 'I want you to go down the coach and pull down all the blinds. Don't leave any up. Say what you like to the group. Use your paddy-field Mandarin if need be, but put the fear of death into them that they must not, on any account, look out.' She looked at me, I could see her mind whirring. 'Now!' I said sharply.

She jumped up and marched confidently up the coach, pulling down the blinds to a rising tide of protest. And as she did so an idea began to form in my mind. We were coming up to the Place Denfert Rochereau, an area which bore a sore memory for me. Many years ago, as a novice in Paris, I had taken a coach down what I had hoped would be a short cut behind the Place St Jacques. I had got the coach stuck. The view from the windscreen had etched itself in my memory as I had sawed the wheel back and forth and wedged myself tighter in the narrow street. But now, if I could find it, it might just do the trick.

I turned down the side of the Parc Montsouris where we had left Nikki to look at trees. It seemed a century ago. The bike closed up to follow. I zigzagged through the road works and up to the Avenue René Coty. We were getting close.

'Hurry!' I shouted up the coach.

Madame Chan had managed to lower all the blinds except one. Monsieur Wong objected. He stood up.

'Do it!' I shouted. I had just seen the street that I needed. It was thirty metres away.

Monsieur Wong began a speech. Madame Chan shouted over the top of him, slapped his face twice, pushed him down into his seat and yanked down the blind. I turned into the narrow alley, hoping it was the right one. It was just as I had remembered it. No sidewalk, just warehouse wall backing directly onto the street.

She stormed back up to the front of the coach, breathing heavily, her face red.

'I'm with you now Simon,' she gasped. 'I've got no future anywhere else. What do we do?' She stared at the right angle bend fifty metres ahead of us.

'Keep them down, keep them out of sight. And tell me what the bike is doing.'

She spun around and hurled short consonants into the quaking men. I had never seen Chinese eyes so wide. In a crouching run she bounced onto the back seat.

'She's stopped at the avenue,' she shouted over her shoulder. 'She's talking into her radio.'

Merde. I needed her to follow me.

'Tell me the moment she enters the street.'

I lined the coach up for the corner. 'Sorry Georges' I thought. I took the right hand rear wheel to the corner wall and began to slowly negotiate the turn to the right.

'She's moving, she's moving. She's coming down!'

She would have to, or risk losing us. I spun the wheel tighter and slipped the clutch harshly. The engine roared, the coach lurched smartly sideways on full lock and with a sickening crunch the two metre overhang behind the rear wheels swung out and engaged the wall on the opposite side of the alley. We were stuck. The bike rider could not get past but, more importantly, she could not see around the corner. And around the corner was the front of the coach.

I banged open the doors.

'Off, off, off, off, off!' I shouted. 'Get them off! Now, now, now!'

Madame Chan thumped on the luggage racks and shouted as she swept down the aisle. As one mass, the terrified Trade Delegation leapt from their seats and scrabbled to the front door.

'Go, go, go!' I shouted at her and pointed through the windscreen. 'You can see where to take them. Get them down and keep them down.'

As they tumbled out into the street I pulled out the cold start tap on the dashboard and revved the engine. Clouds of black smoke filled the space behind the coach as the overrich mixture burned in the hot exhaust pipe. The noise thundered around the blank faced brick walls of the alley. For the ruse to work it was vital that I conceal the movement of the group. As the last Chinese scurried into safety I shut the door and engaged reverse gear. I gave a convincing impression of an incompetent driver wriggling his coach out of a difficult position.

As I reversed to realign the coach at the corner, I could see the motorbike waiting calmly ten metres behind. It was coldly menacing. I made another attempt at the corner and took it wider as I should have done in the first place. I had left some green paint on the brickwork. With a few centimetres to spare either side, I edged around into the other branch of the street. It led directly into an avenue where the afternoon loafers in thin shirts and short skirts were idling before shop windows, unaware of the drama unfolding. Madame Chan had done her job to perfection. The group was nowhere to be seen.

I turned into the main street, praying that the bike would follow. It did. She had taken the bait. She still believed she was following the Chinese Trade Delegation in a coach which just happened to have the blinds pulled down. I accelerated up towards the Seine. I caught occasional glimpses of the black figure as she weaved easily through the loose moving traffic, always positioning herself so that if I jumped the lights she could pull out of line and chase.

I followed the diversion signs, turning right with the other vehicles into the rue de Rennes. Here the traffic had slowed into a knot. We crawled up to the crossroads with the Boulevard St Germain where the weekend tourists on their way to the Latin Quarter blocked the lights as they edged over the junction, one car at a time. I looked at the clock. Three thirty. The Minister would not be pleased if I arrived late. This was the Minister who had scathingly assured me that the group was safe 'with his arrangements'. A sudden, awful thought thudded into my gut. I glanced at the bike as I edged forward another five metres with the traffic. I could see her plainly talking into her radio. 'One of the latest type,' Jocelyne had called it, 'with a little stubby aerial'. Yes, I thought, just the type of radio you would expect the Diplomatic Protection Police to be issued with. As well as black crash helmets and powerful motorbikes. She was part of the Minister's arrangements, wasn't she?

Merde.

I butted my way over and joined the line of vehicles passing down the side of the church of St Germain des Prés. She swayed easily through the traffic to follow me. Oh Simon! Pigheaded Simon Laperche. What have you done? I'll tell you what you've done. You've bullied the Chinese Trade Delegation and kicked them off your coach. You've insulted the Minister of Commerce and Industry, and managed to spirit the group away from the protection he had provided and you have irrevocably lost Madame Chan her livelihood.

Merde.

It seemed that my only success had been to buy Nikki a plastic umbrella. With a sickening stomach I lurched into the street leading to the Quais and nearly collided with a Hertz rental van which was pulling out to join the traffic behind me. The driver looked woodenly through me. Transparent Simon Laperche.

With a numb feeling of dread and disbelief I turned onto the slip lane down to the voies sur berges; down to the level of the river. I automatically checked that the bike was still there. Yes, it was behind the van.

Pont de la Concorde.

I was two kilometres from the televised arrival of my empty coach before the Minister. This was not Feydeau, this was Greek Tragedy. The only way that I could extricate myself from absolute ridicule was to prove myself right. And that would probably kill me. I was wishing my own extinction just so that I could say that Simon Laperche had been right all along.

Pont Alexandre III.

The Seine was high, slopping heavily against the stonework to my right. Above me to my left was the Air France terminal of the Invalides where I had delivered the UTA staff after the mad dash down the runway at Le Bourget. What a lark that had been. My first job for Autocars Fromme. This would be my last.

Pont des Invalides.

Like a great glass slug a bateau mouche was ploughing down the Seine towards the Pont d'Iéna. That was where they turned. Under the bridge, Eiffel Tower on your left, Palais de Chaillot on your right, now we go back to the embarkation point. Thank you ladies and gentlemen, please don't forget the guide. The gawping tourists were crawling over the boat like ticks on a hedgehog. Inside the coach, rows of blank seats jeered back at me under the bland marquee light of sun through the blinds. The sky was blue. Clear blue.

At least I knew why she had silver threads in her hair. I shuddered at the remembrance of her daughter. It was a wonder she was not totally grey. And at least I had told her that I thought she was sexy. I wonder if she had believed me.

Coming up to the Pont de l'Alma. After the bridge is where we take a sharp left up to the level of the Quais so that I can turn at the Eiffel Tower and make my triumphant television arrival for the ego of the Minister.

I heard a sudden screech of tyres. I glanced sharply in the mirror and saw that the Hertz van had swung sideways, blocking the road behind me. I involuntarily flinched as I passed into the black shadow under the Pont de l'Alma and then out into the sunshine beyond.

I did not actually hear the explosion. You don't. Suddenly the back of the Merc erupted in a violent orange flame and a giant boot kicked the vehicle straight through the parapet. I threw my arms up before my face as the blast hurled me through the hole where, a second before, there had been a panoramic windscreen.

The waters of the River Seine rushed up to meet me.

14

Christ the water was cold! But it proved to me that I was still alive. I was buffeted and thrashed in the dark muddiness until suddenly I found myself in sunlight. I gulped a lungful of air. The water around me was boiling with bubbles and steam which brought up antimacassars and odd personal effects, a seat squab and road maps; all that remained to show where the coach had disappeared. I felt as if I were in a giant stewing pot. In an irrational bout of frenzy I swam away towards the middle of the river, away from the maelstrom of foaming debris.

Then the noise and the shock hit me. My limbs became leaden. I kicked myself onto my back. I could hear roaring engines, screaming sirens, the throbbing of a fast marine diesel, the thudding of a helicopter. My hand touched something in the water, I grabbed it. My eyes misted over, they were stinging. There must have been oil on my face. Voices were shouting. 'Over there! There's one in the water! Over there!'

Hands were grabbing me, lifting me, pulling me.

'Alright mate, you're alright now.'

'Get him on the deck. Let the medic see him.'

'Tell Control we've fished out one of them alive.'

'Well he's not a bloody Chinky.'

'He must be the driver.'

'God, what a mess! Nobody else has come up yet.'

My stomach suddenly convulsed and I curled up and retched. 'Only me,' I managed to stutter through chattering teeth.

'Get a blanket on him.'

'Only me,' I repeated.

'Yes, you're the lucky one. You're safe now mate. Here's the medic.'

Confident hands felt me, squeezed me. I caught a hazy snapshot of a bearded face as my eyelid was pulled up and then released.

'One, two, three, lift.'

Something hard was slid underneath me. In the background I could hear the radio chatter of rescue boats searching for survivors. Becoming more frantic.

'Coach was empty. Just me. The driver.'

'I'm giving him a sedative then we'll take him straight to the landing stage.'

'Yessir. I can see ambulances already there.'

A heaviness suddenly began to invade my body. What the hell! I thought. If they want to ignore me then that's nothing new. Let them keep searching.

But I had been bloody well right after all...

The room was cream and brightly lit. I was in bed. I turned my head. A middle aged woman was sitting in a chair nearby. She wore a nurse's uniform. She was reading *Paris Dimanche*. On the front page blazed a lurid colour photograph of a flaming coach hurtling into the Seine.

A bottle was attached to my arm by a long plastic tube. My pyjamas were green striped. On the cabinet lay Nikki's umbrella. That made me laugh.

'Ha!'

The nurse threw the paper to the floor and moved quickly to my bed.

'Monsieur Laperche?'

'That's me.' My voice was weak.

'You're awake then? Good.' She peered into my face. 'Look at my finger.' Why were women always doing this to me, I thought? 'Oh that's good. How do you feel?'

'Tired.'

'You've had a long sleep. The doctor gave you a sedative.'

'What time is it?'

'It's eleven o'clock, Sunday morning.'

'What's the bottle for?'

'It's a drip feed. To help you over shock.'

'Anything broken?'

'Nothing. You've got cuts and abrasions on your face and some truly monumental bruises on your thighs.'

'Something to add to my collection.' I vividly recalled the wrench when the blast tore me out from under the steering wheel. I looked at Nikki's umbrella. 'How did that get here?'

'You would not let go of it. It arrived with you on your stretcher. Once it had come into the hospital it had to be logged into your effects.'

I remembered my fingers closing around something in the water.

'It's for Nikki.'

'Right,' she said, as if she knew whom I was talking about. 'I'll get you something to eat shortly. You'll feel a bit brighter after that. And then there is somebody waiting outside to see you.'

'Thank you.'

She smiled. It was not a professional smile. It was a genuine smile. It made me feel nice.

I have no idea what I ate. It was a slurry of some sort. She sat me up and wheeled the table over my bed. I insisted on feeding myself. I wanted to make absolutely certain that every bit of me was working properly.

I did feel stronger after eating. When I had finished I asked for her paper and read the report. Apart from a dramatic photograph of the flaming Merc it was very thin on text. Apparently it had been a bungled terrorist attack. The silly terrorists had fired a mortar at the wrong vehicle. They had hit an empty coach. Silly terrorists. The hand of the censor was heavy. No suggestion as to what the correct target might have been. No certain identification of the terrorists nor explanation of their fate. I read the report twice and finished with the impression that if it had not been for the embarrassing fact that the Press and television had been able to witness the incident, then it would have been reported as a traffic accident.

I had a sour taste in my mouth and it was nothing to do with the food.

'Finished with the paper?' The nurse began to clear up. I handed it to her. 'I'll just do this and then you can have your visitor.'

With my free hand I surreptitiously tidied my hair and straightened my pyjama jacket. I need not have bothered. Police Inspector Nahon of the Anti Terrorist Brigade had seen worse sights than me. He took my statement. To be exact, he questioned me about what he had been detailed to find out, ignored any observations which fell outside these parameters and refused to answer all of my questions. He then told me that he had been delegated directly by the Minister of the Interior and was to report back to him and that I was not to speak to anybody, and certainly not the Press, about the incident. He never said 'well done Monsieur Laperche' but then I suppose that was outside his mandate. But just to show that officialdom had a humane and caring side, they had detailed a policeman to sit outside my door and deny entry to visitors. Their kindness knew no bounds.

The nurse had been quite offended when Nahon had peremptorily told her to leave us alone for our confidential chat. She returned immediately he left and began fussing around me.

'I expect that nasty little man tired you.'

'Is it true they've put a cop outside the door?'

She nodded.

'He keeps going outside for a quick smoke. Some security!' She finished rearranging the bed and then stepped back and inspected me. 'You're very quiet for a hero.'

'Who says I'm a hero?'

'Everybody does.'

'Read the newspaper. There's nothing heroic about being blown up by mistake.'

She snorted.

'I've got eyes in my head. You don't think we believe newspapers do you? We make up our own minds.'

'When can I go home?'

'The doctor will come tonight and examine you. If he is happy with you, I expect we'll kick you out tomorrow.'

'And good riddance?'

'And good riddance,' she laughed. 'Now, you take my tip. Get a good sleep in now and you'll be sparkling with energy when he does his rounds. He'll just have to discharge you.'

Indeed, I did feel weary. The effects of the sedative had not entirely dispersed and the frustrating one-sided interrogation had proved to be quite gruelling. I drifted off to sleep.

I do not know how long I slept but I was awakened by a commotion outside the door. A woman's voice was raised in outraged anger.

'Don't you tell me I can't go in!'

The nurse was standing, looking at the closed door. I could hear the mumble of a man's voice.

'You can't deny a wife access to her husband!' the voice shouted. There was a thud. The door flew open and in burst Monique.

'Sisi!' she screamed and threw herself on me.

'Nikki!' I said, when I had recovered the breath that she had knocked out of me.

The policeman appeared in the doorway without his cap.

'Madam, my orders are...'

The nurse stepped smartly across, put a hand on his chest and walked him out backwards. She closed the door, leaving us alone.

'Stuff your orders,' she said. 'Go and have a smoke.'

I tried to prise Nikki from my chest. She was sobbing.

'Oh Sisi, I was so worried. I saw it on television. They showed it on the eight o'clock news and again at eleven. Are you all right?'

'It's a bit late to ask me that now that you've jumped on me,' I pointed out.

'Oh yes.' She unlaced her arms.

'I am utterly untouched. Apart from some more bruises on a part of my body which I do not intend to show you. How about you?'

She pulled the chair up and sat down, holding my free hand in hers.

'I'm all right,' she said. 'But I was worried about you. I like you, Sisi.'

'Despite being too old and too poor?'

'Nobody's perfect.'

I inspected her outfit. She was wearing a modest skirt and a crisp blouse.

'Not working today then?' I said.

She giggled and stood up.

'Do you like my outfit?' she twirled gracefully.

'I didn't know you had clothes like that.'

'I haven't. I borrowed them from Adèle in the flat below me.' She sat down again. 'I had to look like your wife if I was to get in.' She pulled up the skirt. 'I'm even wearing knickers.'

'Yes, thank you, Nikki,' I said, indicating that she could lower her skirt. 'I'm not so much concerned about people knowing whether or not my wife wears knickers. I am more concerned about the sudden existence of a wife.'

'Oh Sisi, don't be annoyed. It was the only way I could get to see you.'

I squeezed her hand.

'I'm not annoyed. Thanks. It's great to see you. Look, I've even brought you a present.'

'Oh Sisi!'

She took the umbrella. It was now a sorry looking affair.

'It's been in the wars, I'm afraid.'

She opened it up. With a twang, two of the spokes curled up like claws, the plastic flayed in tatters. She pulled a face. We burst out laughing.

'It's brilliant, Sisi. Just what I've always wanted.' She spun it carelessly. Then she became serious. 'This must have been in the coach with you, then?'

'Yes. As I hurtled headlong through the windscreen towards the welcoming waters of the Seine I thought, "Must grab Nikki's pépin before I go. She'd never forgive me if I left it behind."'

'But you brought it all the same.' She looked at me

and sighed. 'You're one hell of a guy, you know. It's a pity you're so old.'

'And poor.'

'I'll hang this pépin over my mantlepiece like an ancient firearm,' she announced.

'You don't have a mantlepiece.'

'I will have. One day,' she asserted. Her voice was wistful. She looked at me, tears welling up in her eyes. 'Oh Sisi, I'm so glad you're safe.' She put her arms around my neck and kissed me on the mouth.

The door opened quietly behind her and the nurse's head appeared. She rattled the door handle noisily.

'Come along now, you mustn't tire him out madam. He's had a busy day. He'll probably be home tomorrow and you can do all your catching up then.'

Nikki stuck her tongue in my mouth and winked. Then she primly stood up, turned, blew me a kiss and walked out with her eyes demurely downcast.

If I was one hell of a guy, she was one hell of a girl.

They discharged me on Monday morning. I walked out into the street wondering if this was what prisoners felt like upon release. I was wearing clothes provided by the hospital — my own had been damaged beyond use. The blue denim jeans were too long and too hot for this weather. The shirt was tight across the shoulders. It was like being back in the army. I went into the nearest bar and telephoned the garage. I thought that an explanation was the least I could offer my employer.

Madame Aurélie answered. I asked if Monsieur Fromme was there.

'Who is speaking?' Her voice was guarded.

'Laperche.'

'I thought so.' Her voice was excited. 'Hang on.'

I could hear her call echoing in the garage as she summoned Monsieur Fromme to the phone.

'Laperche?'

'Yes Monsieur Fromme.'

'Are you all right? They wouldn't tell me where you were.'

'I've just been discharged from hospital. I'm fine thanks.'

'Good. That's good news.' Before I could say any more he continued. 'Don't come to the garage for a couple of days. We are besieged by the press at the moment. They will have to go away eventually. We can't tell them anything. We don't know anything. I should go and hide somewhere if I were you. It'll soon blow over. Drop in on Wednesday morning.'

'OK. Thanks. I'll do that.'

'See you Wednesday.'

Well, he had not fired me.

I had always promised myself that one day I would read some Zola. I bought a cheap edition of *La Bête Humaine* and spent two days hanging around bars where I knew I would not be recognised and sitting in parks where I would not be disturbed. I drank my morning coffee at a pavement café. I found a bench in the nearby garden and read. From time to time I would lay the book down, close my eyes and turn my face up to the sun. I lunched where it pleased me and in the afternoon I walked to a different square and found another bench. I read until the shrieking of the children leaving school reminded me that I could drink a beer.

I was not recognised by strangers. Nobody accosted me. I purposefully ignored the events of the last few days. I refused to speculate on their outcome. It was as if I, also, would have preferred it to have been a mere traffic accident. I immersed myself in Zola and on the Tuesday evening when I finally closed the book, it did not upset me in the slightest to know that Zola's express train was thundering, driverless, to its own destruction. I drew no parallels. It was just a story. Another story. And it was finished.

Noel saw me first. He put down his broom and walked across the garage towards me. He silently shook my hand, his eyes studying my face.

'Hello Noel,' I said.

'Come for a beer. I'm dogsbody this morning.'

'I've got to see the boss.' I nodded towards where I could see Monsieur Fromme working at his desk.

'Oh yeah. Yeah I suppose that's normal. When you start throwing Mercs in the river you can expect a bollocking.' He was still holding my hand. 'I'm glad you've come back Simon.'

'So am I.'

'Come and have a beer afterwards. Don't worry, We're not allowed to talk about it. Some bloke in a suit came and told us all to keep quiet. Daft. We don't know anything. Talk about raising suspicions. If he had said nothing I would have assumed like all the others that it was just your usual lousy driving.'

'Thanks Noel.'

I tapped on the office door. Monsieur Fromme glanced up and then hurried to the door and yanked it open.

'Laperche. Come in, come in.' He shook my hand vigorously and ushered me into the office. 'Madame Aurélie,' he called. 'Go and have a coffee.'

Madame Aurélie muttered something unintelligible and clanged the filing cabinet drawer shut. The noise rang a bell with me. It was the noise that I had heard coming from this office on the day that I had been told about the Chinese transfer.

'Ah Monsieur Laperche!' she said when she saw me. I held open the door for her. 'How are you?' She laid a gentle hand on my arm.

'I'm fine. You?'

'Oh it's my back. I've got three crooked vertebrae, the specialist said, that's the latest. If I could...' Monsieur Fromme cleared his throat. 'I'll go and have my coffee,' she said. 'Yes.'

'Take your time,' Fromme said.

I closed the door behind her. Fromme pointed to the chair opposite. I sat. He placed his elbows on the desk and rested his chin on his thumbs. He rubbed his moustache with his index fingers whilst he inspected me.

At length he said, 'Georges is livid about his coach.'

I stared at him. After all I had been through all he could think about was... The ends of his mouth were curling then he suddenly roared with laughter. I had never heard him laugh. It frightened the life out of me. I grinned stupidly.

'He saw it on the television in the bar. He was leaping up and down, shouting his head off. "I knew it," he kept saying. "I knew it. Laperche would go to any length to stop me from checking my coach over." He bellowed with laughter again and then took out a handkerchief and dabbed at his eyes.

I stared at him in disbelief. His best coach had just been blown to smithereens and sunk in the river and all he could do was laugh. He finished drying his eyes.

'Let's be serious though. Were you injured?'

'Bruised, that's all.'

'Enough for an industrial injury claim? They'll have to pay it if you claim. I'll support you. It's not as if witnesses are lacking.' He stopped suddenly and seemed to recall the television picture. The picture that I, of course, had not seen. 'My God you must have been terrified. I was, just by watching it.'

'I didn't really have any time to be frightened. It just happened. I'm sorry about your coach. It was the best one.'

He shrugged.

'I can easily get another one. Good drivers are more difficult to find. Are you staying with us?'

'Have I still got a job?'

The phone rang. He picked it up.

'Yes you've still got a job.' He spoke into the receiver. 'Fromme.' He never said 'Autocars Fromme' on the telephone. All the others could say that. Only the boss could say 'Fromme'. He listened for a second and then glanced across at me. 'I've got him here this very minute. I'll pass him over.' He handed me the phone. 'Monsieur de Mello for you.'

I listened to Raoul de Mello, President of the Coach Operators' Federation. I wrote down what he told me. When he had finished speaking I said, 'Yes, thank you very much, I would be delighted.'

'Well?' Monsieur Fromme said, as I replaced the receiver.

'I am invited to dinner tonight with Monsieur and Madame de Mello. Apparently Monsieur Gilbert de Maine wishes to meet me.'

'The Minister of the Interior?' He raised his eyebrows. 'You're moving in exalted circles now.'

'It's all a bit above me,' I was feeling a little dazed.

'You'll cope.' he said confidently. 'Now let's turn to practical matters. I presume we lost the agency card?'

'Yes,' I grinned wickedly, 'And the float. But don't worry too much about the latter because I only had about two francs of it left. I had to pay cash for fuel in Lyon. The agency card didn't work.'

'Why didn't you go to another garage?'

'I'd put the fuel in the tank.'

'Hmm. Awkward.' He made a note on his pad.

'Who paid for the hotels?' he said.

'In Lyon I slept in the coach.' He opened his mouth to say something but changed his mind. 'We could only find one room,' I explained carefully.

He nodded then smiled quietly to himself.

'Arnay le Duc?'

'I never saw the bill. Madame Chan organised it directly with the hotel.'

'Good. That makes it simple,' he said. 'Madame Chan? Is she somebody we would work with again?'

'She's very efficient. Speaks God knows how many languages. Yes, she's good at her job. And she can read a map. I could easily do without the Minister, though.'

'Couldn't we all? Knopf was down here on Monday afternoon. What a silly bugger that man is. He insisted on talking to as many drivers as he could to instil in them the need for absolute secrecy and discretion. I cannot think of any action more likely to make a driver gossip.'

'So you know nothing?'

'Not a fingernail.' He looked squarely at me across his desk and then fiddled with his pen. 'I'm glad you're back, Laperche. We could do with someone like you in the garage. We don't really want to lose you.' He was embarrassed. It made me feel uncomfortable. He looked out as Pradel walked by. 'I'm going to make some changes here. It's long overdue. I must have let things slide a bit. Shall we put you on normal roster as from tomorrow?'

I nodded.

This man had given me a job against his better judgement, had entrusted me with his best coach and I had written it off and refused to give him any explanation.

'Monsieur Fromme?' He looked up. 'They told me that I was not to talk about it but I consider you are entitled to know all that I know.'

He sat there, unspeaking, for half an hour whilst I told him everything. The beating up, the Peugeot, the fire, the motor bike. At the end he looked at me silently, then he said,

'Thank you for that Laperche. I appreciate the confidence. Raoul De Mello always was smarter than me. He did see something in you. Talking of which,' he interrupted himself, 'Have you got evening dress?'

'Evening dress? What, dinner jacket, black tie and all the works?'

'Yes. It will be a butler at the door and candelabra on the table tonight. You'll have to dress.'

'But I don't have anything like that!' I panicked. 'I'll phone and say I can't go.'

'You'll do no such thing.' He pulled a roll of banknotes from his pocket. 'Go down to Maison Sebag, you know, in the Boulevard des Italiens.' He peeled off a generous sum. 'You can hire a complete outfit.'

'I can't afford...'

He held up his hand. 'You are representing the firm. I'll claim it against tax.'

'I'll tell you my special news as soon as I've done this, Sisi. Just hold still.' Nikki was attempting to knot my bow tie. 'Oh, it's no use, she said. Where would I have learned to tie a bow tie?'

'Or me.'

'I bet your lady friend in the coach would know how to do it. She looked as if she could do anything.'

'What? Madame Chan?'

'Rather a chic girlfriend for you wasn't she?'

'She was the guide for the group, Nikki. She was not my girlfriend.'

'I know.' She giggled. 'That was why I called her that when I met her in the coach. You should have seen her face!'

'Right, young lady!' I cried.

I grabbed her by the wrist and spun her around. She squealed.

'No Sisi! No!'

I held her over the padded arm of the bulbous chair and began to soundly spank her bottom.

'No Sisi, stop, Stop!' She kicked her legs to no great effect. 'I apologise! I didn't mean it.'

I stopped, my hand hovering over her squirming buttocks. A lady was standing in the doorway staring at us. She was about forty five. She had mousey brown hair and wore tailored cotton trousers and a sports shirt.

'Oh, have you stopped?' Nikki said, wriggling her bottom in disappointment. 'I was just beginning to enjoy it.'

'We have company,' I said.

She twisted around.

'Oh Adèle. Come in.'

'Sorry, are you working?' Adèle said, shooting me a swift glance.

Nikki snorted into the upholstery.

'Oh thank you very much,' I said.

Nikki stood up and pulled down her skirt.

'Adèle, you do say some awful things. This is my friend Sisi. Simon.'

Adèle held out her hand to me and, without moving her eyes from my face, spoke from the side of her mouth at Nikki.

'What did I say wrong?' she hissed.

Nikki winked at me.

'Nothing Adèle, I was teasing you.'

'Oh I see,' she said in obvious relief. 'She's such a joker,' she confided to me. We shook hands. 'Pleased to meet you.'

'Charmed.'

'Are you going to the theatre?'

'I beg your pardon.'

'Or perhaps a dance?' She pointed at my dinner jacket.

'Oh, just dinner.'

'With the Minister of the Interior!' Nikki bounced on the seat. 'Isn't it exciting?'

'Oh. He is a friend of yours?'

'No. It's er... business really.' This woman was unnerving me.

'Oh how nice. I hope you have a lovely time.'

'What did you come in for, Adèle?' Nikki's voice was gentle as if talking to a child.

'What did I come in for?' she repeated.

We waited.

'Do you know I can't remember!'

'Never mind, Adèle. It's nice of you to pop in.'

'Yes, thank you.' She turned to me. 'Don't forget your tie. Even if he is an old friend of yours, he's still a Minister you know.' She stepped up to me and in a few rapid twists of her wrists, produced a perfect bow. 'There, that looks better. Well, have a good evening.'

She waved happily and left by the same door. I stared after her.

'Nikki,' I said. 'Why don't you lock your door?'

'I've given Adèle a key. She has nightmares. She likes to come in and talk.'

'What? During the night?'

'Yes. Any time during the night.' She looked sternly at me. 'You have to be kind to people like that, Sisi. She's not had a very easy life.'

I felt very chastened.

'So what's your good news then?' I asked.

Her face lit up.

'Sit down.'

I sat. She curled up in the armchair and hugged her legs.

'You'll never guess.'

I looked at my watch.

'I'm sorry for keeping you waiting Monsieur le Ministre but I got involved in a pointless guessing game with a...'

'I've got a boyfriend. No, a real boyfriend, Sisi. I met him at the hospital.'

'When you were pretending to be my wife?'

'Yes, but he didn't know that bit. He's a doctor.'

'Are you sure, Nikki? There are lots of people in hospitals who wear white coats and who are not doctors.'

'He's a surgeon. He was just out of theatre. His name was on his gown. I've looked him up.'

'A surgeon! How old is he?'

She smiled coyly.

'About your age.'

'Well if he is a surgeon at least he won't be as poor as me. So that lets me off the hook does it?'

'Oh Sisi, I am sorry and you do look scrumptious in your dinner jacket and tie, but he is rather sweet. The problem is, he obviously thought I looked really attractive when I was wearing Adèle's clothes. I can't keep raiding her wardrobe.'

'And you think pink bolero and no bra isn't his style?'

'What I really need, is somebody refined to take me out shopping. A lady. When will you be seeing your guide lady friend again?'

'You can forget that!' I said. 'You are quite capable of ensnaring an innocent man without any help whatsoever. Now pass me the phone so that I can call for a taxi.' She pouted at me and pushed the phone across the wooden floor with her foot. 'And Nikki?' She looked up. 'I am really pleased. And I shall expect to be invited to see my umbrella hanging over your fireplace.'

15

'Nice house,' the taxi driver observed as I paid him off. I nodded silently.

It was a town manor house. Its massive *porte cochère* — the carriage gateway — fronted a small street which ran down from the Avenue Foch. This was not a district for paupers. There was a personnel door let in to one of the pair of massive wooden gates. As instructed by the engraved brass plate, I buzzed the electric lock and pushed the door open. It led through to the internal courtyard. This was paved with rounded cobbles that had been old before the Revolution. Opposite, a short stone staircase led to the glazed outer door of the main wing. Despite the summer evening light, I could see the twinkling of a chandelier in the hall. These courtyard manor houses could be quite dark inside.

Parked at the foot of the steps was a black Citroen. It had a small tricolour cockade at the top of the windscreen. The driver wore a dark blue suit and was sitting behind the wheel. A man wearing a grey suit was leaning against the wing, watching my approach. He held a notebook in his hand. He glanced in it, looked at my face and then nodded to me.

'Simon Laperche,' he said.

'Good evening,' I replied equably.

He waved me up the steps. The door opened as I reached it. I had always imagined a male house servant — a butler or such like — would be a doddering old man with a cadaverous face and a nervous tick. This man was about forty and looked like somebody's grocer.

'Good evening sir.'

He addressed me as if he expected to sell me a cauliflower. 'I'll take your coat. The cloakroom is through that door there sir. When you are ready I shall take you to where Monsieur and Madame and their guests are having an apéritif.'

I fumbled with the unfamiliar summer coat. He feigned not to notice.

'I'll just er...' I looked at the cloakroom door.

He inclined his head.

The wash basin was a lozenge-shaped chunk of porcelain the size of a war memorial. I looked at my reflection in the gilt framed mirror. I dared not touch my tie. I prayed that Adèle knew her stuff. Did I feel intimidated by all this splendour? It reminded me of the luxury hotels where Madame Chan had appeared so at ease and yet had assured me that I did not look out of place. I took a deep breath and went out into the hall.

'Please follow me sir.'

Why was my heart thumping? For a horrible moment I thought that the servant was going to throw open the double doors and announce my name to the assembly like they did on the films but as soon as he swung back the narrow panelled door, Monsieur de Mello came over, with his hand outstretched.

'Monsieur Laperche!' he said. He was affability itself. His squared, muscular body in his black dinner jacket made him look like a particularly tough beetle.

'Monsieur de Mello,' I said as I shook his hand. 'It was good of you to invite me.'

He turned to his wife.

'Evelyne, you may remember this young man helping me change the wheel on the car.'

I remembered her. The last time she had seen me she had inspected me as if I had been a biological curiosity. She was wearing pale blue again but now with something sparkling looped around her neck.

'It was very gracious of you to assist my husband,' she said. I longed to tell her that I had only done it to hide from the police. 'He has this fault of thinking he can do everything better than anybody else.'

'I'm afraid men are like that,' I said. It sounded rather patronising.

She sucked on the inside of her cheek with her tongue.

'How refreshingly candid.' She said as she turned to her husband. 'Did you hear that, Raoul?'

'I'll pretend I didn't,' he growled. 'Come and meet the others.'

We were in a small ante-room — high ceiling, decorative cornice, tall windows overlooking the courtyard. He thrust a small glass into my hand.

'White porto,' he whispered disgustedly. 'Woman's drink. Pour it into the potted plant when nobody is looking.' He propelled me towards the Minister of the Interior. 'Gilbert,' he said, 'This is Simon Laperche, the coach driver.'

I was impressed by de Mello not only remembering my first name but by his being on first name terms with Gilbert de Maine. This minister was utterly unlike the Minister of Commerce and Industry, Van der Leeuven. He was in his sixties, balding, thin, with a bony face and as I shook hands with him I had difficulty suppressing the scandalous observation that had he opened the street door to me I would have handed him my coat and walked gaily into the house. He looked exactly like the archetypal butler of my cinema.

'Monsieur Laperche, I am pleased to meet you. We will have a talk after dinner.'

I tried to arrange an expression on my face to convey that I knew exactly what he meant. His wife was a dumpy lady with red lipstick, dark ringlets and a double chin. I think he said her name was Anne-Marie but I was not listening. I was rudely looking elsewhere.

Monsieur de Mello said, 'And of course you know Jocelyne — er... Madame Chan.'

She was wearing a straight silk dress in flame orange, decorated with Chinese dragons. It had a slit up from the hem in Oriental style, giving glimpses of her tanned legs. She had dressed her hair up on top of her head and pinned it with a dark wooden comb.

'Good evening Monsieur Laperche.' Her hand was cool. It always was. 'It's a pleasure to meet you again. I do hope you are well.'

I stared into her brown eyes and stuttered, 'Er... yes. Yes. I'm... er very well thank you. You look...' I began enthusiastically. Her eyes widened in alarm. I stopped myself just in time. 'You look well. As well.' I felt and sounded an utter idiot.

A tiny smile played around her eyes. My heart was thumping again like a tom-tom and I told myself that I had no idea why.

It was an intimate dinner. 'Just three couples, how convenient!' Madame de Mello had observed, as if the guest list had been a fortuitous but unexpected surprise for her. Gilbert de Maine and Raoul de Mello sat opposite each other and argued fly-fishing passionately from hors d'oeuvres to dessert. They had an easy relationship which suggested to me that they had been acquaintances since childhood. Evelyne de Mello and the Minister's wife, whose name was probably Anne-Marie, discussed theatre and actors with a familiarity that betrayed an abundance of leisure time. Madame Chan and I listened politely.

Monsieur Fromme was wrong in his prediction of the dinner setting — there being no candelabra on the table. But there was an entire battery of silver utensils laid around each diner's plate. I viewed it with dismay. I was not a great fan of shellfish and the last time I had eaten oysters had been on the beach at Cancale. You don't worry about etiquette there, you tear them from the shell with your teeth. I looked at my oysters and toyed with a small spoon.

'Tell me, Monsieur Laperche,' Madame Chan said, as she discreetly waved a short fork at me, 'why did you become a coach driver?'

I dropped the spoon as if it were red hot and casually picked up my short fork. I can't remember what I replied. I thought the question utterly asinine but from then onwards I watched her every move. She led me through the meal with the skill of a mountain guide goading a granny across a glacier.

After the dessert, we moved into what they called 'the salon' to be served our coffee. Despite the lofty spaciousness, the glittering miniature chandeliers and the oil paintings, the room still exuded a lived-in cosiness. A newspaper lay unfolded on one of the armchairs, the toes of a pair of mules poked out from under the ormolu bureau. I sat in an armchair and bathed in the warm glow produced from having consumed some rather good wine. I looked secretly at Madame Chan and wondered why the distance had opened up between us again. Or had there never been a rapprochement? Had the closing of the gap been an illusion?

'Perhaps,' Gilbert de Maine proposed, his pale eyes twinkling, 'when we have enjoyed our coffee we could prevail upon Madame Chan to play us a little something? Hmm?' He indicated the baby grand piano which was placed diagonally by the window so that the daylight could fall upon the keyboard.

Madame Chan glanced warily at me and protested. 'Oh I don't think you really want to listen to...'

'Oh but we do,' the Minister insisted.

'Now, come along Jocelyne, don't you be shy,' Raoul de Mello said.

I found that the easy use of first names between the hosts and guests blurred the relationship. It suggested that they had worked together on many previous occasions. And it emphasised for me that I was an intruder. I wondered if I would ever again be able to call Madame Chan, 'Jocelyne,' with the familiarity that I had done.

She finished her coffee and moved to the piano.

'What would you like me to play?' she asked as she turned back the lid. 'Any requests?'

She avoided my eye. I tried not to look at her legs under the piano. It was difficult with that dress.

'Is Brahms a bit heavy for a summer evening?' the Minister enquired. He was quickly shouted down.

'Why not let Monsieur Laperche choose?' Madame de Mello smiled sweetly at me. There was a little viper in there somewhere. She still saw me as the wheel-changing coach driver that I was.

'Evelyne, I don't think that's fair on Jocelyne.' Monsieur de Mello tried to unspring the trap. 'He is hardly likely to be familiar with her repertoire.'

'Oh I'm sure Jocelyne could play anything that Monsieur Laperche would be likely to suggest.'

The heavy allusion to my presumed musical ignorance almost tempted me to prove her right and ask for *'Swing Baby Blue'* played on the black notes.

'I've chosen,' Madame Chan declared. 'You're like a load of politicians. You can't make up your mind.'

'Touché!' Gilbert de Maine winced.

Without further ado, and, I noticed, without recourse to a score, she launched into a piece. I watched the top of her head as she teased the music from the keyboard. She must have felt my eyes burning into her because she suddenly looked up and met my gaze over the top of the piano. She smiled and shrugged and then looked down again. How many languages could this woman speak? And play the piano? And what could I do? Drive a coach.

I listened, enraptured, to the end and then I applauded enthusiastically with the others whilst she bobbed a miniature curtsey.

'Chopin's Grande Polonaise,' I said quietly. 'You can't go better than that.' She had remembered that it was one of my favourite pieces. She was still kicking footholds in the glacier for me. I wondered why.

Madame de Mello looked me up and down and then glanced across at Madame Chan. Madame Chan gave a tiny nod.

'Yes, I thought I recognised it.' Madame de Mello fussed with a cushion. 'Thank you Jocelyne, that was delightful.' She turned to the Minister's wife. 'Anne-Marie, don't you think we could leave the men to their business?'

'I would love to.' She stood up and looked across to Madame Chan. 'You play the piano like an angel, my dear.'

'Thank you.'

We gentlemen stood to see the ladies out.

'You are staying, Jocelyne,' Monsieur de Mello said. He looked at her sternly. 'I learned today that this concerns you as well.'

'I'll stay.'

Her voice was pert, almost rebellious. He frowned at her and indicated a chair. She ignored him and sat on the chaise longue. We sat.

'Go on then Gilbert, get the pompous bit over and done with.'

'I would like to express to you, Monsieur Laperche, the gratitude of the Government of the French Republic for your remarkable achievement in bringing the Chinese Trade Delegation safely to Paris in the face of such difficulties. You displayed a courage and a perseverance quite out of the ordinary.'

'Hear hear!' Monsieur de Mello said, warmly.

'Just a minute,' I got up smartly from my seat. These platitudes grated on me. 'Before you start throwing bouquets around; some of the difficulties we had to overcome were caused directly by your inefficiency. Well perhaps not yours, personally, Monsieur le Ministre, but that of your government.'

Madame Chan closed her eyes and put her hand over her mouth.

'Hear hear!' De Mello said, even more loudly. 'What do you say to that then Gilbert?'

'And another thing,' I continued with the force of the wine behind me, 'It was not "me", but "us". I could not have succeeded in anything if I had not had Madame Chan with me.' I swept my arm around to her. 'She was efficient, caring, a superb navigator, a brilliant linguist, an inspired diplomat and a brave woman. I could not have had better.'

Monsieur de Mello seemed overcome. Perhaps, like me, he was also appreciating the wine. He stood up and grasped my hand.

'That makes me very happy to hear that, Monsieur Laperche. Very happy indeed. What do you say, Jocelyne?'

'I think that Monsieur Laperche has a misplaced modesty.' She was blushing bright red. I could not tell if it was from embarrassment or anger.

'I agree,' Gilbert de Maine declared. He must have felt sidelined. 'I have read the inspector's account of how you saved the delegation from the fire.'

'Me?' I said. I turned and pointed at Madame Chan. 'I don't speak Chinese!'

'Mandarin,' she said.

'Chinese! Mandarin! Who cares?' I snapped at her. 'Who was it who stood up in front of all those flames and calmly shouted to the Chinese to lie down?' I turned to the men. 'It wasn't me. I couldn't do it.'

'Who was it who told me to shout it?' she retorted. 'I didn't know what to do!'

'But to stand up there. In front of... and those flames... You could have been hurt you silly girl!' I was shaking with rage.

She came off the chaise longue like a panther. De Mello and De Maine were forgotten.

'Hurt?' she cried in my face, 'Hurt? If it hadn't been for you, you idiot, we would have been burned alive.' She prodded her finger on my chest. 'It's not "hurt" we're talking about, Simon. They tried to kill us!'

'Oh!' I said in an exaggerated manner. 'And when did you learn that, I wonder? Every time I tried to explain it to you, you threatened to call the doctor to get me my head examined.'

'Well we wouldn't have needed the doctor at all if you had not been fighting with that stupid woman on the motorbike.'

'Stupid woman on the motorbike? You mean the darling who tried to put her boot through my windpipe? That was another thing! You never believed me when I said she was following us.'

'I did.'

I caught her wrist and shook it.

'You did not!' I was scandalised.

'I did, Simon.'

'Oh! Oh!' I was almost speechless with disbelief. 'I had to get myself blown up to prove I was right. Hurtling headlong into the Seine in a flaming coach and at last, at last!' I threw my arms up like an evangelist preacher, 'Madame Chan believes me!'

She gave a gasp and buried her face in her hands.

'Don't say that, Simon. Don't say that! It's just too

terrible to be believed,' she whispered.

I stood there, awkward. I wanted to hold her and calm her. I wanted to reassure her and console her. My arms dropped. I dared not.

'I'm sorry. I say things without thinking. I didn't mean to upset you.' I looked at my host. 'I'm afraid I've made a bit of a spectacle. I would ask you to excuse me.'

The two men were standing watching us. Monsieur de Mello with a glint in his eye as if he had just proved himself right, once again. Gilbert de Maine had lost his eyebrows, they had dissolved somewhere up in his scalp.

'I think you should both sit down,' Monsieur de Mello said, pointing to the chaise longue. We sat. 'You're both excused. You have been through a terrible time together. When I recommended you for a job with Artur Fromme, Monsieur Laperche, I had a premonition that I would hear about you again.' He smiled. 'You're not the kind of chap who passes unnoticed.'

Madame Chan looked at Monsieur de Mello and then said to me, 'Is this the man whom you said you could never repay for backing his hunch and getting you back into coaches?'

My embarrassment brought the colour to my face. Monsieur de Mello chuckled.

'That's the one,' I said briskly. I didn't care now. 'Don't you remember I told you that you didn't have the monopoly on good connections?'

'Good connections?' she exclaimed in derision. 'My father?'

My mouth fell open.

'You didn't know did you? Thought not.' Monsieur de Mello laughed heartily.

'So you are Jocelyne...?'

'Jocelyne Chan, née de Mello.' She smiled and gave that little shrug that she had given me at the piano.

'Our only child, Monsieur Laperche. A secretive little girl who does not always keep her parents up to date with her activities but we think she is rather precious all the same. If a little headstrong. As for your never repaying me, I can never repay you for saving her life. Twice.'

'Oh don't let's start all that again,' I pleaded. 'I didn't mean to save her life. I didn't mean to save anybody's life. Not really. Actually, she was a pain in the neck most of the time.'

'Well if you think you're so easy to live with!'

'Children! Children!' Monsieur de Mello wagged his finger. I got the impression that he was enjoying himself.

'Monsieur de Maine.' I addressed the Minister who had moved to the piano stool in order to study the cobbles in the courtyard. 'You said we would have a talk after dinner. I would like that talk now.'

'With pleasure.'

He stood up and crossed to join us.

'Shall we have a little cognac?' Monsieur de Mello rang the bell.

'As long as you don't ask Simon to pay for it,' Madame Chan said. She grinned at me. 'You should have seen your face at the Seignerie when you got the bill for our drinks! You didn't have any money did you?'

'I am glad you thought it was funny.' I turned to the two men. 'Whilst Madame here enjoyed a five star hotel in Lyon, I had to sleep in the coach because I had been obliged to spend my hotel money on diesel. Oh and on a packet of sweets for the guide of course.'

'Oh,' she said, 'I didn't know that. But you're daft, I could have lent you some money. Why on earth didn't you ask?'

'I'm not certain we were talking at the time.'

The men exchanged glances. The cognac arrived and the manservant moved to close the shutters.

'Oh, can we leave them open for a while?' Madame Chan turned to ask. 'It's such a lovely sky.' I could feel her leg against mine. She did not move away.

Monsieur de Mello nodded and the man withdrew.

'What I want to know,' I said bluntly, 'is who the enemy was, or is. Were they caught?'

The Minister rubbed his jaw and looked at me.

'If you don't tell him Gilbert, you will never drink my cognac again,' De Mello said. 'Worse, I shall encourage Anne-Marie to go on your fishing trips with you.'

The Minister brushed these threats aside with a majestic sweep of his hand.

'You really can be quite petty, Raoul. I am a Minister of State. I cannot be coerced or blackmailed.'

'And I'll suggest she takes the dogs.'

Monsieur de Maine grimaced.

'That was a bit underhand.' He looked at us, sitting side by side on the chaise longue like a couple of children awaiting a bed time story.

'You understand that what I tell you now, must not be spoken of outside these walls?' We nodded. 'The anti-terrorist brigades of the major European police forces have been exchanging intelligence with each other for some years now. We got information that a cell of the Baader-Meinhof had been established in Metropolitan France. We managed to identify a courier and bit by bit she led us to other members of the group. We kept them under surveillance and a few months ago it became apparent that they were planning an attack. Money was moving in, known weapons experts were visiting them — that sort of thing. At this stage we had no idea what, or indeed where the target was.

'I give operational autonomy to the brigades. I don't believe that one person can direct and control so much. He can obtain an overview but to take command and direct every operation would just not be possible. The system, thankfully, worked. When the terrorist force suddenly moved into Orly airport, the brigade commander acted immediately, without awaiting my permission. Well, you read the result in the papers.'

'Didn't need to read it. We were there, Madame Chan and I.'

'Yes,' she said, 'if I remember rightly you were ogling the air hostesses and looking for a "Chinky guide".'

The Minister held up his hand. We fell silent.

'Siggi Hanaps. German. He was the cell leader. We caught him but the others got away. Hanaps of course refused to talk. He still refuses. We now know that their target was an airliner. The China Airways. They wanted to shoot it down as it landed.'

'Christ!' I exclaimed. 'So they were only saved by the air traffic controllers' strike?'

'Exactly. We caught Siggi Hanaps. He was the most important but the others escaped. We rather rashly assumed that their first concern would be their own safety. We closed the borders. We had miscalculated. They went after you. They had no commander but they were still armed.'

'So it was not just a chance target?'

'No.'

'But why the Chinese Trade Delegation?'

'For the propaganda value. Can you imagine the recriminations? An entire delegation wiped out before it touches French soil? The publicity value would have been enormous. We already knew that Baader-Meinhof was worried about losing its credibility, its status amongst the world's terrorist organisations. This coup would have put them right back up at the top.'

'So when you got the special flight laid on to the military airfield that was not just to avoid the strike?'

'Quite. The air control was handled by the Italians and the French Military net but it did also mean that we could have a secure arrival.'

'Except that they followed us down there?'

'Well, we don't think that they did. Not initially.'

I thought of the Peugeot and said,

'I hate to disabuse you but... Ah!' I flinched and gasped with pain. Madame Chan's knuckle was digging urgently into my thigh. It was right on my bruises.

'Oh I'm so sorry!' she said, visibly shocked at my reaction.

'No, my fault, my fault.' I breathed out. 'You could not know. I'm a little tender as a result of a recent rapid exit through the windscreen of a coach.'

'Jocelyne,' Monsieur de Mello said, 'if you can't stop fidgeting I shall have to ask you to sit elsewhere.'

She put her hands into her lap and blushed like a schoolgirl. But she still managed to throw me a warning look. She was right. Where did the Peugeot fit in to the story?

'You were saying, Monsieur Laperche?' the Minister prompted.

'I was about to say that they found us at Arnay le Duc. How did they know we were there?'

The Minister looked down and sucked his lip.

'Tell it like it is, Gilbert,' de Mello warned. 'You owe this man a lot. We both do.'

'Oh I agree, I agree,' he admitted. 'My difficulty is that we are not exactly sure. From our preliminary inquiries it would seem that an official in the Ministry of Commerce and Industry, a certain Monsieur Knopf...'

'Oh we know Monsieur Knopf,' I said.

'Quite. It would seem that he received a call purporting to come from *Le Monde* newspaper enquiring as to where the Trade Delegation might be. Now my... er... colleague the Minister, Monsieur Van der Leeuven...'

'Yes we've met him as well,' I added.

'He is... er ... very keen to work with the Press and the broadcast media.' I thought that was a generous understatement. 'And Monsieur Knopf, knowing this, told them where you were.'

'Easy, isn't it?' I was disgusted. 'But if you knew the group was in danger why wasn't Knopf told to keep his trap shut? I would have thought that was elementary security.'

'We didn't know that the group was in danger.'

'Well the threat of having its plane blown out of the sky is fairly indicative, isn't it?'

'We did not know that was the threat when we arrested Siggi Hanaps. In fact, rather regrettably, we were not informed of the expected arrival of the group, nor of its programme. At Orly Ouest, you knew more about the group than we did.'

'But surely, as Minister of the Interior, you would have been consulted on security?'

'In the normal course of events, yes. But Monsieur Van der Leeuven chose not to inform us of the impending arrival and to make his own arrangements.'

'The man's an idiot, Gilbert. He wants your job. What a fool!' De Mello swirled his cognac angrily in his glass.

'Please,' Gilbert de Maine lifted a thin hand in supplication, 'You are talking about one of my colleagues.'

De Mello threw him a mock disgusted look. He then grinned conspiratorially at me and said, 'You could no more be a politician than me, eh, could you Laperche?'

'He certainly couldn't be a diplomat,' Madame Chan observed. I looked from one to the other and said nothing. 'Monsieur De Maine. Might I ask a question?'

'Please, my dear.'

'This is not meant as a criticism, but if you as Minister of the Interior did not know that the group was arriving, how did the terrorists?'

This girl could certainly use her brain.

'That's a good point,' he said. 'The departure of the delegation from Pekin would have been given quite a high profile in the Chinese press and we assume that they had a contact there, probably provided by the JRA — the Japanese Red Army — who followed their movements and reported their departure.'

'Surely the Commercial Attaché at the French Embassy in Pekin would have reported it also.'

'He almost certainly did but the Ministry of Foreign Affairs would not bother to mark it for our attention, they would presume we already knew. As I said, my colleague Van der Leeuven decided for his own reasons that he wished to keep it as a domestic matter, something to be handled just by the Ministry of Commerce and Industry.'

'So how did he propose to ensure the security of the delegation?' I asked.

'He has within his department, a small commercial enforcement branch. They undertake surveillance duties and investigations to gather the evidence for prosecutions, usually for fraud. He used two of his investigators to tail you. They didn't have much success unfortunately. Their radio support would only work in the Paris region. That would have been OK but of course you disappeared off to Lyon. And then, when they caught up with you, they had the misfortune to write their car off in an accident.'

'I expect they were given something unremarkable to drive such as a Peugeot, in a nondescript dark colour,'

Madame Chan observed to nobody in particular.

The Minister looked at her, which was just as well because my face must have been a picture.

'I'm sure I don't know,' he said.

'You idiot!' she hissed at me from the side of her mouth. 'You idiot!'

I felt inclined to concur with her opinion. The only protection that had been provided, I had disabled in the first hour. Thankfully the Minister continued.

'Their misfortunes were only just beginning. An off duty policeman tried to arrest the driver, and so his companion punched him. Along came reinforcements and they were both carted off to the commissariat. The driver tested positive for alcohol. His mate was put in the same cell for assault. Nobody was going to phone the Ministry of Commerce and Industry on their behalf. There was a great deal of bad feeling on both sides. By the time they had sorted it all out, you were on your way to Fontainebleau and they were still in Lyon with a wrecked car and worried that they might not have a job either. So they packed up and came home by train.'

'Dedication to duty. And that was the extent of his "arrangements"?' I asked.

'It would seem so.'

'So the security protection, or whatever you care to call it, packed up and went home whilst the terrorists stole a pick up truck and set the forest alight. How did they plan that?'

'We don't think it was actually planned, we think it was opportunist. Don't forget, these terrorists go to school. They learn their trade. They are encouraged to identify opportunities and exploit them. This is when they are at their most dangerous. As I said, Knopf had already told them where you were, he had also mentioned the outline arrangements for the reception at the Palais de Chaillot. We believe that they intended to shadow you to Paris and make the attack there but when they arrived at La Seignerie what did they see? The Chinese Trade Delegation standing in the middle of hectares of inflammable material. It was an opportunity too good to miss.'

Madame Chan bowed her head, 'It was horrible,' she said, her voice almost a whisper. 'Horrible!'

The Minister looked at her with compassion.

'I would have given anything to have spared you that experience, my dear.'

'Yes, I realise that. I'm sorry.'

'So where does my girlfriend...' Madame Chan looked at me openmouthed. '... with the motorbike fit in?' I finished.

'We have numbered the active members of the cell at four or five. Numbers one and two in the pick up truck, once the fire had failed, went straight to Paris to assist numbers three and possibly four in preparing the attack at the Pont de l'Alma. Number five, the motorcyclist, her job was to keep tabs on you and report your position.'

'Pretty easy when its motorbike versus coach. Not much of a contest really.'

Madame Chan laid her hand on my forearm.

'Look, nobody's blaming you, Simon. Don't be so sensitive.'

'And having a radio bug fixed to your coach made it even easier,' the Minister added.

'Of course, that was what she was doing!' I thought of the figure crouched by the front wheel. 'She was fixing a bug on the coach. What a fool I was. Why didn't I think of that?'

'Yes, and you even listened to it!' Madame Chan gave an ironic laugh. 'Don't you remember all that rubbish you spouted about German FM radio receivers and how great they were? And what did you pick up? Hissing and bleeping. You were listening to our own bug giving us away.'

The Minister nodded.

'The motorbike was discovered abandoned in a supermarket car park in Péronne on Sunday morning. Our experts examined it. It was a Kawasaki, stolen in Belgium some months ago and carrying false French plates. It still had the pulse direction indicator strapped to the top of the tank. The frequency it was tuned to indicated that the bug they fitted was working on FM. Madame Chan is right. You could easily have picked it up.'

'I didn't know you were a radio expert,' I said to her.

'I'm not, but you would not have believed anything I might have said.' She looked at me coolly.

'You can talk!' I protested. How many times did I have to tell you that the bike was following us?'

'Children!' Monsieur de Mello bellowed. 'Will you stop squabbling?!'

'You heard what your father said,' I muttered from the side of my mouth.

I had forgotten how pointed her elbows were.

Monsieur de Mello said, 'One thing intrigues me about this affair, Gilbert. Why did the terrorists blow up an empty coach?'

'It wasn't empty!' Madame Chan grabbed my arm again. 'Simon was in it.'

'That's all right Monsieur de Mello, I'm used to it. Throughout this whole business I could not get away from the belief that I was transparent. It was like a surreal tragedy. I was looked through and not seen, heard but not listened to.'

'Yes. I'm sorry, I didn't mean that you did not count and as for not being listened to, well, I'll come back to that in a minute. But my question remains unanswered. Why did they continue to shadow what they knew to be an empty coach?'

'They didn't know,' Madame Chan said. The Minister nodded agreement. He had read the report. 'Simon got the group off the coach without them seeing.'

De Mello looked to me for an explanation.

'Actually, it was Jocelyne who got them off the coach. I don't speak the language. Jocelyne could get them to do whatever I needed. We simply pulled down the blinds so that the tail could not see what was happening in the coach and then I jammed the coach around a narrow corner so that the bike was stuck behind and could not see the group getting off the front. After that it was easy.'

'After that it was easy.' Monsieur de Mello's voice was dry and emotionless. 'You consciously made yourself the target for the attack.' He looked across at the Minister. 'I hope you are listening to this testimony, Gilbert.'

I laughed shortly. 'I didn't really think I was making myself the target. In fact, just before the explosion I had convinced myself that the motorbike was the Diplomatic Protection Police and that I had lost Jocelyne her job and was about to present the Minister with an empty coach.'

'Now that would have been embarrassing.' De Mello got up and went to the bureau. 'But I think we should listen to this, just to put things in perspective.' He slipped an audio cassette into a tape recorder. He fiddled with the volume and a buzz came out of two speakers which I had not previously noticed because they were disguised as potted plant stands.

A disembodied voice filled the room. It was mine.

'This is Simon Laperche.' I winced as Jocelyne tightened her grip on my arm. 'I changed the wheel on your Rolls. You got me a job. I'm doing it now. I've got a Chinese Trade Delegation at Fontainebleau to take to the Palais de Chaillot. Somebody is trying to wipe it out. They have made one attempt and are still following me. I don't know who they are. I've tried warning Van de Leeuven — he thinks I'm insolent. I've tried telling the guide — she thinks I'm deranged. Before it all goes nastily wrong I just need somebody, somebody to know that I tried. I did try.'

The tape clicked off. Shocked silence in the room.

A hot tear dropped onto my wrist.

Jocelyne's hand was grasping so hard that her finger nails were cutting my skin. The utter desolation in the final, desperate, 'I just need somebody, somebody to know that I tried. I did try.' was still resonating in all our heads. I was back there, in the petrol station, alone, frightened, frustrated.

Suddenly Jocelyne gave a sob, got up and ran out of the room. We watched her from our seats as if watching a play. Unreal. Then the spell was broken.

'Young man... young man...' the Minister stuttered. He was lost.

'You got my message then?' I said to Monsieur de Mello. I tried to make my voice sound bright. It sounded just like the tape.

'Yes... Yes,' he said with a quiet irony. 'When I got

back that evening. After I had seen it on the television.'

'No matter. There was not much you could have done,' I said.

De Mello glanced across at where his old friend, the Minister of the Interior was looking very uncomfortable.

'When you're playing your politics, Gilbert, when you're taking your light decisions, just remember that message. Just recall the sound of despair in the voice of one man whom your colleagues and your system had repeatedly failed but who went on to put his life on the line.'

'Well, let's forget it shall we?' I said quickly. It was not benevolence, it was not modesty. I did not want perpetual reminders of the affair. All I really wanted to do now was to get on with my life. 'Feeling a mortar shell hit my coach is an experience I am trying to forget.'

The Minister got heavily to his feet.

'One would not think that I could be any further embarrassed tonight but... it was not a mortar shell.'

'Oh?'

'That is what the press were allowed to publish. It was actually a ground to air heat-seeking missile.'

'Good God!' Monsieur de Mello exclaimed.

'It was what they had intended to use on the plane. They launched it from the back of a rented truck. It was parked above you.'

I was stunned.

'Are you certain?' I said. 'A ground to air missile would surely have blown me into the next world.'

'It should have done. What they did not know was that they had been traded a training missile. It was a dud. It had no warhead.'

'So what produced the explosion?'

'The unspent fuel in the rocket. There was ample to provide a decent explosive.'

I pointed at the tape recorder.

'I was at the service station when I telephoned. I had just filled up the tanks. We were carrying at least two hundred litres of diesel. I suppose that would have helped.'

De Mello was frowning in thought.

'But at least the coach was the latest Merc wasn't it?'

'Yes, that must have saved me to some extent.'

The Minister appeared baffled. De Mello explained.

'Engine at the rear. If the missile was heat seeking it would target the motor. That put ten metres of padded seats between the point of the explosion and the driver.'

'I could have done with a bit more than ten metres,' I said.

'I would have wanted ten kilometres,' De Mello admitted fervently.

My thoughts went back to the attack.

'So the hire van behind me was also a terrorist?' The Minister nodded. 'And his job was to clear the road directly behind me by blocking the traffic, so that I would be the only hot target for the missile to hit?'

'That was how they planned it. The moment he stopped the traffic, the van driver jumped out, got on the pillion of the motor bike and they rode the wrong way back up the voies sur berges to escape.'

'And did they escape?'

'As I said, they dumped the bike at Péronne and stole another car. Yesterday, the German police informed us that two persons answering their descriptions failed to stop at a police check. The police gave chase, shots were exchanged and the suspects crashed at one hundred and fifty kph into an overbridge on the autobahn. We will not learn anything from them, I'm afraid.'

'And the truck? The one that launched the missile?'

'He got away. We're studying press photographs.'

'Radio bugs? Missiles? Where do these people get hold of such stuff, Gilbert?'

'The terrorist groups engage in trade. We think they got the missile from the Middle East.'

'From a Middle East terrorist group? From the Palestinians?'

The Minister shrugged.

'Even if I knew I would not be wise to tell you. I can say that we know that the Baader-Meinhof group have got a stock of blank German passports that they have collected from various raids on provincial town halls. These would be viable trading currency. Arab groups certainly have access to the vast amount of hardware that gets thrown at the Middle East by all the peacemaking countries.' He made a hopeless gesture with his hands.

'And so we can soon expect Arab terrorists to turn up with German passports and French missiles?' I observed.

'They may trade the passports on with another group for something else. We just don't know. Not very reassuring, I'm afraid.'

The manservant came in and spoke quietly to Monsieur de Mello. He looked at his watch and nodded. Outside, the darkened sky of Paris was being regularly swept by the revolving searchlight on top of the Eiffel Tower.

'I have to take my medicine, gentlemen. And the ladies are making noises.'

They looked at me as if awaiting my permission.

'Have I answered all your questions, Monsieur Laperche? Is there anything else I can tell you?'

'I thank you, Monsieur le Ministre, you have been very open and I appreciate it.'

He shook my hand and looked me steadily in the eye. I could see the weight of responsibility and knowledge therein. It was a weary burden for him. Raoul de Mello put his arm around both our shoulders.

'Well, Gilbert, you're not a bad old stick. And you...' He studied me for a second. 'I think you're more scared of my daughter than of terrorists.'

'Don't you believe it.' I laughed uncomfortably. It was too near the truth.

We stood in the hallway in an untidy gaggle of shaking hands and kissing cheeks. It was a warm evening but rather than carry Maison Sebag's summer coat over my arm I slipped it on. I fancied that I would take a gentle stroll home, but not with my evening suit in full view. I was not that brave. The Minister's minder walked him to his car and the streetlight flooded in as the enormous gates were swung open.

Madame Chan appeared in the hallway behind us. I could see that her eyes were red. Madame de Mello looked accusingly at me.

'Well, goodnight Monsieur Laperche.' De Mello shook my hand.

'Goodnight. Thank you for inviting me this evening.' I moved out onto the steps.

'I expect we shall be seeing you again sometime.'

I could not understand his confidence. By her disdainful expression, Evelyne de Mello made it apparent that she could happily cope with never seeing me again. I looked towards Madame Chan. I only wanted to say goodnight.

'I can give you a lift, Simon, I'm going your way.' She had pulled a thin stole over her shoulders.

'But don't you live...?' I looked up at the manor.

'Good God no!' De Mello said. 'Jocelyne's been a free bird since University. Oh, the peace!' he added with theatrical fervour.

She pushed through between her parents, giving them a peck each on the cheek.

'Come on,' she said with authority and took my arm.

16

She held my arm tight as if she was scared that I would escape and we walked out under the stone arch into the deserted street beyond. The night was still warm from the day. The tapping of her high heels echoed back from the shuttered fronts. For some reason I felt contented.

'My car is on the avenue,' she said and turned us towards where the harsh glare of the street lights was filtered by the foliage of the trees in the Avenue Foch.

'It's very kind of you to offer me a lift,' I said, 'but I had intended to walk home. I was actually looking forward to a stroll.'

'Good. So was I. Which way shall we go? I think we have things to talk about.'

'Yes, I suppose we have.' I made my voice sound non-committal. 'Our paths haven't crossed for a few days. The last I saw of you was when you jumped out of the coach at St Jacques.'

'What's the matter?' she asked.

I had suddenly been assailed by the memory.

'Oh, nothing,' I said.

'Simon! When are you going to stop clamming up on me? Tell me!'

'If you must know, I was just remembering that when I saw you getting out of the coach I wondered if I would ever see you again, that's all.'

We turned into the avenue.

'Did you want to see me again then?' She looked straight ahead as she said this.

'Oh it wasn't just you I wondered about, it was everything. I did not know what was going to happen.'

'Oh, I see.'

Her voice was suddenly abrupt.

She pulled her arm out from mine and searched in her purse for her key. 'My car is here. Get in.' It was the Volkswagen. She pushed the passenger door open. I laughed. 'And what is so funny?' she asked as I squeezed in beside her.

'Your parking! You've got one wheel on the kerb. That's how we first met.'

'I remember distinctly. You were incredibly familiar with me. I thought how rude you were.'

'I remember distinctly too. You were incredibly inept. I thought how pretty you were.'

'Liar! You didn't even notice me. You were too busy showing off your prowess with a steering wheel.'

I stared out through the windscreen. It was coated with a fine layer of city dust. I said, in a conversational voice, 'You were wearing a silk blouse under a two piece suit in beige material which looked like linen. You had strappy sandals with high heels, heaven knows how you drove with those on. Your hair was loose and hanging, not tied up as it is now. When you looked over your shoulder it swished from side to side. I noticed that you had deep brown eyes, freckles on your nose, suntanned legs, and a mole at the top of your left thigh. Prove me wrong or believe me,' I challenged.

Silence.

At length she muttered a slow, 'Yes.' Her voice was contemplative. 'I was wearing that suit. Oh, and those sandals.' She shook her head slowly and looked down at the dashboard. 'You've tried this before. Trying to make me believe something you think I want to believe.'

'Oh forget it!' I said. 'That's far too convoluted for me. I just made it up on the spur of the moment.' I nodded at where the slit in her dress had drawn open. 'Even to the mole on your thigh.'

She looked down.

'Oh Simon!' she said and thumped my leg with her fist and then broke into a profusion of apologies as I gasped in pain.

'You never miss do you?' My voice was strained through jaws clenched in agony. 'Right on target every time! One day, when I know you better. If I ever do get to know you better,' I added, 'I will give you a private viewing of my bruises but until then, can you just accept that they exist and are painful?'

'Yes. Sorry. Sorry.'

She started the car and drove out onto the avenue.

'What I am waiting to hear, is what happened to you after you all got off the coach. Did it work OK?'

'Like clockwork. I got them down the métro steps with no problem and I stood at the bottom pushing them through the doors. I thought that we could not risk even one of them being seen. I did just catch sight of the roof of the coach as you drove off.' She paused. 'It occurred to me then that what you were doing was incredibly brave.'

'I thought it was incredibly stupid.' She threw me a questioning glance. 'Just when we had started to get along nicely I chuck you off the coach,' I explained. 'Not very clever was it?'

'It saved our lives, Simon.'

'Well that's alright then,' I dismissed it. I did not want to start along that tack again. She looked at me as if she wanted to say something else so I quickly said, 'What did you do then?'

'I bought four first class carnets and took them to the Palais de Chaillot by métro. In fact,' she pointed at the street corner, 'we came up there. Trocadéro. It's direct.'

I had not really been paying attention to our route.

'I hope you weren't late. You know how the Minister hates people to be late.' I was trying to be flippant.

'We were on time.' Her voice was smug. Then her face suddenly changed to a mask of anguish. 'But you were early,' she whispered. 'We did not know what had happened when we came strolling along the pavement. You should have heard the noise! People were running everywhere, police cars were screaming! It was awful. They wanted to know, "Was this the Trade Delegation? Why weren't we in the coach?" That was when I realised that something had gone wrong.'

I snatched the wheel straight.

'For heaven's sake, Jocelyne, pull over.'

She bumped the car to the kerb under the trees at the Place de l'Alma. As soon as it stopped she buried her face in her hands. I leaned across, switched off the engine and yanked on the brake. I opened the door and got out, leaving her crying in the driving seat. She would get over whatever was bothering her. And she was bothering me.

I crossed the road and strolled down towards the Seine. It was funny; I had not been this way since it had happened. A small gaggle of people were leaning on the parapet. From this height they had a good view over the river. I joined them and gazed out, trying not to think of Madame Chan and her brown eyes and the mole on her thigh. I focused on the floodlit pontoon for some seconds before I realised what we were watching. A cloud of exhaust fumes burst from the crane and a second or two later the noise of the engine reached us from across the water. I leaned my forearms on the stonework and goggled just like the others.

'It's coming up now look!' A man with a walking stick pointed.

'Oh yeah, I can see it,' said another.

Like a leviathan from the depths, the tangled mass of blackened metal that had been the rear of Artur Fromme's best Mercedes coach, slowly emerged, glistening and dripping into the floodlights. I was transfixed by the gothic nightmare of it.

A small arm slipped under mine and Madame Chan pressed against me. She was shivering. I put my arm around her and drew her closer. Her eyes were two dark orbs of staring horror, glued to the wreckage. As it climbed higher, the river water poured out of it in muddy cascades.

'Oh my God!' she whispered.

'Shh!' I said and squeezed her as one would comfort a small child.

The man with the stick turned to me and remarked, 'I bet that buggered up his insurance!'

'Yes,' I said.

'They say the driver was drunk.'

'No, I think it was drugs,' a voice further up added.

I put both arms on Madame Chan's shoulders and firmly turned her away from the wall.

'Simon!' she squirmed, 'Didn't you hear what they said?' She tried to pull free. I marched her further towards the car. 'Don't you care?' she blazed.

'No,' I said, 'I don't care what uninformed ignorant people want to believe about somebody they don't know, cannot recognise and will have forgotten by tomorrow morning.' I looked at the car. 'Can you drive?'

She hesitated then she handed me the keys.

'No, you had better drive if you are so nervous.'

I scowled at her and opened the passenger door. She caught me looking at her legs as she got in. It made her frown.

I drove in silence along the Seine to the Place de la Concorde. I liked the majesty of Paris and the night was the best time to see it. The twinkling lamps around the square; the occasional green glow wavering amongst the trees of the Tuileries Gardens; the jewel-like red and yellow lights of the cars circling the Arc de Triomphe at the top of the Champs Elysées like fireflies clustering around a bud; it was fairyland to me.

'There's Le Guennec.' I indicated the Saviem in the colours of Autocars Fromme which was turning up the Champs Elysées. I flashed my headlights at him and then realised what a fool I was. He would not recognise the car.

'I didn't know they worked so late,' she said.

'He's doing one of the night club tours.' I looked at my watch. 'He's done the eleven thirty Moulin Rouge and now he's taking them to the Lido for the half past one show.'

'Goodness! What time will he finish?'

'By the time he has delivered them back to their various hotels, about three thirty.'

'That must be exhausting. Do you ever have to do that tour?'

'No. I'm what you might call, "at the bottom of the pile". The only reason I was given your group is because the idiot Minister asked for me.'

'Yes, I think you made an impression on him.'

'I wasn't trying to impress him.'

'Who were you trying to impress?'

'I wasn't trying to impress anybody, Madame Chan, I just felt sorry for you. God knows why! You've been nothing but trouble.'

'There might have been less trouble, Monsieur Laperche, if you had not forced our bodyguard off the road the moment you saw them. I never understood why you did that. They weren't going to hurt us.'

I stared at her and the car slowed down. With an angry blast of its horn the bus on the all night service swept by on the inside. I let it pass then pulled over to the side.

'What's the matter?' She looked scared. 'Don't look at me like that, you frighten me.'

'Why did I do it?' I pondered aloud. She shook her head at me. 'No, you're right Jocelyne. Why did I do it? Listen. I thought they were after me.'

'But they weren't. You're paranoid. They had been assigned to protect the group.'

'But I thought that they were the two who had beaten me up a few days earlier didn't I?'

'That's what you said.'

'I can't imagine Van der Leeuven, for all his faults, instructing his investigators to rough me up, can you?'

'Of course not.'

'So who were the two in the other Peugeot, the first Peugeot, who attacked me at St. Lazare?'

'The ones who gave you all those horrible bruises on your chest.' She contemplated. I waited. 'Why do you think they chose you rather than anybody else? I mean, could it not just have been a random attack?'

I thought back to the nod that one man had given the other. I shook my head.

'No,' I said. 'They knew who they were looking for. One of the men looked at me, recognised me and nodded to the other. And then they laid into me.'

'Did they say anything?'

'You mean, apart from begging me for mercy?'

She gave an exasperated sigh.

She looked pretty when she did that. I grinned.

'And you didn't recognise them?' she said.

'No but...' I stopped.

'Go on. What?' she prompted.

'Well, I am not an expert in common asssault but they seemed sort of, amateur.'

'What do you mean?'

'The bloke behind me knocked me down. I fell to my knees. But the one in front tried to kick me in the face.'

'Oh, how horrible!'

I shook my head dismissively.

'No, the point is, he should have used his knee. It was right in front of my face. He could have laid me straight out. But what did he do? He tried to lash out with his foot. To do that, he had to take a step backwards and, by doing so, he threw himself off balance. It was a daft thing to do.'

'How can you sit there and analyse it so objectively? It sounds awful.' Her eyes were big and round again.

'I'm only doing what you told me to do.'

'Who could it have been, then?' I shrugged at her. 'You don't owe anybody any money?' I shook my head. 'No jilted girlfriends out for revenge?'

'Hundreds,' I said, 'but like you, they don't know where I live.'

'So how did your attackers?'

'What do you mean?'

'Despite your inaccurate and intentionally sordid reference to me as, "another one of your ignorant jilted girlfriends", I do know that you live near the Gare St Lazare and so did your attackers. They were waiting for you. Where would they find your address?'

And as she said that, I heard Madame Aurélie's filing cabinet drawer slam shut. I put the car in gear.

'You're brilliant Jocelyne, brilliant. I always thought so!' I accelerated away.

'Where are we going?' she asked in alarm, and then added, 'two minutes ago you said I had been nothing but trouble and now you say I'm brilliant.'

'Well you are that remarkable type of woman who can be both at the same time. We're going to the garage.'

'In my car?'

'Oh, er... with your permission?'

'Well, I was doing nothing else with my evening,' she said in a resigned voice. 'Why the garage?'

'I've just remembered something. You jogged my memory. I've had a bit of trouble from one of the coach drivers, a chap called Pradel.'

'What sort of trouble?'

'Oh, he keeps referring to my accident. Calls me "widow-maker Laperche" and that sort of thing. I didn't take much notice.'

'Because you're tough?'

I glanced at her. She had that exasperated look again.

'No, because I'm not clever like you. This chap Pradel is a nasty little weasel. I remember that a couple of days after Monsieur Fromme had carpeted me for carrying your group, I came back early from lunch into the garage. I heard the filing drawer being slammed shut in the office. I assumed that it was Monsieur Fromme or Madame Aurélie but they both walked in later. The only person in the garage was Pradel. And in the filing cabinet are the personnel records. If somebody wanted to find out my address without asking me or anybody else, that is where they would look.'

'Simon, slow down. Why the hurry?'

We were racing up the rue Lafayette whilst all the lights were green.

'You saw Le Guennec? The coach at the Concorde? Well there will be two others out tonight. One will be poor old Noel in his clapped out coach meeting a charter train at the Gare de Lyon to pick up a group of schoolkids returning from a holiday camp; the other will be Pradel. He will be doing the other night club tour.'

'What do you hope to do?' Her voice was full of a brittle anxiety.

The tyres suddenly thundered on the cobbles as we crossed the boulevard de Magenta.

'Oh, just ask him a question or two,' I said, as I recalled the solid fists thudding into me. 'In a nice and gentlemanly fashion.'

There was a space outside Chez Jean so I slotted the Volkswagen in there. I turned to thank her for the lift.

'I'll wait,' she said.

'Oh, there's no need, really. It's not your problem. Thanks for the lift. The garage is just there.' I pointed at the blackness of the open doors. 'I would rather you went home, Jocelyne. You get some funny types around here.'

'Like coach drivers?' she smiled. 'I'll wait.'

I got out of the car and slammed the door.

'Go home!' I said.

Pradel was still out but Noel was already back. His coach was parked at the far side. The most difficult slot to get out from. The hierarchy of a garage even extended to where you parked your coach. The old Saviem looked even more decrepit and abandoned than ever. Its doors were open and a mop leaned drunkenly in a bucket by the front fender. Noel was kneeling inside, cleaning the floor. I went up to him.

'Working late?' I said and as I did so, I puzzled over the soles of the shoes. Leather. The driver turned, saw me and a look of alarm crossed his face. It was Pradel.

'Ah, Laperche.' His voice was uncertain.

I recovered quickly from my surprise.

'I was hoping to find you. I think we have some things to talk about, don't you?' I tried to sound as menacing as I could. I looked into the coach where he was disgustedly sponging up children's vomit. 'Doing a job for Noel are you?'

He backed awkwardly down the steps. He had splashed vomit onto his trousers and his shirt was marked with grease where he had rubbed against the hinges of the door. He presented a stark contrast to my immaculate dress. He stood up and backed defensively against the side of the coach.

'This is my coach now.'

I looked at him and recalled Fromme's assertion that he was going to make changes. I grinned maliciously.

'And Noel?'

'He's got the new Saviem.'

I noticed that he didn't say, 'my Saviem.'

'It couldn't go to a nicer chap, could it?' He did not respond. 'Could it?' I insisted.

'Noel is a nice fellow.' His voice was neutral. It was hurting him and I didn't care.

'Tell me about your friends who drive a dark coloured Peugeot.'

'They're not my friends.' His sharp face twitched. It made him look even more like a weasel.

'But you know them.'

'I wasn't responsible for what they did. It wasn't me.'

'What did they do then Pradel?' I asked smoothly. Then my arm stabbed out into his stomach. He collapsed with a grunt to the concrete.

'Don't hit me,' he gasped. 'Don't hit me.'

I had no further wish to hit him. He was already beaten. I grabbed him by the collar of his shirt and hauled him up against the side of the coach. He whimpered and covered his head.

'Yes, you cover your head, Pradel. It's easy when there's only one attacker. It's not so easy with two. Who were they?'

'It wasn't me, it was Madame Grignon.' The name meant something to me but I could not recall what.

'Go on.' I prompted and banged his head against the coach. 'I'm listening.'

'She saw you in a coach and asked me... She thought that you hadn't been punished enough. She thought you had got off too lightly.'

'Grignon,' I said.

'The mother of the girl. The one who fell out of your coach.'

'Oh yes.' I did not remember the mother but then that was not surprising. I had avoided looking into the public gallery during the enquiry but she would have seen me. Her daughter was in a wheelchair and I had walked away from the tribunal. The shock must have caused the hatred to build up. Papa Coursamel was the real villain. By his criminal negligence and ignorance he had caused the accident but he had come over as a lovable, lost, confused figure. A tragic figure, which had assumed a disproportionate dignity after his suicide. I had stood up there in the prime of life and in full command of my faculties and had thus become the target. Poor woman. But when was I going to rid myself of this curse?

Pradel was scared enough to want to talk. I let him.

'She asked me to get your address. She said that she would send a couple of her friends to visit you. She said once would be enough.'

'Would you like me to send a couple of my friends to visit you Pradel? I can get your address from the filing cabinet just like you did mine.'

He made a strangled noise and pulled away. He overbalanced and fell, thrusting his arm into the bucket. It tipped and sent him sprawling into a spreading flood of slops from his coach. I suddenly lost interest in him. He would be no more trouble to me and the misguided woman was satiated. I did not need any of this anguish in my life. I turned and walked out of the garage into the Paris summer night. I knew what I wanted in my life.

The sound of the racing Volkswagen engine died as I reached her.

'I can't get it out of the space you put it in,' she said through the open window.

'I could get a bus out of this space! Move over,' I sighed heavily.

'No. Get in the other side and tell me how to do it.'

'I haven't got all night.'

'Most of it has gone already, Simon. Get in.'

I walked around the car. How did she manage to put the rear wheel so far onto the sidewalk? I got in. She turned and smiled at me. I said,

'Turn the wheel the other way. Edge forwards a bit. Go on.'

'We'll bump the car in front.'

'You're a hundred metres from the car in front. Anyway, nobody will see you. They were probably all asleep until you started revving your engine.'

She began to edge forward.

'Oh,' she gasped.

'That thud was only your back wheel slipping off the sidewalk. Now turn the wheel the other way. Reverse. Centre the wheel. Right, now you are straight and can start again.'

'Thank you,' she said, and cut the motor. 'Now we can talk.'

I looked at the impish expression on her face. She had trapped me on purpose and she did not mind me knowing it. The minx!

'So what is it you want to talk about?' I asked.

'I've got some things I want to say to you and I would like you to listen.'

'Are they going to embarrass me?'

She ignored my question and stared down the street.

'What you said on the telephone message — that the guide thought that you were deranged — upset me. It was not true.'

'Was that why you ran out of the room?'

'No it was not! I ran out because... because... Oh Simon, you sounded so desperate, so utterly alone. I felt so ashamed.'

'I was alone. I left that message at the service station at Fontainebleau. You weren't believing anything I said.'

'But I did believe IN you Simon. I still do.'

'I'm glad somebody does.'

She sat forward and hugged the wheel.

'Simon, I would like us to remain friends.' Her voice was wary. As if the declaration carried another, unuttered suggestion.

'Have we become friends then?' I slipped my arm around her waist. The silk of her dress was very thin.

'If we are not careful, we will become more than friends.' She looked pointedly at my arm.

I withdrew my hand from her waist. It had been too good to be true.

'Why shouldn't we be more than friends?' I felt truculent. Now that she was slipping away from me I knew that I wanted her.

'Simon, I like you very much. You have your faults...'

'Good of you to point that out.'

'And that is one of them — speaking before you think. But your qualities far outshine your defects. I think we should be truthful with each other.' She paused over 'truthful' to emphasise the sense.

'OK,' I agreed. I took a deep breath. 'I think you are excellent in your job. I have never worked with a better guide and, on a professional level, I would hope that we could overcome our mutual antagonism should we have to work together in the future.'

'Simon, I didn't mean...'

'On a personal level,' I said, 'I find you gracious, intelligent and irresistibly attractive but irremediably irritating. This is a great pity. Perhaps not for you, because you want us to be "just good friends", but for me, who, I realise now, had been hoping for something more. There now I have said it. And that was more frightening than being blown up in a coach.'

'Simon, don't say that.' She shuddered.

'Well what did you expect from me?' I kicked my heel into the rubber floor mat. 'I can't get you out of my mind, Jocelyne. You're just there all the while.'

'Simon. I feel very fond, dangerously fond of you.' She turned in her seat to look me in the face. 'But I can't get involved with a married man.'

I looked at her and blinked. Had I heard straight?

'Why are you telling me this?'

'I know, Simon.' She nodded at me with a look of infinitely sad encouragement at me. She desired and yet dreaded that I would confirm her belief.

'I am not married, Jocelyne. And it appears that I have no current girlfriend,' I added bitterly.

'Simon, I found out through the Department which hospital you were in. I wanted to see you. I had things I needed to say to you.' She gazed out at the steel shutter on the café without seeing it. 'I thought I had things to say to you,' she corrected herself.

'Jocelyne, you were the only visitor I really wanted to see,' I admitted. 'But you never came.'

She turned quickly.

'I did come,' she contradicted. 'I did.'

I thought back to the hospital and the policeman posted at the door to deny my visitors entry.

'But you couldn't get past the policeman?' I laughed. It was just too ironic. 'Didn't your facilitation card work?'

'I didn't try it,' she said quietly and looked down at the hub of the steering wheel. 'When I got to your room they told me that your wife was in there with you.'

'My...?'

'Yes, Simon,' she sighed sadly. 'Your wife. I was so disappointed in you.'

Suddenly everything clicked into place.

'Bloody Nikki!' I exclaimed. 'It was Monique!'

'Monique? And she is your wife?'

'My wife? My wife! No she is not my wife!' I was almost shouting. 'Listen, you've met Monique but you don't know what she is capable of.'

'I can imagine.'

'Oh no you can't. The Prefect of Police of Paris puts into place a security operation to protect the life and liberty of Simon Laperche, coach driver. Did he think it would stop Monique? She turns up at the hospital — God knows how she found out where I was — and demands to be able to see her husband. The policeman refuses so she punches him and walks in. Simple. It's a good job she's not in the Baader-Meinhof!'

'Oh.' She looked uncomfortabe but relieved. 'So you're not married?'

'Not married. Never have been. And am sitting next to an unbeatable argument for continued celibacy. I would not refuse an apology, were it to arrive.' But before she could say anything, another thought struck me. 'Just a minute!' I said. 'Don't you think you are being a mite hypocritical, saying that you cannot get involved with a married man, MADAME Chan? Hmm? It seems to me that I must be careful that I don't get mixed up with a married woman! You are still married aren't you?'

'Well, yes and no.'

'I can't wait to hear this explanation.'

'Simon, I'm sort of glad that I was wrong.'

'Am I to accept that as your apology?'

'And as for my being married, well, in China I suppose I am still married because we never got divorced — I just walked out — but the marriage is not recognised in France. I did not get it registered at the consulate.' She looked down into her lap and absently closed the panel of her dress again. 'I use my married name to keep a distance from people... men.'

'That would work better if you weren't so damnably attractive.'

'It always has worked up to now, Simon.' She looked up at me. Her eyes were dark and lustrous, heavy with meaning. 'You must be special.'

'If I am that special, can I have my first kiss?' I drew her towards me.

'Not your first,' she said. 'You've already had that.'

I sat back and looked at her. I was astounded.

'I have not.'

'Oh yes you have.'

'When?'

'I am quite hurt that it made so little impression upon you.'

'I would have remembered if I had kissed you!' I found that I was speaking with rather more fervour than I had intended. 'I have been wanting to kiss you for days.'

'You have only known me for a matter of days.'

'Well that must prove that I am telling the truth.' The reasoning was abstruse but I knew what I meant.

'I never doubted you in that.' She put her head on one side. 'Don't you remember the fire?'

'I could hardly have forgotten it. What has that got to do with it?' I thought rapidly and then said, 'Ah no, I didn't kiss you, I gave you a hug when I found you, not a kiss. I was just so relieved that you were safe.'

'Oh, I think that was obvious to everybody, Simon. Not only do you sometimes speak without thinking, you act without thinking, and a crushing great hug from a man in filthy shorts is not something to be passed over lightly.'

'But it was only a hug,' I insisted.

'Didn't you want to kiss me at that time?' she teased.

'Of course I did.'

'But you were frightened of me?' she nodded in a mocking comprehension.

'All right Madame Chan, if that is what you want — the absolute humiliation of Simon Laperche. Yes. I was frightened of you. And the way you are behaving now only reinforces my belief that it was a sensible emotion.'

'So that was why you kissed me behind my back?' She looked at me, a challenging smile puckering her cheek. 'You don't remember!' she accused. 'Well I remember, Simon, because I had been wanting you to kiss me for ages.'

'You could have said so.'

'That's not the way it is done.'

I suddenly remembered the kiss.

'You never felt that!' I accused her.

'Ah, now you remember. But if I didn't feel it, how did I know it happened? Who would have told me? Not you.'

I shook my head dumbly.

'No, not me.'

'You lay on top of me to save me from the fire. Remember?' I nodded. 'I know what happened. Don't think I didn't notice afterwards that you had scorched all the hairs on your legs. And when the fire had passed over us, you kissed the back of my neck.'

'And you told me to get off you.'

'Well, you were creasing my suit.'

'I'll crease your dress. Come here.'

She was warm and luscious and melting. It lasted a long time but still not long enough. I breathed in her perfume, I revelled in the touch of her body against mine.

'And did you really believe that Nikki was my wife?' I whispered in her ear.

'She fancies you. She has good taste and I'll tell you something else.'

'What?'

'She's right. You do have a nice bum.'

I pulled away, scandalised.

'I've got a...? How do you know?'

She started the car and put it into gear. She looked very, very, smug.

'The bathroom of the Majestic Palace Hotel, Lyon? You are not the only person in the world who knows how to use a mirror. There was a full length glass on the wall behind you.'

In one insultingly easy manoeuvre she swung the car out into the avenue.

'Now, which way? I want to be the first of Simon Laperche's girlfriends to find out where he lives.'

THE PASSPORT

The History of Man's Most Travelled Document
by Martin Lloyd

Published by Sutton Publishing
288 pages   55 illustrations

The passport is a document familiar to many, used and recognised worldwide and yet it has no basis in law: one country cannot oblige another to admit its subjects simply by issuing a document. But the state, by insisting on the requirement to hold a passport, provides for itself a neat, self-financing data collection and surveillance system. This well illustrated book tells for the first time the story of the passport from its earliest origins to its latest high-tech developments. Handwritten documents adorned with wax seals, modern versions in plastic covers, diplomatic passports and wartime safe conducts, all drawn from the author's collection, complement the exciting exploits of spies and criminals and the tragic real life experiences of refugees. Whether recounting the birth of the British blue passport of the 1920s or divulging the secrets of today's machine readable passport, Martin Lloyd has written an informative and engrossing history book which is accessible to everyone.

"...a lively and thoughtful book..."
Sunday Telegraph

Martin Lloyd has recorded The Passport *as a talking book for the blind. RNIB catalogue no: TB 14107*

The Trouble with France

Martin Lloyd's new international number one blockbusting bestseller

"...makes Baedeker's look like a guidebook..."

When Martin Lloyd set out on his holiday to Suffolk why did he end up in Boulogne? What caused Max the Mad Alsatian to steal his map and what did the knitted grandma really think of his display of hot plate juggling? The answers to these and many more mysteries are to be found in THE TROUBLE WITH FRANCE

THE TROUBLE WITH FRANCE contains no recipes and no hand drawn maps. It does not recount how somebody richer than you went to a part of France that you have never heard of, bought a stone ruin for a song and converted it into a luxurious retreat which they expect you to finance by buying their book.

Nor is it the self satisfied account of another ultra fit expedition cyclist abseiling down Everest on a penny farthing but Martin Lloyd attempting an uneventful ride on a mundane bicycle through an uninteresting part of France... and failing with outstanding success.

THE TROUBLE WITH FRANCE is destined to be a worldwide success now that Margaret's Mum has been down the road and told her friend Pat about it.

Published by Queen Anne's Fan

Martin Lloyd has recorded THE TROUBLE WITH FRANCE as a talking book for the blind. RNIB catalogue no: TB 15323

What they said about **The Chinese Transfer**
(now reprinted)

"...not quite right for our list..."
Rejection slip, Piatkus Books.

"...not quite what we're looking for..."
Rejection slip, Constable & Robinson.

"...not suitable for our current publishing programme..."
Rejection slip, Hodder Headline.

"...I fear it would disappear without trace..."
Rejection slip, Time Warner Books.

"...not going to pursue your project to publication..."
Rejection slip, Harper Collins.

"...It is old fashioned both in content and style..."
Rejection slip, Random House.

"...we don't talk to authors..."
Rejection, Penguin Books.

**"...a compelling story with a strong and
exciting plot. I curled up in a chair and
stayed up late to finish it."**

Mrs. P. W. – a lady who actually read the book.